STONES
IN THE
SEA

how came those strange, baffling stars?

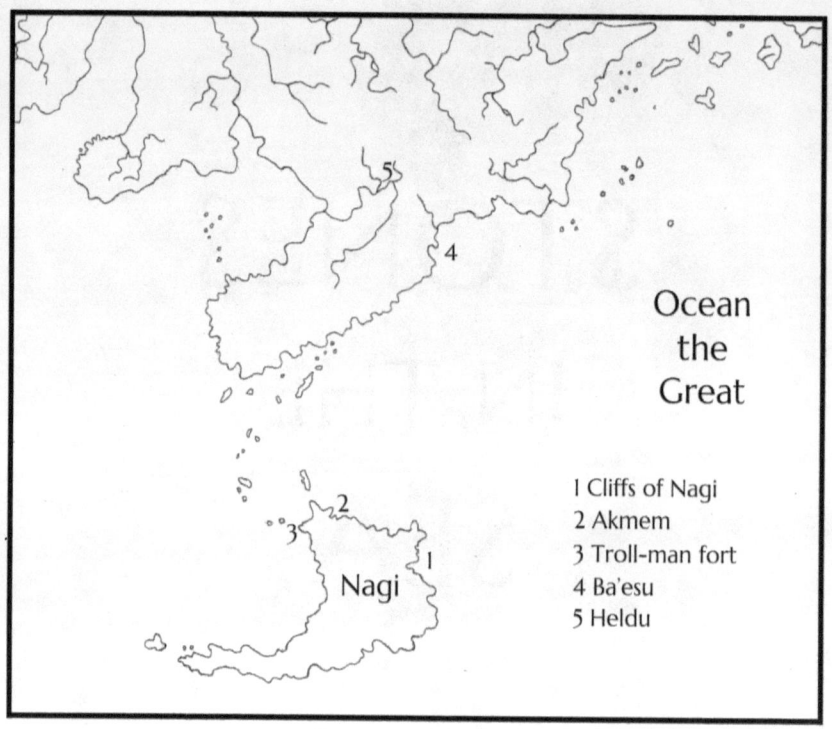

Ocean
the
Great

1 Cliffs of Nagi
2 Akmem
3 Troll-man fort
4 Ba'esu
5 Heldu

Nagi

THE LANDS AND SEAS ABOUT THE ISLE OF NAGI

STONES IN THE SEA

STEPHEN BROOKE

Arachis Press 2023

Stones in the Sea
©2023 Stephen Brooke

ISBN 978-1-937745-88-2

Arachis Press
4803 Peanut Road
Graceville, FL 32440
http://arachispress.com

I. RIDDLES

One

There would be no profit in telling of the road that led me to Juan Fernandez. Suffice it to say I ended up a prisoner there, the only American among a population of Latin cutthroats. The soldiers treated us like the dogs we were, working us hard, kenneling us in caves in the mountainsides. There was no escape from this island prison; so all believed.

So they believed until those Chilean prisoners rose up and murdered their guards. I knew nothing of what had been planned, if it had been planned. Perhaps it simply happened. I did know it would be best to separate myself from the others. I was the outsider, the target for any scoundrel with a grudge, and I doubted one man would lift a finger to aid me. When the others fled to the mainland, I found a small boat and sailed west.

Yes, a foolish thing to do. But what could await me on the South American mainland? I would be hunted down and executed, whether I had aided my fellow convicts in their uprising or not. The nearest English-speaking population was on the other side of the continent, beyond Cape Horn, on the Falklands. There was no way I could reach them. I'll circle out into the Pacific, I told myself, and try to make land further north, Peru or even Colombia. There would be vessels at the Isthmus of Panama, American vessels that might carry me home. I had no illusions of being able to cross the vast ocean, of reaching New Holland or any other shore.

The winds are treacherous around Juan Fernandez, as are the seas. My intentions of sailing north were continually thwarted. I was carried further and further out into the Pacific until I began to think my only hope would be to find some island before my meager supplies were depleted. An island in all this expanse of water! The proverbial needle in an exceedingly large haystack, that would be.

Had I not been a sailor, I might not have recognized this. But had I not been a sailor I would have had no chance at all. I gave up all thoughts of turning back to the continent behind me, risking all —but all was very little at that point. I was gambling with empty pockets.

Navigation? I carried no instruments, no sexton, no compass. No, not even a way to tell the time, save by the transit of the sun. The stars offered little, save to tell me I remained below the equator. Surely I had passed beyond Easter Island and had no chance of sailing north in hopes of finding it.

Indeed, all I knew was that it lay somewhere north. Everywhere I might wish to go lay somewhere north, but the winds and currents did not favor my progress in that direction. Might I not do better to let them carry me west in hopes of reaching land, any land, before my supplies gave out? Ha! At any time those winds might turn another way, might they not?

All about me, water. Green or blue or gray, depending on the vagaries of sunlight and cloud. At times, great waves rose, born in some distant storm; at times, the Pacific lived up to its name, as calm as a bath. And the sky, the vast sky, arced above. Even here, near no shore—no shore of which I knew—one saw birds. I could but sail on, seeking to nest on some shore of my own.

It was not a bad little boat, the one I stole, cat-rigged with a single gaff sail. Oh, it could have carried more sail; I might have added at least a jib. To what use its owner had put it, I knew not, but it seemed unlikely it had ever voyaged further than the coast of Chile, perhaps to Valparaiso. My journey would be much longer.

But I was losing track of time, as one day followed another, and night just as surely. Each dawn seemed the same. My supplies dwindled; I rationed what water I had, managing to catch a little rain once to replenish it. Was I five weeks out, or six, when I first glimpsed the darkness, off toward the north?

Two

Hurricane, cyclone, typhoon—whatever one named it in these waters, it was surely a storm of the tropics. I saw now the lightning playing along its dark belly, as it crept inexorably closer.

It was no boat for one man to row, wide of beam and high of freeboard. I set one of the long oars near the stern, to use it to both steer and propel the craft. Without sail, the rudder would be useless.

For now, however, I remained under sail, running before the storm. Shouldn't it track southerly? And toward the east, backwards from the hurricanes I had known in the Caribbean. If I could angle north away from it, around it, I might have a chance. Northeast, northwest, it didn't matter which.

But only if it followed that typical route. Storms are notoriously fickle. It had already proven that by being here. Or was I further north than I had believed?

That mattered not in the least. I was where I was, somewhere in the Pacific, in a boat of some twenty feet of length. Alone, save maybe for the God to whom I had not prayed since I was a boy. I would not now; he had jumped ship somewhere on my voyage through life.

Soon, I saw I would not be able to dodge the storm. It filled the horizon and half the sky, towering to nebulous gray heights. "Best take in sail, captain," I told myself. Captain at last, captain of this insignificant vessel. My first and last command, most likely.

What sail I had billowed and strained as the wind grew ever stronger. It would surely split if I didn't strike it, but that would leave me completely at the mercy of the storm. There was little I could do with one oar; I much doubted I could even keep my craft from going broadside into the great swells. Great and growing greater, they were. The first sheet of drenching rain overtook me as I lowered my own sheet.

The tiniest of rags I set on a line to the prow, adding a sort of jibsail at last. Maybe that could do some good, allow me to continue running before the tempest. Run and maybe angle out on the far side. It was unlikely, I knew.

Yes, I knew it deep in me but had no time to think about it. All my effort, all my attention, was given to keeping myself upright and headed in the proper direction. I would need to bail, wouldn't I? But I couldn't leave my oar for a moment. I reached down with one arm, scooped some of the water gathering about my feet with a cup, and tossed it into the raging water outside the boat. I would be at that as long as I was in this typhoon and could only hope to stay ahead as rain and wave attempted to fill the boat.

An hour? Two hours? I know not; time meant nothing as I labored. There were bands of lesser wind, of lesser rain, to give me respite. It grew ever darker, though night was yet far away. Above me, churning cloud. Below, churning sea. All around, wind, howling as I'd never heard wind howl before, howling like all the damned in hell.

And lightning. Its crashes rose again and again above the wail of those winds. I saw it flicker here, there, but not close. Not at first.

What was that? Something had of a sudden plummeted from the darkness, into my boat. A great albatross? It could be; it was large anyway, and white. "A place to rest, eh?" I addressed it. "You are welcome to it, mate." As long as it remained afloat. I did not add that; no need to alarm my passenger!

The storm gathered strength again, blew more violently than ever, and the lighting now was close. Thunder rumbled almost steadily, its voice merging with that of the winds. "This may be it," I announced, to myself, to the bird. Then I said no more, struggling to keep my vessel headed as I wished. The bit of sail I had improvised tore apart, disappeared into the darkness, another bird taking flight. Only my oar remained to me.

It would not be enough. Around and around we went, near capsizing time and again yet managing to remain intact. Whether my steering played any part in that I can not say. It might have been no more than luck. Then all was still.

The eye of the storm. Great ramparts of cloud rose all around, disappearing into blackness. Nigh continuous lightning lit up those walls. Sooner of later they would again engulf me. I did not expect to survive when they did.

I looked to the bird huddled in the prow. No albatross nor anything like one, but some sort of eagle it was, white with dark wings. "This would be your chance to get away," I informed it. Fly high, if you have the strength. Fly and leave me.

No, it had not the strength. No more than I. I sat and waited, sat and watched. The lightning in the storm walls seemed to whirl, even as did the winds, becoming almost one light all about me. Then, one great crash that seemed to come from no one direction but lit up all the sky and sea, blinding me for a moment.

When I saw again, the seas were calm and the sun was rising.

Three

There was no mistake. I was north of the equator. Could I have been carried so far off course? Did such storms even cross into another hemisphere?

And how had evening turned to morn in the blink of an eye? I must have been knocked out, I told myself, lost consciousness for hours, and the boat somehow drifted to safety without my hand to guide it.

The eagle hopped onto a forward bench and stretched its wings. Long wings they were, dark though its body was white. I had never seen such an eagle before but I knew little of the Pacific. My ill-fated trip to Chile had been my first acquaintance with the ocean.

"So where from here?" I asked it. It screeched in reply and took to flight. I watched it disappear, winging west. As good a direction to go as any, I decided. I soon had my sail up and followed, bailing what water remained in the boat as I went. That took some time.

Too bad it was at least partly brine. I might need more drinking water before this voyage ended. Not that I was badly situated there; I had filled every container I could when the rain first came. Food was another matter.

I should try fishing again. There had been lines and hooks aboard the boat but I had found no luck when I trolled with them. But these were new waters, were they not? New waters and new luck. Luck seemed to be with me, at last.

A pewter spoon had been among the items aboard. I had already managed to poke a hole through it and tie on a couple of hooks, one smaller and trailing the other. To this I attached strips of cloth, white and yellow. I could have used some of that eagle's feathers, maybe, but these might do just as well. What a fish might mistake it for, I knew not. A squid? A sardine?

It did not matter. I tossed it out aft and sailed on. Slowly; neither wind nor current favored the direction I had chosen. Those should be better south of the equator, should they not? I was not certain but I was doing far too much cutting back and forth here for quick progress. It might be as well to go south as well as west.

So I let myself trend southwestward, not that it was likely to take me anywhere more quickly. My line. It was taut and shifting back and forth. I had hooked something at last! Not something small, I realized, as I began to pull it in, hand over hand. Before I had my catch aboard, I noted the bulging head, the rainbow colors, as it darted here and there beneath the surface, attempting to find its freedom. A dolphin. We had those in the Atlantic. Wasn't there a gaff hook somewhere aboard?

Yes, there. I heaved the fish–a good yard long–into the boat. I would have to eat it raw, wouldn't I? So be it. I clubbed it and it lay still. I soon had a knife to it. Those entrails, the head, could be saved as bait.

A moment later, the eagle lit just before the mast and turned a fierce eye toward me. "As lost as I am, are you?" I asked. "Here." I tossed it the filleted carcass. I did not begrudge my shipmate his share.

Stars began to fill the clear sky. Stars I did not recognize. How could that be? I knew the heavens both above and below the equator. Some looked like constellations I knew, but not quite the same. There. That was Mars, wasn't it? It shouldn't be quite where it was.

Things moved about; I knew this. Even the stars, slowly, imper-ceptibly, shifted over the eons. I could not believe they had moved since yesterday but had no other explanation. Foolishness, I told myself, and fell into slumber, too weary to concern myself further with stars.

In the morning, the stars disappeared and bothered me no more. I did see the morning star–or a morning star–and that was reassuring. And the sun rose as ever it did.

As it did the next day and that after. Nights continued to baffle me, not that there was anything I could do about the stars. Some-times I wished I could reach up and set them right. I lay on my back, watching the wheel of heaven slowly turn against the infi-nite black distance, and fell into sleep.

Four

The skies remained clear. That was good for a while but I hoped for some rain—or at least clouds—eventually. My luck held when it came to fishing. I pulled in catches two or three times a day, though none so large as that first dolphin. My feathered friend approved. At least, he returned for his share after launching into the sky each morning. He sought land, I was sure, just as did I.

Or she sought it. I wasn't sure. I might have named my comrade had I known its gender. Instead, I got in the habit of calling it Mate.

I was certain I edged closer to the equator. No longer being certain of the season—that is, if time had somehow changed—I could not rely on the sun to position myself. How did I know if it were spring or autumn? Be that as it may, I felt following the equator a safe course. I called up charts in my mind and tried to determine where I might eventually make land.

If I didn't hit some other island first—and it seemed likely enough I would—I would fetch up in the Dutch Indies. There were head-hunters there, weren't there? Maybe cannibals too. I'd rather find some other harbor first. My supplies might not last that far anyway.

And if I did not expire of boredom first. These days, each as the one before, were becoming more than just tedious. They might well drive me mad in time. Maybe they already had and those stars were an hallucination.

Oh, probably not. But it might be better if I were mad. Something on the line, I noticed. It was jerking back and forth, going taut and slack. Ah, I could actually feel the jolt as it hit the end of its length. It must be large. I began to pull it in, slowly, with a rag in my hand to prevent the line from cutting into it.

Another dolphin. Larger than the last, I estimated. I would let it tire itself out a bit. 'Mate' dropped out of the sky to alight upon the gaff. It looked an uncomfortable perch for so large a bird. Lopsided, too.

Hand over hand, I drew the dolphin closer. It was weakening, I could tell, but might have another run or two in it. Then, a great gray bulk rose from the water beside it, a huge maw lined with rows of sharp teeth engulfed the fish, and both sank beneath the surface. My line hung slack.

A shark—that I could tell, but far larger than I had ever seen or even heard tales of. It might well have been twice the length of my boat. More even, but I will not strain your credulity further. Gone? So it seemed.

So it seemed for a few seconds. It rose again, directly beside my boat, and sort of nudged it, perhaps trying to figure out what it was and whether it was good to eat. We tipped over far further than I would have liked, me holding on as best I could, the eagle launching itself with an aggrieved shriek. The monster plunged and did not return. I watched for quite some time to be certain of that and found myself glancing toward the water hours later.

And the next day too, yes. This encounter started me again thinking. No such shark swam the seas. This I knew of a certainty. Could I be, as far-fetched as it seemed, in another time? The past? The future? I would not know until I reached land and spoke to another human. I did hope humans existed in whatever time or place I now found myself.

"I'll have to make up a new bait and line," I told Mate. "It's a good thing there are more hooks."

Mate undoubtedly thought so too. I was fishing for both of us, after all.

Five

To the south they lay, more than one of them, mountains rising from the ocean. My mate had winged off that direction earlier in the day and not returned. Maybe he had found a place to roost and I would not see him again.

Him. I had decided it was probably a male from its size and the white of its feathers. Females were likely to be drabber, weren't they? Not that I did more than guess about this and if he never came back it didn't matter. It might not even matter if he did come back.

A chain of islands. Could they be the Solomons? That seemed no better nor worse guess than any. There would be people there if they were. Or even if they weren't. People who might be friendly, people who might put a spear through me. I had spied no boats so far. No smoke from fires, either, but I could be too distant yet to spy that. It might be safer to wait till dark before approaching.

Approaching over what might be treacherous reefs. No, that was not a good idea. Even more so if forty-foot sharks lurked.

Not that smaller ones wouldn't be every bit as willing to take a bite of me. I would remain offshore tonight and scout, watch for fires so I would know where villages lay before attempting to land. Best to do so well away from human habitations until I learned more of these isles.

This was a good-sized boat. I could not simply run it onto a beach. One man wouldn't be able to get it off again. I would need a place to harbor, to drop anchor or dock.

Three large islands I could spy. The little ones lying between them were too numerous to attempt counting. Whether more lay beyond sight I could not then say, but later found they did, a long chain of them extending southwestward.

I sailed past, keeping well offshore. If anyone saw my sail, they did not act on it. I saw not one sign of inhabitants. Toward evening I swung around the furthest of the three large isles and sailed back east. There. Lights. Maybe these people all lived on the southern sides of the islands. As it grew darker, I fell further away from land, not wishing to risk any reefs or rocks. Through the night, I spied a fire here or there. Not many.

I would land somewhere in the morning. Maybe on the northern coast, unseen. Yes, that was a good plan. I gazed toward the dark bulk of the mountainous island, at the little lights flickering near its beaches, and waited. No sleep. It would not be safe to drift in the night, as I did in the open ocean. Carefully, I did work my way south, thinking to come around again to the other side at dawn.

It was not to be. At first light I saw a triangular sail heading my way. Soon after, I could make out the large canoe beneath it and a dozen men at paddles. It might have been possible to outrun them with a little more breeze. I sat and waited.

Solomon Islanders were black. This, at least, I knew. So I could not be in the Solomons for the men in the approaching canoe were golden-brown of skin. Where then? Samoa? I was certain these islands were too far north to be the Societies. But these were almost certainly kanakas. I had met only a few in my voyages, for they did not often find their way to the Atlantic.

Their vessel fully was as long as mine, appearing all carved from the trunk of one tree and with an outrigger. The men sat and looked at me, expressionless, as they pulled alongside. A sudden outcry by one and then all began muttering to one another, their eyes cast upward, toward my sail. I turned to look.

Mate had returned and was perched up there as before. I greeted him with a smile and friendly word. An old friend—one who could do me not the least good but who was good to see at an uncertain time like this. I returned my gaze to the kanakas. One gestured toward the shore. Rather deferential, he seemed.

There was no other choice for me. I nodded, though these people might not know the meaning of the gesture, gave him a little bow, and turned my attention to my sail. Mate dropped from his roost to the forward bench. "I've nothing for you this morning," I told him. In a minute or two, I had the boat turned and was following my hosts toward a landing.

Good it was to have someone to follow, for I might not have been able to thread the reefs myself. A wide, placid lagoon lay before me and, beyond it, huts and houses at the mouth of a valley. A village, a stream flowing by it. The canoe was pulled partway onto the dark sand; I dropped my anchor a little off the beach, dove in, and swam to shore, as Mate launched himself and soared away.

I knew it not then but I would never see him again. Farewell, shipmate!

Six

Big men they were, for the most part, and all carried spears, spears with hooked heads carved of some bone. Fishing spears, I conjectured, though they would go into a man readily enough. A crowd gathered; the leader of my escort gave a long incomprehensible speech to them, pointing to the sky.

Who might know what notions they had of me? And of Mate, for that matter. I was burnt as dark as they from my trip beneath the equatorial sun. Possessing no mirror, I could only guess how my beard and hair looked. My only apparel was a pair of ragged trousers. The knee-length loincloths these people wore, both men and women, looked more comfortable. The nakedness of the children looked more comfortable yet.

His tale completed, the man turned to me and spoke in a language of which I knew not a single word. I shook my head—again a gesture these folk might or might not understand—and answered in English, receiving only blank looks in reply. I then essayed Spanish, which I knew fairly well. Neither language made any impression on any of them.

I intended to try out the few words of French I knew, when he called a fellow forward who addressed me in what seemed another tongue. I was as ignorant of it as the first.

My host—or captor—only laughed, and pointed to himself. "Maviki," he proclaimed. Probably his name. Or that of his tribe?

I could have told him I was Richard Brown, the name I had used until recently. "Dick," I said, placing my hand on my chest. "Call me Dick." There was no point in anything more.

"Dika," he repeated. It was close enough. Maviki nodded. Apparently they did use that gesture. I understood the next gesture too. He was inviting me to eat.

It seemed the entire village took their breakfast together, a communal meal, around mats of woven fronds. I followed him to one of these, where Maviki took a place at its head. He must be an important man here. He motioned for me to take a place at his right hand. The men all sat on that side and the women on the other.

Women. It was good to see them again! They had been nearly as scarce on Juan Fernandez as at sea. And just as much out of reach. As the men, they tended to be large. Both sexes wore many tattoos and not much else.

The man who had been called to attempt translation squatted a little behind and to one side of Maviki. The chief passed him back food now and again, and exchanged the occasional word. His chore seemed to be to teach me their language. Each food he named to me. I repeated the words to better remember them. Much of the meal consisted of various starchy pastes. And fish. Of course, there was fish.

Following the meal, all went their varied directions. Some to work, some to loaf, some to garden, some to fish. My teacher took me in hand. "Ruheyo," he said, indicating himself. Up the forested valley he led. I saw that many of the trees were not wild but fruit-bearing sorts that had been planted here. There were many breadfruit. Breadfruit I had seen in the West Indies.

We gathered a bit of an entourage, curious children for the most part. They joined in my lessons, pointing to this and that, chattering more names than I could hope to learn this morning.

I would learn. It would be good to rest here for a while and do nothing else. In time, I should know enough to ask where I might find Europeans. Or a ship might stop by. I still suspected I had touched land at Samoa but I also knew I could be completely wrong. The Marquesas, maybe? Neither seemed to jibe with what bearings I had been able to take.

And the night sky remained strange.

"Kuru," spoke Ruheyo, pointing to a breadfruit.

"Kuru," I repeated.

Seven

The name of this place—or these islands—was Aru. This, I learned, meant nothing more than 'rocks.' That is what they were, essentially, rocks rising from the ocean. Volcanic rocks.

I had been on these stones in the sea for a couple weeks now. Nothing was asked of me in the way of work or service, other than the learning of the language. The people of Aru themselves did not work all that hard. Not even those Ruheyo assured me were slaves.

A handful of nobles, of which Maviki was one, ruled the place. None of them seemed to be in overall charge. Maviki's wife, named Mire, was a large woman, a heavy woman, with many tattoos. I was not overly surprised when informed she was also Maviki's sister. Such was known of some kanaka rulers.

No, I shall not name them kanakas again. These were Aruans. Women did not seem to wield much power here but Ruheyo let me know that all inheritance was through the female line. A good reason to marry in the family, I suppose, though it supposedly kept their bloodline pure. These nobles seemed to be seen as semi-divine.

If any woman did wield power, it was the mother of Mire and Maviki. This fat old woman, named Ti'ine, sat on a raised porch before her house most of the time, gossiping or simply watching others go about their affairs. Sometimes I noted her painting designs on the bark cloth that all wore. I did too, by now. I had seen it being made from the bark of the breadfruit trees. The kuru was a staple of these people.

Ti'ine appointed herself one of my instructors. She could appoint herself pretty much anything, I gathered. Much of her instruction consisted of telling long-winded stories while I sat and listened, there in front of her post-and-beam, thatched-roof house. Maybe she was doing no more than taking advantage of a new audience, one that had never heard her tales before. It was not a bad way to learn, even if I did not understand many words.

"My great-grandfather was one of those who led us here," the old woman told me. "They had lost a great war, far away." Her eyes turned east but she might not have truly known the location of that lost homeland. "Yes, they lost a war in the land of the Mora, and took many canoes away with their families and their slaves."

I attempted a question with my broken and inadequate Aruanese. "Land of Mora. Sail to can?" I had never heard of such a place but it would be good to know.

She only shrugged. "Ruheyo might know. He sails far and trades." My tutor nodded. So that was how he knew a second language. I quizzed him on it later, as best I could.

"I have not sailed as far as the Mora lands," he told me. "They lie that way." His arm extended toward the northeast. He pivoted to point southeast. "But I have visited the mainland there. Twice, where a great river empties into the sea. It is said the gods live at its source." His smile suggested disbelief. "Those who live there say it."

"Was language Ruheyo spoke me day come?"

"No, that was the tongue of those who dwelt here when we first arrived. I trade mostly with them, on other islands."

I would have to learn more of this. In time. A great river and land to the southeast? Maybe just another island but apparently more substantial than these Arus. I tried to think of what that land might be. Somewhere in the Dutch Indies, maybe? Or New Guinea? That would make more sense but I should not be near those places.

"See, um, men like Dika there?"

He solemnly—mock-solemnly I was sure—shook his head and answered, "No one has ever seen a man like Dika."

That was not encouraging. "What trade?"

"Here in the islands, I carry bark cloth and trade for pots." He glanced at a nearby earthen crock. "We do not make pots. Other things, too. There is not much to trade for on the far side of the sea. That is why I have not journeyed there again."

I noted a pair of women eyeing me as we walked along. I did not mind eyeing the women of Aru myself, even if they tended to be robust. Some had done more than eye me but, so far, I had not yielded to temptation.

I did not know how to say 'proposition.' "Women, um, Dika me, um—" I didn't know at all how to say what I was trying.

Ruheyo was amused but answered seriously. "They wish to share in your mana. You are believed to be a great noble by some. Or a messenger of the gods. Who else would travel in the company of a sacred eagle?" My companion then snickered. "They think you good to look at, too."

I was certainly more presentable than when I had arrived. "Share mana?" I had read of mana, though my understanding of it was nebulous, at best.

"By coupling with you. If they have a child, all the better."

Oh. Ruheyo seemed to think nothing wrong with this. I could not be so certain of husbands or fathers. I did not know this people well enough yet.

Nor was I inclined to become entangled with them. I was going to sail on, wasn't I? But why? The Aru Islands might be as good a place to spend my life as any. Maybe with one of those young ladies giggling over there.

There was little back in the States I truly missed.

Eight

"I, um, second on big canoe." The term 'first mate' would mean nothing to him. "Sail far, uh, men–" I searched for a word. "Men bad." The word I had found referred to spoiled fruit but I felt it would get the meaning across. "Men bad fight."

Ruheyo smiled at my usage. "Enemies," he supplied.

"Enemies." I nodded. "Enemies kill chief, Dika make slave. Escape. Away sail!"

"Did you slay many first?" asked Maviki. Nearly a month into my stay, he was finally asking into just who I was.

"Killed all." Which was truth, even if I didn't do it personally. I had nothing against those Chilean guards, even though they were a brutal bunch. The men who had cheated and betrayed us, killing the captain, accusing the rest of us of piracy–those I hated. I doubted I would ever find revenge.

"You will come and fight with us," the chief said. "We too have enemies." He looked me over. "Dika should have tattoos," he stated.

Though a sailor for some dozen of years–since a boy–I had no ink. Tattoos marked one as a common seaman, I felt, and wouldn't do for one who expected to captain a ship someday soon.

On my next voyage, I had hoped, but I ended up only captaining a twenty-foot boat.

"At least one to identify him as of our tribe," opined Hevarua, another of the nobles.

"Maybe Dika should have a wife, too," interjected Ruheyo. He was not part of this little council but seemed willing to offer advice. "He has been trying some out."

Maviki laughed deeply at that. "So I have heard! A noble girl for Dika, yes, but not until he has his tattoos so she will recognize him as an important man."

I was to be important? "Maybe eagle?" I asked, and ran a forefinger across my upper chest. I might not mind that. All three noblemen there began to jabber at each other at once, too quickly for me to follow. Maviki, at least, seemed amused by the suggestion.

He turned back to me and stated, "The great sea eagle is sacred to Marahina, the Woman of the Moon. It is rare for a man to wear her symbols but we think it would be right for you." One of his companions whispered something to him. "Yes, yes. We must speak to the priestess first." Maviki paused and considered and then, seemingly satisfied with the decision, asked, "With which weapons are you most skilled, Dika?"

For a moment, I thought I might claim to be a trader like Ruheyo, not a fighting man. Only for a moment; I recognized it would not jibe with their idea of me being noble.

"We know you can not throw a spear," said Ruheyo.

Not a fishing spear. I'd given it a try and decided to stick with a hook and line. Could I claim proficiency with any weapon? I'd never had call to use anything more than a marlin spike. But like any sailor, I had carried a knife. "Um, knife maybe," I said. "Or cutlass. Them like big knife. Club some maybe."

I was a bit surprised that answer satisfied them. I told them some of my home, mostly that it was very far away and I was not certain how to get back. That satisfied them too. Then Ruheyo and I wandered down to the lagoon. I liked to check on my boat from time to time, though I had not lifted its anchor since arriving.

It was a broad and shallow lagoon. Shallow that is in the distance out to the reefs, not in the depth of the water. I doubted it a safe harbor in any sort of real storm. That did not matter to these Aruans; they simply dragged their canoes well up onto the sand. Even the biggest ones.

Those were of a length with my boat, more or less. Most were smaller. All had outriggers, always to the left side though no one could explain why. It was always done that way and most felt it would be somehow wrong to do otherwise. It might even be a taboo. There were many taboos, not that most were enforced in any manner. People just knew they should not be broken, that it would be unlucky not to follow the rules. It was not good for their mana.

I waded and swam out to the boat, pulling myself in over the stern. Ruheyo followed me; as a traveler, vessels held an interest for him. As I extended an arm to help him aboard, I asked, "Shark any water here?"

He swung an arm in the direction of the horizon. "On the reef. Mostly small." A crooked grin. "But not always."

If big sharks visited the reef, they could certainly swim in closer to the beach as well. I peered into the crystalline water but saw only small darting silver fish. "Big big shark see sailing. Boat long two."

The man raised his eyebrows at this. "And you live."

"Bump canoe. Go away."

"Few encounter Ni'inoe and survive. He is sacred to Wanga, the shark god." Ruheyo gave me a long, appraising look. "Twice you have been marked by messengers of the gods."

"Twice enough," I informed him.

Nine

It was now debated whether my tattoos should identify me as an adherent of the moon goddess or of the shark god. Wanga, it seemed, had a strong cult among these people.

I had heard of a number of gods by this time and undoubtedly there were more of whom I had not heard. Tu was important to the nobles. He was considered the source of their authority—and of their mana—as well as being the deity of warfare.

Neither Tu nor Wanga appealed to me. Nor did Ra, the god of the sky and supposedly the father of them all. The creator god. I'd had enough of creator gods when I was young.

Ruheyo was guiding me now, if I understood it properly, to meet some sort of high priestess. A priestess of Marahina. For the first time, I had left the valley of his tribe and traveled across the ridges. It was a rugged path.

"Maranua, she is named," he told me. "It is both title and name, not her birth name but one worn by she chosen to lead the priestesses of the moon."

"Seen no other, um, tribes. Will we visit?"

"We could. There are villages in many valleys." He paused a moment. "Your speech improves, Dika."

I thought so too but knew I was still clumsy in the language of the Aruans. It was a complex and baffling language, and I might never be truly fluent. "Are you a, um, numerous people?"

"We are not. Not so many came here and not so long ago." We trudged on a bit, through a steeper section of trail, before he continued. "Even before the war, sailors found these islands and some came here to live, to follow the old ways that had been discarded among the Mora. More came after the fighting, refugees, four or five generations ago. There was already a people here but they were not many, either. They still are not."

"Two peoples live peace? Um, in peace?"

"I do. I trade with them. The nobles would rather fight them." There was no mirth in his quick, sharp laugh. "When they don't fight each other."

The forest gave way to scrub, high on these rocky ridges dividing the valleys. It looked difficult to push through, if one had no trail to follow. So I mentioned to my companion.

"Dangerous, too," replied Ruheyo, "to stray. One might be speared as an enemy. It is always safer to approach our neighbors from the sea."

"But safe here?"

"Yes. Attacking those who walk this trail is a taboo. As is using it to go to war."

Most of the fighting here, it seemed, consisted of small skirmishes and ambushes. That was the fighting between tribes, between valleys. I had heard tales of actual warfare, of voyaging to other islands to raid enemy villages. More than one tribe might join together for that.

I wanted no part of either sort of conflict. To live in peace in these Aru Islands would not be bad at all. Some might call it a paradise. It was certainly pleasant. I reminded myself a ship full of white men might show up any time. Would I leave then? Or might I just set off in my own boat one of these days, seeking?

We descended into another valley, much like the one we had left. My guide took a trail that branched off to our right, up its length, between the high ridges. We crossed many small streams rushing down from them through the jungle. I saw no other humans but many birds of many colors. These sang and called all around, their voices rising above a drone of insects. Then we crossed over the valley, grown narrow here, and began to climb again, our path steep, at times up what was almost a cliff. The rock was dark and much eroded, crumbling. One had to be wary of ones footing.

That ridge, too, we crossed, to reach what seemed more a ravine than a valley. I spied a high waterfall at its far end. Waterfalls of one size or another were common here, where it rained much and the land rose and fell sharply. "Beyond the falls," announced Ruheyo, "lies the Valley of the Moon."

Ten

A lake? Yes, a little mountain lake. A stream ran down the bowl-like valley from it to the falls we had passed by. Now we stood on a low ridge, looking toward what might be a small village beside the water. Cultivated fields could be made out here and there along the banks of the stream.

"This is some sort—?" I couldn't come up with a word.

"A shrine," said Ruheyo. "It is a shrine. A sacred place."

"A sacred place," I repeated. It looked it—an idyllic setting if ever there were one. At once I felt an urge to linger in this valley. Perhaps to never leave it.

We set off toward the village. "Maranua is a very high noble," Ruheyo said after a while. "Be careful around her and try not to break too many taboos. I know you will break some for you are most ignorant."

"Why see priestess I?"

"Better ask why the priestess is seeing you, Dika." He gathered his thoughts for a moment. "Most are willing to see you as noble. You made an impression on your arrival! But Maranua must agree before you can be accepted."

"If not?"

"Then a commoner like me. Better than being a slave. Ha, freer than both noble and slave, I am!"

Being a commoner did not seem so bad. They'd probably expect me to work some, though. Not that I was staying. "Could trader be like Ruheyo. Have boat already."

"The nobles impose much on us, Dika. I could be about business rather than attending some stranger the ocean brought by." He chuckled after that but I suspected there was truth in it.

The buildings ahead, once I could better see them, proved to be of the sort with which I was already familiar. Posts and beams, walls of woven mats, roofs of thatch. Rectangular. None were particularly large; one stood as high as the dwelling of Maviki—or of Ti'ine, maybe I should say—but was not as long. There were a number of carved wooden statues about, some taller than me. I had seen similar effigies at the coast, though not so many together.

A woman emerged from the largest house as we approached it. Ruheyo at once crouched, hands and knees on the ground, forehead in the dirt. I figured a noble such as I should not debase myself. At least not quite to that extent. Rather, I gave her a deep bow, as I might some Spanish lady.

"That's enough, Ruheyo," she said. "Do get up."

He scrambled to his feet. "My lady, this is—"

"I know, I know. This is the eagle man." She looked me over. I looked her over at the same time. Short for an Aruan, quite young and undeniably fat. The typical kilt of bark cloth hung from her hips, as a short cape did from her shoulders. Feathers. It was made all of feathers, mostly yellow but some green.

The nobles had sometimes worn peaked caps of feathers, crowns of a sort, on ceremonial occasions. Yellow and red those were.

A handful of women, of varied age, stood behind the high priestess, giving us curious looks. Probably giving me curious looks. "Walk with me," spoke Maranua. "You too, Ruheyo. We might need you."

She set off toward the lake. I fell in beside here; Ruheyo followed at a discreet distance. "My lady," I asked, "lake sacred is?"

"One might call it sacred if one wished. And address me as Maranua."

That being a title, it was probably just as good as 'my lady' or any other. Maybe better. "Lake very beautiful is."

"Yes, even to I who see it every day. I see dawn's light touch it gently as the sun rises above the mountains. I watch the moon reflected in it. Of these I never tire." She giggled. "I swim there too."

"Is, um, permitted?" I meant for guys like me.

"There is no taboo. There was a truly sacred lake in the land of the Mora. I believe we built our shrine here only in memory of it." More seriously then, Maranua said, "It is told that the priestesses of the moon there, they who dwelt by that lake, prophesied. None of us have that gift but Marahina speaks to me in dreams sometimes. She spoke to me of you, Dika."

I held back any sort of flippant reply, though one came readily enough to my tongue. "Will you tell me of this, Maranua?"

"Later. Ruheyo! Why are you lurking back there?"

"I would not intrude, my lady," came his ready reply.

"Hmmph. You can tell your nobles—Maviki's bunch, right?—that Dika here is definitely of high noble blood. I knew that before ever you arrived."

I wondered if her goddess had told her so.

"But whose tattoos should he wear, my lady?"

"I'll decide that later. Or tell you what I have decided later. Now that Dika has spoken of swimming, I wish to do so myself." We stood on a slab of dark rock beside the lake. "You come in too, Dika."

She carefully folded her cape, doffed her loincloth, and dove in. I followed.

Eleven

"This shrine serves as sanctuary for those escaping fighting or prosecution," Maranua told me.

Ruheyo sat a little behind me, as he had Maviki when I first took a meal with the Aruans. This was the position of an attendant rather than a guest. I had learned no taboo prevented commoners from eating with nobles, though they had to take a place further down the mat. Having an attendant, a man or a woman, seated close by was sometimes handy when nobles took meals.

Never fear that Ruheyo went hungry. Maranua herself would pass him bowls as she chattered on. "They may stay until their trouble passes," the priestess continued. "And they work for us while they are here. Those who can."

"How long stay?" I asked.

"Until we decide they have made amends to the gods. Those who break taboos and such, that is; those who fly from war may return when it is safe."

It was undoubtedly convenient to be the sole maker of that decision. People would stay and work until told otherwise.

"They have the word of Maranua to keep them safe," Ruheyo added. "None would dare go against that."

It was maybe worth coming here and serving then. Good to have her as a friend too. That she had decreed me a noble might or might not be so good.

No refugees attended us here. These were the other priest-esses who served and then sat to eat with us. I counted five but didn't know if that was all of them. We ate in a central room of the largest house; too much rain was falling outside. The roof was supported by great bamboo posts and beams. I hadn't known bamboo could grow so large before coming to the Arus. Some of the posts were veritable logs.

I had thought it a temple of sorts when we first spied it but, no, it was the home of the priestesses. The actual shrine to Marahina was somewhat smaller and was not enclosed within walls.

"Priestesses, um, have no husbands?" I hadn't seen celibacy in this land so far but one always happens upon new things.

"Oh, they don't live in this house. The girls have to go visit their men." Maranua snickered. "Whether husbands or lovers."

"But it is right that we sisters gather for meals," averred one of the women.

"At least now and then," added another. "When we have such handsome guests."

"Ruheyo is always very friendly when he visits!" General laughter followed. Ruheyo had no comment—wisely so, no doubt.

In time, each woman rose and went off to whatever business— or pleasure—she might have. Maranua rose too, and held out a hand. "There is a little house just for me. We will speak there." Down the slope we walked, toward the water, shining in the light of a new-risen full moon. A little way along, she glanced back at the man who followed. "Oh, we won't need you, Ruheyo." He fell aside as the priestess led on to a hut beside the lake.

"Ruheyo won't be lonely," Maranua confided. "Let's talk out here." We sat. No words came for a time, as the priestess's eyes were fixed on the rising orb. "We wanted you here when Marahina is at her greatest," she said at last. "Not that the moon really matters that much; it is not the goddess."

But a potent symbol of her power. I understood that. "She comes you to in dream?"

A little nod, a distracted nod. "I do not truly see her. It may not be wise for a mortal to see a goddess! But she speaks to me; in my dreams I hear her words."

Shamans and priests the world over claimed such things, did they not? I had met those who called themselves mediums back home, men and women who said they could speak to the departed. Charlatans? Or merely the deluded? I did not know, but I was sure Maranua believed her deity spoke to her.

Dreams may be interpreted in many a way, after all. "You are high priestess because Marahina speak to you?"

"Maybe. Or maybe because I am round like the moon!"

It was wise to laugh at her jest. Not too heartily, perhaps.

"She has told me you belong to her," Maranua continued. "Nothing more." She looked again toward the moon. "This would be a good night for dreams. And much else." She was looking at me, now.

And I had no objections. The woman took my hand and led me to her little house.

Later, I asked, "How long claim sanctuary I, o priestess of the moon?"

"As long as you desire." A giggle. "Or as long as I desire you."

Twelve

A flute? A plaintive tune—barely a tune—was rising from somewhere near the lake. Maranua stirred beside me. "That's Arisu. He sought sanctuary here years ago and fell in love both with a priestess and our valley. Now he plays by the water each morning."

Not so bad a life, maybe, in the idyllic south seas setting of many a romance. "Now I bother him not go down to bathe."

"Others will." They were used to him, not doubt, and he to them. "I did not dream last night, Dika. You kept me too busy!"

"Or your goddess not wish to intrude."

Another of her giggles erupted. I rather liked them. I also suspected they might grow annoying in time. "Oh, yes, that is it. She gave little Maranua some time for herself!"

Sudden thunder shook the roof above us. Bits of thatch filtered down, tiny golden flecks in the half-light. "It's raining inside," said Maranua. "Outside soon, I think."

Rain I had come to expect in the Arus. Violent storms I had not experienced.

"A storm brought me here." I still did not understand that storm and how it surrounded me one moment, to be gone the next. Nor did I understand much I had seen since. The skies; the night skies remained an enigma no matter how long I stared up at them.

"Tell me about it. Tell me about *you*, Dika."

So I did for the next hour, as the wind rattled the walls and the thunder crashed and waterfalls pounded the roof. Of my life both before and after the storm I spoke, though I doubted she understood much of it.

"A storm," she said, when I was finished. "My ancestors—the ancestors of the Mora—also came through such a storm. In nine great canoes they came. So say the epics."

"To a land east of here."

"Yes. They named it the Land of the Peaceful Sky, after passing through storm. That is what Mora means."

So it did. I hadn't put that together. "And like you, they found the night sky strange and the stars all in the wrong places. I would not like that at all!"

"It bothers me some does. Has the storm passed?"

"I think so. Let's get some breakfast."

It was still breezy, gusts coming and going, and bringing showers with them. A nearly black sky had given way to gray, becoming lighter from minute to minute. There, a bit of blue broke through for a moment. It might be another fine day in paradise before long.

The mountain peaks remained clad in the mists of rain. What was that speck I saw, dark, emerging from those mists? An eagle? Maybe Mate had come to visit.

As it flew closer, I saw it was larger than any eagle. Nor was its shape like any bird I knew; more that of a devil! It dove straight toward Maranua and me. I had no weapon. No one carried them in this shrine, this sanctuary.

What I did was undoubtedly stupid. I pushed my companion to the ground and fell atop her, in hopes of providing protection. The creature passed close over us, perhaps missing its intended mark. Prey? Were we prey? I glimpsed sharp teeth and long leathery wings as it rose again. It would surely make another pass. "Stay down," I ordered. After, I was not sure whether I spoke it in Maranua's language or mine. I saw Ruheyo rushing toward us as I rose. He had no weapons either.

A loud screech, somewhere along the lines of a steam whistle. I looked up to see the thing hovering, readying itself for another attack, most likely. It could more clearly be made out now. Bat-like wings spread on either side of the narrow, deep-chested body. Clawed feet; the wings sported claws as well. A crested head with a long toothy snout topped it all.

Out of frustration, perhaps, I picked up a rock and hurtled it at the creature. It bounced off its chest and it backed up a bit. Surprised, I think. I followed it with another, hitting a wing this time. It screeched again and climbed higher. It surely intended to dive at me now.

Rocks were not going to do the job. To their credit, some of the folk here, both men and women, were running toward us. I would not blame at all those who ran the other way. That was sensible when one had no way of fighting.

Some of those foolhardy individuals had picked up lengths of bamboo from a nearby stack. "All together here!" cried out Ruheyo. "Like this!" He knelt beside Maranua, holding his own bamboo stave upright, its butt against the ground. The others surrounded us. Down came the beast, to be baffled by this fence. It swooped away again.

But only to once more hover. "It must be very hungry," said someone.

"Or it was sent," said another.

I doubted it had much brains but it changed its attack now, coming in low and knocking the staves aside. Its claws raked one man before it again ascended. Couldn't it have grabbed someone right then if it was after prey?

A broken bamboo lay beside me, its end sharp where it had splintered. I grasped it and stepped away from Maranua, waving my arms. The creature came directly for me. Whether I had been its intended prey all along or I had simply caught its attention now, I could not guess. Nor had I time to think about it.

Would it come straight on with that murderous maw or turn to grasp me with its taloned feet? That I did not have time to think about either, but I suspected the latter. Yes, it did turn, reaching to clutch me, carry me away. To a nest? To its young? Who could know? I drove the improvised spear with all my strength into its body as it crashed into me and then cartwheeled wing over wing to lie broken some distance away.

The impact had been less than I expected. It must be lightly built. That made sense when I had leisure to think about it. We walked over—cautiously—to look at the body. Quite dead it was, the broken wings twisted about it. They would have extended somewhat more than twenty feet from tip to tip when it was in flight. The body was covered with a fine fur, save for the naked reptilian head.

"Are you all right, Dika?" breathed Maranua. "There is much blood on you!"

"Some of it yours," said Ruheyo. "You are cut up a bit. Nothing broken though, is there?"

"Does not seem to be." Not even a finger. That might have been just good fortune.

Ruheyo perused the remains. "A lalun," said he, his voice and manner matter-of-fact. "They nest in the high peaks, in the isles far to the south. The storm winds might have carried it here."

They might well have. Indeed, it seemed probable. But I could not forget that someone had said it might have been sent. Was that possible?

And by whom?

Thirteen

Though my cuts were superficial I was quite bruised up and moving stiffly by that night. This did not prevent me from doing my best by Maranua.

In the morning, she announced, "Marahina has spoken to me."

I did not ask what the goddess had said. Maranua would tell me when and if she wished. She did not seem eager at the moment.

We breakfasted in the big house. "Ruheyo should hear my words," she said, as we finished a meal eaten largely in silence. "And you, my sisters, any who wish," she told the priestesses in attendance. Maybe half of them were there. Maybe all were there by the time Ruheyo came. They were curious.

"First, you must know the Moon Woman claims Dika as hers. You may report that to the chiefs, Ruheyo." Maranua looked long into my face before speaking further. "The goddess of the moon told me also, Dika, that you must seek other stones than these islands. Only that. I do not understand what it means beyond the fact that you would have to leave me."

She must have known I would leave anyway. In time. Maybe this dream gave her an excuse to say farewell.

"I do not wish to see you go. I was only told you must." Having made that clear, she added, "But maybe you could forget her words and stay here at the shrine of Marahina with me. No one would bother you or demand anything of you."

I was tempted. Part of me was tempted. "Aside from your goddess?" That would surely matter to Maranua. Eventually, it would.

"She would be very displeased with me, wouldn't she?" She pondered this but for a moment before fiercely proclaiming, "I don't care!"

Her sister priestesses exchanged meaningful looks but said nothing. Not so Ruheyo. "The goddess did not say Dika could not return, did she?" It was not a question intended for an answer. "We shall go back to the coast for now and see what comes."

"To see what comes is always wisdom," spoke one of the older priestesses.

Maranua only nodded her consent. She would not allow tears to come now. Maybe later. "I know the way here now," I informed her. "I know where to seek sanctuary."

There were no dreams that night; no, not for either of us. Not much sleep either. In the darkness before morning, I set off with my guide, returning to the village of Maviki, to the lagoon where my boat remained anchored.

My boat. I might as well call it that. I owned it now. He who had tied it to the docks of Juan Fernandez might have been killed by the escaped convicts. He certainly wasn't going to come seeking it. And was I going to sail it further? Again, it was best to see what comes.

"The flying beast," I said to Ruheyo as we crossed out of the valley, "what did you name it?"

"Lalun. It is a Ta'i word. I don't know if it means anything; it is just what they call the creatures."

"I would meet the Ta'i."

"You already have. Some of the slaves in the village are of their people. But," he went on, "perhaps you would care to sail with me when I trade with them." A chuckle that might almost have been a snicker. "It would be a start on seeking other stones."

That was so. I was seeking more than stones. I was seeking answers. Where was I? How came that primitive flying reptile here or the shark twice the size of any that swam the seas I knew?

And how came those strange, baffling stars? "I would gladly sail with you, Ruheyo," I said. "My boat or yours?"

He seemed a little surprised by the question. Ruheyo must not have considered that option. "Yours would hold much more than my canoe," he admitted. "It also might scare those we visit. Best to stick with the familiar."

"And what do you carry?" I had the breath to converse now we descended.

"Tools of obsidian and lava rock and shell, and the materials for their making. Pottery, which they make and we do not. Woven mats. Bark cloth. Wooden bowls and other crafts of that sort. That is something our people do." He frowned. "There are not so many trees on the southern islands."

We trudged on a little way before I told him, "I was a trader among my people."

"So I suspected. Don't let anyone know," he advised. "The nobles do not have a high opinion of our calling."

On the second day, we stood again by the ocean. I had mixed feelings as I looked to the horizon, looked to my little boat. I turned and looked toward the mountains. Somewhere up there lay a valley where one could forget strife and seeking.

I would sail away and never see it again, wouldn't I?

Fourteen

"We hear you are a hero now!" said Hevarua.

"A slayer of monsters," added Maviki, "like the demigods of legend."

The third high noble of the village, Hohevi, asked, "Is it true you speared it with a broken bamboo?" His eyes shifted quickly to a stolid Ruheyo, seated nearby, and back. "So we have heard."

"It was at hand," I told them. "I wasn't about to wrestle the creature."

"We have better weapons for you," Maviki said, signaling to an attendant. "You are not a big man—"

"Even if you kill monsters," interjected Hohevi.

"Yes, so we would not give you a heavy club." I had mentioned clubs to them, for want of anything better. The noble was handed a sword of sorts, a flat piece of wood with a row of shark teeth down each side.

"You can bite like Wanga with this," spoke Hevarua. He sounded rather eager to see it happen.

"Although we are told you are not the shark god's. Hevarua," Maviki said, nodding in his fellow's direction, "is our priest of Wanga. You are invited to share in our rites."

I caught just a trace of a grimace on Ruheyo's face. He could not always hide his feelings, despite apparent long practice. "Are they soon?" I asked. It was best to be polite about it.

"Not tomorrow night?" he asked Hevarua.

"No, the next."

Maviki nodded. "We have a spear for you too. You seem to know how to use one after all."

I thanked the men for both weapons and hoped I would not be asked to use them. The valley of Marahina had become more desirable than ever.

They had not mentioned tattoos. I assumed that would come up in time. Wives, too.

"It is best you take their invitation," Ruheyo advised later, "and attend the rites once. That should be enough. We can sail away the next day, if you wish."

That sounded good to me. I wouldn't mind sailing away before this ceremony of Wanga worshipers.

"Be warned," the trader went on, "the rites of Wanga are not for the squeamish. React to nothing that happens, nor take any part in it."

I spent the next couple days helping Ruheyo assemble his trade goods—making certain Maviki and the others knew I was not myself trading but only letting the man show me around. My status, I knew, was still not quite fixed. Was I the equal of the three high nobles here? Was I of sufficient birth to marry into their families?

Two of those nobles, Maviki and Hohevi themselves, came to escort me to the rites of Wanga. Secret rites, I discovered, for they put a bark cloth across my eyes and led me blind. The path led upward and was rocky; that I could tell. When I was allowed to see again, I stood in a torch-lit cave. One side was open to the sea, the moon-lit horizon clear to me but naught else visible. We were high up. Surely this cave was in one of the cliff walls rising from the water.

Both my companions wore grotesque masks now, though their tattoos proclaimed their identities. Twenty men or more stood in the place. Some were surely commoners; Wanga welcomed all, it seemed. Only one other than I was without mask, one I knew to be a slave. He seemed terrified.

Maybe I was too. I certainly had premonitions of unpleasant things to come.

There was Hevarua. Also masked, of course, but not easy to miss, being both a big man and the leader here. He chanted something I could not understand, for the most part. There were occasional responses from the others.

Those others were getting worked up. I noted that all held shark teeth in their hands. They would wave these about. stabbing the air each time they answered their priest now. Hevarua shouted something. Again I couldn't tell what but his followers knew. They dragged the slave forward, two burly individuals holding his arms. The priest slashed the captive across the chest with his shark tooth and, one by one, the others followed his example, leaving the man torn and bleeding from twenty or more gashes. Was this to be like that death of a thousand cuts of which I had heard?

No. The moaning, gibbering slave was dragged to the ledge, held there peering down toward the dark sea. "Feed, Wanga!" cried out Havarua and the man was pushed over the edge. There was nothing to see in the darkness below, of course. Maybe sharks did eat him.

Silently, the cult of Wanga filed out. I followed, my eyes again covered. Not that I would ever wish to find my way here. And I was not sure I would ever carry my shark tooth sword.

Fifteen

"Captured warriors are sacrificed to Tu," Ruheyo informed me. "Especially if they are noble, to gain their mana. Only slaves go to Wanga."

"Sorry I am to say this, friend," I replied, "but your people went down in my, um, estimation last night."

"That happened to me long ago."

Last night's brutality had also led me to question having left Maranua. The woman was not so desirable of herself, perhaps, though I liked her and liked making love to her. It was the sanctuary of her valley that drew me, the place of peace of which she was the personification.

But I had chosen to voyage away with the trader Ruheyo this morning. We were already well out at sea. I was learning to sail an outrigger canoe. There were differences from the boats and sails I knew but the basics I found the same. West and south we sailed, away from the group of islands I knew and down the long chain inhabited mostly by Ta'i. We would cross a sizable gap of empty water first, something of a divide between the two populations.

A divide for now. By trade and by conquest, there would be one people in the Aru Islands one day. A day yet far in the future.

"Much further is to sail to mainland?" I asked my companion.

"Much further, yes. Weeks, not days."

That was not promising. "Not worth trip?"

A shrug. "It can be. I and others have carried flint from the mainland. It is not found in these islands. That and the hides of a beast that lives in the rivers. Like a great lizard, it is. We use the hides for shields and armor."

The crocodile, he meant surely. "What you have to trade in return?"

"Little, I must admit. Obsidian is most prized. The skin and teeth of the shark can be traded, for the people there do not venture much into the sea."

There was seemingly no modern civilization on those coasts, only a stone age culture as his own. No metal. Did Ruheyo know of metal? Surely I had some with me. My knife I had left on my boat.

The fish hooks. I had brought my lines along with me. "Have seen ever you a, um, substance? Material? Stuff like this?" I held up one of the hooks.

He examined it carefully. "Something like it comes from far up the river. They make knives of it, and ornaments." Ruheyo seemed to dismiss the memory with a crooked little smile. "The knives are much too dear for me to purchase one. All my trade goods together would not be enough." He rummaged in the pouch hanging from his waist. "I did get this across the sea. I thought to give it to a woman some day, if I find one I want to marry."

It was a not-so-tiny bead of solid gold. "Rus, they called it there," he told me.

It did not seem so valuable here as it would have in other places and times. "Make sure she deserves it."

He only laughed and returned the trinket to his pouch.

Days indeed passed before we came to our first harbor. These islands were lower than those we had left, worn down perhaps by eons of tropical rain. Yes, I knew the world was a very old place; I was not one of those who believed it created six thousand years ago. I was not inclined to believe it created at all.

There were more open fields here, and more coastal marshes. Mangrove grew along the shores in many places. The people, the Ta'i, built houses not too unlike those of their neighbors, save placed high on stilts.

Ruheyo sailed boldly in and strolled into the village, trusting these Ta'i folk to know him and that he came to trade in peace. The ubiquitous pigs and chickens of Aru villages scratched and rooted around and under the houses here, as well. "It is said we brought the first domesticated animals to the islands," Ruheyo said. "The Ta'i had no chickens, no pigs. No dogs for that matter."

The people themselves looked little different from the Aruans I already knew, a little darker of skin, a little slighter of build. No one denied there was Ta'i heritage among the commoners of the Arus, and even more among the slave class. The women's skirts were longer, the men's hair cropped shorter. Aruans let it grow long and often tied it in a knot behind the head.

At once, Ruheyo began chatting with them in their own language. That it was a start to buying and selling seemed certain but none of his wares, nor those of the Ta'i, were yet produced. All being apparently satisfactory, we turned back to our canoe.

"It will be useful to have someone help me carry things on this trip. The Ta'i are curious about you, of course. They can see you are not of my people."

What he had told them he didn't let me know. "They seem friendly to you."

"Here, they are friendly. Do not doubt that an ambitious Ta'i warrior might try to overtake us on the open sea and rob us all we carry. Including our heads."

We began carrying Ruheyo's trade goods into the village. Apparently the thievery he feared on the sea would not occur here, for he was willing to leave them unattended. His wares included many utilitarian tools and vessels, formed of the soft volcanic rock which underlay pretty much all the islands. It was relatively easy to work and as durable as any other readily available material. This was one of the items he traded for Ta'i pottery.

It was also heavy! It took a while to carry many lava rock bowls up to the village. Worse, we had to take them up a ladder to an elevated platform of bamboo, before one of the big houses. Communal houses, it seemed. They were of bamboo as well.

We slept on the platform that night. The next day we carried everything back to our canoe, what we had taken in trade, what we had not been able to trade, and set sail again. It all happened again that afternoon at another village.

"I do not carry goods to the inland villages," Ruheyo explained. "There are Ta'i traders who will do that, and make a further profit on what I have brought them."

We sailed on, day after day, down the long chain of islands, stopping and trading until all the Aruan had brought was gone.

Sixteen

"The way home is quicker," said Ruheyo, "with no stops. And the current will be with us. The winds—probably. The prevailing winds."

It seemed that current and those winds would be more favorable if we sailed further south, away from the islands, and made a wide loop back to our place of origin. Or maybe he felt it was safer. We remained north of the equator. I could make that out but nothing more of our position.

"Your trading has gone well, hasn't it?"

"It has. Maybe I can afford that wife now."

"And stay home for a while so you can have many children?" A thought that had come to me before came again. "They would be of your status?"

"A woman's status determines that of her children. If she is a commoner, they will be commoners, even if the father is the highest noble of the land."

"And if commoner like you marry noble woman?"

"Her kin would probably kill me." He laughed but I believed he spoke truth. "But not all children come from marriage, after all. A noble woman has noble offspring, though they would be handicapped if they have no father of rank to help them find a place. Such tend to end up serving as warriors, and not always for their own village or tribe."

Knowing men and that they are the same all around the world, I suspected there were more than a few noble children with fathers of commoner blood. Despite their many taboos, the Aruans seem to find few objections to love-making. But I had learned they felt relations between those of unequal rank—or equal, for that matter—had its effects on the mana of both.

The sailing proved as easy as Ruheyo had promised. It was a big canoe for one man to handle. Maybe Ruheyo had taken along other helpers on his previous trading voyages.

It was on the second day we spied the snake. I spied the snake and pointed it out to Ruheyo, not recognizing at first what it was. I thought it maybe another school of flying fish, as we had frequently seen in these waters.

"The great sea snake," he commented. "I have seen one only once before."

It was a snake, its undulating black and white striped form appearing and disappearing as it passed through the waves. Stretched out, it might have had thirty feet of length. My immediate question was, "Is it a danger?"

"I think not." Ruheyo sounded reasonably confident. "The small sea snakes do not attack men, though they sometimes bother divers. Only curious, I think those ones are. Or seeking mates, and mistaking arms and legs for other snakes!" His eyes remained fixed on our visitor for some time. "I am sure even the giant ones eat nothing nearly as large as a man. I do not expect him to try to swallow us."

But the snake did not leave us, paralleling our course through the day. It made even the imperturbable trader nervous. "Yet another omen to attach to you, Dika," he joked. "The eagle and ni'inoe and lalun and and now the great sea snake. This is the stuff of the epics."

I desired no more such signs, nor to appear in any epic of the Aruans. I could not help but think the snake—a true sea serpent— was watching us. Watching me.

As ever, we took turns at watches through the night. My sleep was fitful when I tried to lie down. All that had been put aside these weeks I traveled with Ruheyo, these peaceful, thoughtless weeks, returned, clamoring, vying for my attention.

In the morning, the giant sea snake was gone and all seemed to return to normal. It had not; not for me. Soon I would be back in the village, facing once again the decisions I had put aside. I was half of a mind to set out at once for Maranua and her shrine. I had sought other stones, had I not? It might be enough to satisfy her, to think I had done as she believed her goddess bade me.

And marry her? I did not know what customs and taboos might apply there. It would be enough to be with her. I looked to the empty horizons all about me. My other love, my first love—the sea. I might never again look upon it if I chose that sanctuary in the mountains.

"You have a woman picked out for a wife?" I asked Ruheyo. It was on my mind now.

"There are possibilities. More than one young woman would accept a wealthy trader as her husband." That seemed to be all he would say but after a long pause, he stated, "There is a Ta'i woman I love. I may marry her and make her village my home."

"But continue trading."

"Yes." This time, he said no more.

A Ta'i village would not hold him. Nor one of his own people, for that matter. I considered bringing up the woman in every port idea but wisely–I believe–held my tongue. As did I, Ruheyo had choices to make.

I dreamed that night. Perhaps I had Maranua and her words on my mind, for I dreamed of stones. Of gems. Four they were, each of a different color. They floated a while in the darkness and disappeared.

Seventeen

"You speak better now," observed Maviki.

"I had nothing to do but talk to Ruheyo all day. And night."

"Ah. You will have things to keep you busy now," Hohevi informed me.

"Yes. We are going to war!"

My thoughts, inevitably, went again to the shrine of Marahina and the sanctuary to be found there. "War? With one one our neighbors?" Those sorts of little raids occurred from time to time. Sometimes, someone actually was killed.

"A great raid against the Ta'i," announced Hevarua. "Many tribes come together for it!"

"The Ta'i? What do they have that you might want?"

Maviki actually spat. "Pah, we want nothing of them."

"Maybe their land," said Hohevi. "Some of the young men need more room."

"Yes, yes, maybe. But war is to prove ourselves to Tu and to gain mana."

I felt a bit sick to my stomach. Not that I had any particular liking for the Ta'i but they had seemed good enough folk. And peaceful, at least while I had been with them. "You, ah, take captives?"

Hevarua nodded with considerable enthusiasm. "We keep the women as slaves and feast on the men!"

"None are worthy of sacrifice to Tu, being only Ta'i dogs," added Maviki.

I felt sicker now. And I made a decision. "I should take my boat. It would hold many warriors."

"Yes," agreed Maviki. "We all must prepare."

Prepare I did, checking over my craft carefully, its hull, its sail, and then provisioning it. Provisioning it well, for I would be carrying many warriors, would I not?

Ruheyo came down to the black sand beach as I busied myself. He watched for a while before speaking. "The nobles like the idea of you having your own large canoe full of warriors. Such things mark one as a high noble and suited to their company." I will not deny there may have been some sarcasm in his voice.

"I am glad they approve." I did not hide my own sarcasm. "I ask something of you, Ruheyo. I ask you to carry a farewell to Maranua, if you should find your way someday to her shrine. Tell her—tell her I seek stones."

"Do you make a farewell to me as well, Friend Dika?" The trader could guess what I intended.

"I think I do, Friend Ruheyo. Who knows? I might find my way again to this shore."

He shook his head, slowly, pensively. "I would hope it is so."

But we both doubted it. Ruheyo placed his right hand on my left shoulder and I the same with him, the greeting of equals among these people. Then he turned and left.

The next day, all was in readiness. It was an hour yet, maybe, to sunset. "I must give my boat a trial run before the fleet sails." I announced to those there, pretending to ponder the sun, low in the sky. "I should be back before dark."

Outward I sailed, across the reefs, toward open ocean. There was a good breeze. I set my sail and set my course, set it westward, the sky growing dark behind me, the mountains fading into distance. Before me? I knew not; perhaps answers to the riddles those strange stars asked me. They now appeared, one by one, in the sky above.

I took up the shark tooth sword I had been given and cast it into the ocean, before sailing on into the deepening night.

PART II. ANSWERS

Eighteen

For days I trended southwest, crossing the equator. There I picked up a prevailing wind and current that carried me west. Where I was going I knew not.

But my progress was good and my provisions still plentiful. I would surely come on inhabited lands if I followed this course. Lands where I might find answers. Or white men for that matter. That seemed less important now.

The Arus faded in my memory, a dream from which I had awakened. Maranua, too, would fade. This I recognized. New worlds lay ahead, to crowd the old ones from my mind. I hoped the priestess would find new dreams of her own and only remember me fondly as one she knew for a few days.

I had some concern about my sail. No replacement existed for the day it would inevitably wear out, rip somewhere in some wind. Nothing resembling canvas had I found in the islands. The sails of Aru canoes were woven of the fronds of some plant. That worked well enough for their craft but did not seem so adaptable to mine. Ah, I did not know what I might find ahead. My sail might not need get me much further.

Or it could last years longer. There was no point in worrying and no canvas to be found where I was! Only water, meeting the sky in every direction.

Yet I had a sense that something did lie ahead. No more dreams had come my way, not that I put any stock in those. Something—pulled me. I who believed in little, believed this.

At times I fished, without much success. Plenty enough dried fish was in my stores, along with dried coconut and fruit. After three weeks, they were not so plenty and my dwindling stores began to concern me.

Then I spied it, a lone isle, in all the vastness of the ocean. What chance brought me to its shores? Mountainous, it was, but not as the mountains of the Arus, with their many valleys and ridges. This isle rose like one great monolith, its heights barren of any green.

Around it I sailed, and spied no other islands. For the better part of a day I sailed, for it was not small, seeking a landing. Cliffs rose from turbulent waters along much of its perimeter. Such beaches as I did spy were protected by rock reefs on which the waves crashed. Was there no safe place, no harbor?

Between cliffs, an opening appeared, a narrow passage. A fjord, one might name it. I peered into its black depths. Nothing to be seen. Yet it was sheltered from the power of the surf and seemed easy enough of entry. Yes. I took in my sail and made my way with the one oar, standing, facing fore so I might see where I steered my vessel. Clumsy and slow was the progress but in time the walls of stone rose high on either side of me, closing out the fierce light of the tropical sun.

Now and again I rose on a wave, much dissipated in power, that rolled into the passage. Above I could see a ribbon of sky, all cloud. The way remained wide; a much larger boat could have entered here. The cliffs rose dark, barely to be distinguished from the shadows they cast, the shadows that surrounded me. Granite, I thought they were. Now the passage widened more, becoming a sort of lagoon, and more light found its way to the water. At the far side yawned a cave, that water disappearing into an inky unknown beyond its high arch. A shelf of rock jutted beside the opening, barely above the level of the water. At another tide, it might well be immersed.

No, Dick, I reminded myself, there would not be much of a tide here in the middle of the ocean, near the equator. I rowed to the mouth of the cave. I was not willing to row further into that blackness; not yet. Torches were among the supplies I had brought on my voyage. There had been little use for them till now, though a few times I had wanted a light in the night, and I had nursed an ember for when I needed fire.

I retrieved now the stone jar in which I kept it, added a little fuel from my meager and dwindling supply. Enough. A torch, its end wrapped in fiber anointed with coconut oil, ignited readily. I fastened it in place near my prow and cautiously rowed toward the ledge, lying in half-shadow. Could I tie up? There seemed no place to fasten a line.

Nor was I likely to drop anchor here, into those dark depths. Ah! An actual hole through the rock, worn by the inexorable action of the water over the ages. I ran a line through it, tied it off with a midshipman, and stepped ashore. If one could call that bit of rock a shore.

At least it was solid ground once again beneath my feet. Sailor though I am, I welcome its feel from time to time. I approached the cave, torch held high. The shelf extended into it, further than I could see. Nothing could be made out beyond the glow of my torch. So the torch must move forward, mustn't it?

Though I had no particular need to go further. I sought nothing on this rock in the ocean. Fresh water, yes, and maybe food, though I could sail on weeks more with neither replenished. What I sought, in truth, was answers. Answers to the riddles the stars asked each night. They might be here as well as any other place.

I would not expect to find white men. Perhaps no men of any sort. It seemed an inhospitable place. Never the less, I should be prepared if I met any. I had the heavy fighting spear still I had been given by the Aruans. It seemed too useful to cast overboard, as I had my sword. With its shaft in one hand, torch in the other, I went forward.

Here I splashed through shallow water. The end of my rocky pathway, perhaps. No, I could see it rise above the surface again a few yards ahead. Something touched against my leg, coiling itself about it. I lowered the torch to spy a striped sea snake, writhing at my ankles. Another over there? The light seemed to discourage it, for it turned and undulated away into the dark water.

I was relieved to step again onto dry rock. The ledge now widened before me. A faint light could be spied ahead. Shortly, I entered a great cavern, sunlight filtering in from a narrow rift in its distant rocky roof. Here ended this arm of the sea, thrust deep into the rock, in a sort of lagoon. It appeared one could walk all the way around it, save where flowed the channel I had followed.

Damnation! I had blundered into a spider's web. Thick it was. What sort of insects might a spider hunt in this place? I held my torch aloft, peered upward to see the husks of bats entangled in the strands of more than one web. Though I could not make out the roof, I surmised the fliers roosted up there.

And I imagined the size of the spiders that might ensnare them. Were they scuttling along their shadowed webs, just beyond the illumination of my torch? I went to edge of the pool to gaze into its depths. Only the reflection of my light could I see, masking what might lie below. I walked on at the water's edge, waving the torch before me, lest I blunder into more webs.

A wind flowed through this place, coming in by the way I had and exiting through the rent in the cave's roof, forever sighing and whispering as it went. But did another sound echo here? A sound arising from the shadows? Just the bats, I told myself. I must have disturbed their slumber with my torch, the fall of my footsteps. I walked on, keeping close to the water's edge but looking ever into the darkness, searching for another way out.

Were I more willing to plunge into those shadows, perhaps I would have come on such a way. Best it is I did not! From the corner of my eye, I glimpsed a movement, then another, here, there. From the blackness, creeping on eight legs, came creatures of nightmare, black spiders as large as mastiffs. Each had a pale, sickly green hourglass figure on its back, that might have faintly glowed in the dark. A web shot toward me, warded barely in time with my torch.

One scuttled around to my right, hoping to flank me. To the edge of the water it went but no further, for a giant sea snake, like to that which I had encountered with Ruheyo, shot from the water and seized the creature in its jaws before slithering back into the depths. But that had done little to even my odds; a half dozen or more still menaced me.

Taking to the water myself might be my only chance. I doubted the snake—or its smaller cousins—would bother me. As for what else might lurk, it could be no worse than the monsters I faced.

I prepared to turn and dive when a voice rang out.

Nineteen

A woman's voice it was, and in a language I did not know. A hooded figure raised one hand and again commanded. She seemed then somehow larger, and of a different shape. Surely, an illusion of the moment, a play of the flickering light.

The horrid arachnids scuttled back into darkness. She turned to regard me for a few seconds, before nodding. "This back door is not the best way into my home."

It took me a moment to realize what language she spoke. "You know English?"

"I took it from you. I see another—one you name Español—and the language of the Aru Islands. This is not the time and place for explanations. You have a canoe?"

"A boat."

"Boat." She considered that. "Yes. Take me to it and I shall show you the way to a better landing."

I asked no questions. Better to be gone from this cave and allow explanations to come in their time. "You were going to escape in the water, were you not?" she asked. Her voice had a detached feel to it, as if she were speaking of something far away, something that had nothing to do with either of us.

"I was."

"The best choice and it might well have worked. Most who blunder among the spiders allow their fear to keep them from it. So they perish." A pause, perhaps thinking of those unfortunate predecessors. "You did not need to find out. I awaited your coming, though I was not certain just where and when it would be."

We waded through the shallows. Ahead I could glimpse the light of day. "What do the creatures eat when men are not available?" I asked. One question wouldn't hurt.

"The largest take their share of bats, but also catch fish. Sometimes they eat my snakes."

"*Your* snakes?"

"I think of them as my pets. They serve me, in their limited way. Or I should say they serve me in my task here." Whatever that task might be, she sounded as disinterested in it as all else. "As do the spiders, in a sense. They guard my door."

We stepped into the sunlight. My boat was as I had left it. My companion stood and looked it over before nodding. "Yes, a boat." She threw back her dark, enveloping hood at last, revealing a torrent of curling, fiery hair falling about a black face.

Obviously not a European nor any race of which I had ever heard. Yet her features were such as might be called classical, the face of a Greek goddess. Eyes of emerald took me in, interest seemingly aroused at last.

"What do I name you, traveler?" she asked, stepping into my vessel as I undid the hitch.

"Dick will do."

"I suppose it will have to. I am Kesarra. Kess, since we seem to be using monosyllables." The woman laughed for the first time. "Turn right when we exit this inlet. Starboard, right?"

"Right, right," I answered. That got no laugh.

I raised my sail, which elicited some interest. "I have seen sails pass by my isle, but never one quite like this," she told me. "You can sail close to the cliffs now. It is safe."

It was as well to trust her. She would know these waters better than I. More than one small waterfall came over the cliffs, streams making a final plunge to the sea. "The wisest sailors replenish their water here and make no attempt to land," was all Kessara had to say of them. "See you the arch ahead?" she continued. "Go through it."

It was a natural arch, connecting cliff to a tower of rock rising from the water. Rough was the water around it, yet the passage appeared safe enough. Through it, we entered a small bay shielded by a number of large standing rocks—sentinel islets, breaking the force of the great waves. A crescent of dark sand lay to our right.

Waves, much dissipated, tumbled onto the beach. The cliffs, not so high here, rose above it. Vegetation clung to their base; I could spy the ubiquitous coconut palm of the south seas. This shallow bay seemed a poor anchorage to me, nor was I going to run my boat onto the sand. Or rocks; such might well be hidden. My guide pointed to a jutting point. Rounding it I discovered a wide, clear stream. A river, call it. The flow was sluggish enough I believed I might progress against it with my one oar. For now, the sail could still be used.

Until we reached the mouth of the cave from which it issued. "Again?" I asked.

"These are the doors of my home," she stated. I could read nothing in her tone. "If you prefer, you may leave your boat here and climb the cliffs. There are ways up."

I looked toward the dark opening before me. "Any spiders?"

"Not a one." A smile at last. "Or not one you need fear unless you are a fly. There is a place you may moor your boat within."

Very well. There appeared to be plenty enough clearance for my mast—I would want to keep a watch—but I struck the sail, propelling us with the oar. Shortly we entered an open lagoon, walled all about by cliffs, with a waterfall tumbling into its far end. A dock lay to my left, with a pair of modest canoes tied alongside.

I rowed my way to it. Bamboo it was, all of it, and floating rather than fixed to the bottom. That bottom, I suspected, was rock and possibly quite far down. I tied my own vessel beside the others. My host stepped onto the dock without a word; I followed. Set in an alcove in the rocks was a heavy wooden door, the first door I had seen in many months. Its fittings were all of wood, too; not one bit of metal was to be seen.

Beyond it lay a tunnel through the rock. Whether man-made or natural I could not say. Perhaps some of each. "Welcome to my home, Dick," she said, leading me up the dark hallway. Had the door been shut behind us, I doubt I could have seen at all.

"I thank you for your hospitality, Kess. But where is your home? What is this place?"

"This is the Isle of the Stones. Some, not understanding the origin of that name, call it the Isle of Stone—for it looks like a great rock—or simply the Stone."

"I was told to seek stones," I ventured.

"So I understand. But you do not understand, do you?"

"I do not. There is much I have not understood recently. The world became strange to me."

"You are no longer in your world but another, one of the infi-

nite worlds that are. Or can be—that makes no practical difference."

It seemed as good—or poor—an explanation as any I had come
up with. "How?" was all I could ask.

"You passed from yours to this one through a gate, opened by
the power of a great storm. I have heard of your world from other
travelers; it is one with few such gates and little magic. Yet
through two gates have come the ancestors of most of the
humans who dwell here."

"Your ancestors?"

Kess laughed. "Who said I was human?"

Twenty

Stairs lay ahead, cut from the rock. So did a dim light, filtering from above. Kesarra called out in a tongue I did not know, and another answered. A man's voice it was.

We turned aside into a small chamber, its gloom but poorly dispelled by a single oil lamp. Kesarra doffed her hooded cloak, tossing it carelessly aside. Beneath, a simple tunic of silvery gray clung to her shapely, slender form, belted at the waist with a ribbon and falling below her knees.

I could have spent some time looking at her but a man entered at that moment, a tall man, beardless, with long black hair tied at the back of the neck. A white man. He but glanced at me before entering a long conversation with the woman. They might have been arguing, though, if so, there was little passion in it.

Finally, Kess told me, "Dick, go with the, hmm, guardian. Yes, that would be as good a word as any. He will get you squared away. Ha, I like some of the expressions from your language. It is too bad I shall not need it again!"

The man turned without a word and left the cell. I followed. He was dressed as Kesarra, save for the broad leather belt at his waist. A sheathed dagger hung there; I wondered of what metal its blade might be. My own good−speaking relatively−steel knife remained at my side. Lean and straight he stood, taller than me by perhaps a couple inches; that did not make him a particularly tall man, admittedly. I was fairly certain he was of no nation I knew.

No nation I knew existed here, were I to believe what Kesarra had told me. Another world−I did not believe, not truly, but accepted it as a possible answer to some of my many questions.

Up more stairs we went. I thought perhaps we had wound our way back toward the cliffs. That thought proved true when we entered another chamber, a larger one, with a window admitting light. A window, I call it, but it was practically a tunnel, a good six feet of rock separating the room from the outside air.

This chamber was somewhat better furnished than the last. There was even a sort of rustic luxury to its appointments. The man turned, addressing me in the Aruan tongue. "Kesarra say speak Aru? Know some." He gave me a thorough perusal. "Not Aru."

I answered in the same language. "I stopped there some time while on my way here. How long I stop here, I know not."

There might have been a faint smile. "Does any? Teach you other, mm, words. Need." He shrugged. "So told. Name me Var."

Lessons began at once in the language of a people he called the Heldu. Why their tongue was chosen I did not understand, for my hosts did not speak it to each other. This room I shared with Var. I could walk to my 'window'–the opening was tall enough–and look out over the basin where my boat was moored. We seemed to be about halfway up the cliff. There was little to see but I welcomed the sunlight.

I learned soon Var's name came from a Heldun word, varu, meaning something along the lines of guardian or, more precisely, one entrusted–one under an obligation. Kess had called him guardian when first we met and I realized soon 'the Guardian' was a title he wore.

As Kess was 'the Hand.' Of her I saw little; she came and went but we spoke of nothing of importance. She and Var spoke only the Heldun language to me. "Why this tongue?" I asked Var, when able to form the question. "Why learn? You Var Heldu?" I didn't think so but it didn't hurt to ask.

He laughed outright at the question. I did not understand why at the moment. "You are to go to the Heldu. So Kesarra has been told." He did not seem overly pleased with that. "Kesarra's father was Heldu. A mortal man. Her name is from a word of that people, a word meaning 'hand.' She styles herself the Hand of Banat."

"Banat?" The obvious question.

"The chief of their gods. It would be far better is she tells you of all this someday. When you can speak better."

I could have pointed out Kess and I could speak English to each other perfectly well. How this was so, I did not understand at all. Another thing it would be best to ask the woman. "So what nation of you are, Var? You if not mind question."

The word he used to describe himself I knew not, nor did he offer to explain it, so I asked no further. But I pondered his use of the term 'mortal man,' and remembered Kess implying she was not human.

Our servants there were not human either. Their presence went far toward convincing me I was truly in another world. Short, they were, standing but a little higher than my waist, with spindly arms and legs, and large heads. The ears were definitely pointed. Goblins.

"A tribe of goblins dwelt here when first I arrived," Var told me. "I ignored them. In truth, I should say I avoided them, for they would surely have killed and eaten me were I careless. But Kess insisted on befriending them and recruiting some to serve us."

"Before Kess here you were?"

"Yes, for a few centuries I was sole Lord of the Stone." Var did not sound entirely happy when he added, "Now I must share authority."

Centuries. I decided not to ask of this, either. What I did ask was, "Is safe it me to venture from these caves?"

"The goblins would not bother you. Kesarra very much put the fear of the goddess in them. Other dangers? If you keep to the open you should be safe enough."

But I would retrieve my spear from the boat first, I decided. I should check my craft over anyway. I retraced the way I had come up to his apartment, carrying a stone lamp—not much different from those I had seen in the Aru Islands—to cast a faint light before me.

I reached the door. A stout bamboo shaft was placed as a bar to opening it. Or to entering it—I was exiting, wasn't I? So I lifted it and pulled the heavy wooden slab inward, to glimpse the lagoon. It was peaceful down here; I wouldn't mind sitting on the dock a while. Swim? No, I was not overly tempted to test the dark waters. There should be places above the high waterfall, shouldn't there? I would have to find my way up there.

I found my spear, the heavy fighting spear of the Aruans with its obsidian point. The fishing spear, my lines and hooks, I checked over. Who could say when I might need them again? Best they be ready. For all I knew, some reason could arise to flee the Stone tomorrow, next week, next month. An hour from now. All seemed shipshape. I clambered back onto the floating dock and sat a while, cross-legged, contemplating the water. What was that? A dugong perhaps?

And another. Women. A pair of sleek, fat women who floated regarding me. Mermaids, I could only assume. Why not mermaids in this world? When one dove, I could see she had two short legs, not the fish tail of legend, and her feet were broad and paddle-like. One spoke to me in a language I could not understand.

I answered in one she could not understand. She blinked her yellow eyes and said something to her companion. Maybe commenting on how handsome I was? Or asking whether she thought I would taste good. I had heard conflicting tales about mermaids. They had slowly moved toward me while increasing the distance between them. I understood what that meant. I was being stalked by mermaids.

At once, I leapt to my feet, bolted toward the safety of the cave. They moved surprisingly quickly, launching themselves with one powerful kick. One reached and grabbed my leg, tripped me but could not hold on. I jabbed with my spear as she reached again, pushing myself backward along the dock without rising from my arse. They were big girls! Wide, open mouths displayed sharp teeth.

Could they follow me onto solid ground? I suspected the answer to be in the affirmative. Not far, maybe, not quickly, but perhaps well enough to cut me off from the door. Already, one was squirming her naked bulk up onto the rocks.

I rolled away from the one threatening me, came to my feet. I should charge with the spear. If necessary, use it. If necessary, kill. That was when the giant sea snake rose from the water, undulating toward the mermaid climbing ashore. She dove, disappearing into the depths, as did her sister.

Again, this monstrous serpent had come to my aid. After a fashion. It was one more thing I did not understand.

Twenty-one

"Var has made love to one or another of the mermaids from time to time. With sensible precautions, of course," Kess told me. "I would not recommend it to you."

I'd had no thoughts of it. Not since I'd first spied them. "Stick to humans will I." Though some of the goblin women didn't look bad at all. I wondered if Var had made love to any of them. Or to Kesarra, for that matter.

"I am half a human, you know," she said. "Or so I believe. Var has told you a little of me." I only nodded so she continued. "But I am also a goddess. A minor goddess, a demigoddess. Name me as you wish, but I am immortal and that makes me divine."

"Your father was a man the Heldu of, no?"

"Most likely. I know not his name nor aught else about him. Chances are he was one of my mother's devotees, perhaps a priest, or he may have been some random man she seduced when he took her fancy. He may or may not have survived coupling with the goddess Dekata."

"Dekata. Your mother?"

"Goddess of the Dark Moon, goddess of witchcraft and of madness. My dark skin is Dekata's legacy; she is like a piece of polished obsidian. Beautiful in her way." Kess's voice trailed off as some memory took her elsewhere.

"But innately evil. Some of her children—those she doesn't eat before they reach maturity—become the worst sort of lamias and vampires. One could make a case that I am a lamia myself. I escaped her cave while quite small, and the father of the gods, Banat, took me in. He saw that I had the free will of a human, that I could choose good or evil. Eventually, it also became evident that I was immortal. Not all demigods are; some live longer than men yet perish still."

"And that make a goddess you."

"It does. Banat saw other things in me too, things hidden. He named me his Hand and, when the time came, sent me here to do his will."

"And the great sea snake does your will?"

"The spiders and sea snakes serve as guardians but I do not truly command them. I have enough sorcery to sometimes direct one at a time. Only enough sorcery." That brought a brief smile, one I could not read. "Despite my deity, I can not match the great human sorcerers. Not so long as I remain in this world, in this mortal form."

I was willing to accept all this but not necessarily believe it. And certainly not understand it. "What of the Guardian?"

"Oh, all his people have some power. None are truly great." Disinterest and condescension mingled in her voice.

"Told me he the name of his people but the word me meant nothing."

"Hmm. In your English you would say elf. Fay, maybe too? Yes. Var is of the High Fay."

An elf. Why not? "How you know English I ask?"

"It is easy for a god to take language from a mind. Little else— we are not mind-readers. Not most of us. No mortals can do this, even the most gifted, but for a god it comes with barely any thought. Your words float at the surface, ready to be scooped up and made ours."

I may have looked dumbfounded.

"Ah, you wonder how this is done. You have no sorcery in you, Dick, so it is difficult of explanation. All wizards work their magic by entering other worlds—sending a part of their physical being elsewhere. If two send themselves to the same space, they can share their minds and knowledge. But it is dangerous! We gods do something similar to read language, by sending ourselves into another world and then back again to be, um, within someone. We can not truly merge at all with you that way but it is enough to glean language. Hmm, and maybe some broad emotions," she added.

"So do giant sea snake with?"

"Exactly! I stayed with its mind for a time while it watched you sailing. Very boring. Mostly, I just remind it now and again to keep an eye on you." The look she gave me implied I needed that. "That does not work well with more intelligent beings; the snake is almost too smart. Also, I have to send a part of me underwater to be with it. Most unpleasant."

I thought to ask whether she had to hold her breath. Other questions pushed their way to the front. "Human sorcerers there are? Many?"

"No, not many. It is a gift with which one is born and most of those in this world descend from a single sorcerer who found his way here from another, some thousands of years ago. He yet lives, somewhere on the other side of the world, the most powerful of all mortals." Did I sense awe? He must be very powerful indeed to impress a goddess. "Hurasu is his name. He avoids any contact with those such as I."

"That would seem wise," I ventured.

"It does," Kess admitted, taking no note of the jest. "I do not bother him, either. But the occasional wizard does find their way to the isle, intending to possess that which we keep safe here. Most fall to the guardians." Now she did smile. "As almost did you, more than once."

"That which you keep?"

"Yes. You will learn of it soon. It is why you are here. It is why you learn the language of the Heldu. You are getting good at it, by the way."

Better, anyway. "If one of your sorcerers I were, you give it to me directly could, could not you?"

"Yes, but I would not. Too many other things might be learned. Things that belong only to me." The goddess lingered only a moment on that thought before saying, "You have grasped the concept of sorcery. That may prove useful."

"I hope not."

"Ah, but you have already been noticed. I do not think you can avoid sorcery." She rose to her feet. "However, you can avoid merfolk and spiders and other nasty creatures. Let me take you up out of these tunnels."

We had been sitting in the little cell to which she had first brought me, speaking by the light of my lamp. The scent of the coconut oil it burned filled the room. I did not think Kess lived in this barren space, though there was a sleeping mat. Now she led me to the stairs and upward, past the chamber I shared with Var.

More stairs. Ways and rooms opened to one side or another. There was more such up here than lower. Goblin-folk went about their duties and errands, most giving my companion a little bow before scurrying away. At some point I recognized I stood not on rock but on a floor of bamboo. We reached another door like the one at the base of the cliffs. This one stood open. Beyond lay a meadow. To my right, the cliffs fell away; to my left rose rocky slopes. I turned and looked behind me. A house, rose there, a small house of stone. The tunnels had led upward into it.

"There was only a hole and a ladder when I arrived here," Kess told me. "Var was not ambitious about building. But I set the little folk to work." She smiled. "And others."

I did not think I would ask about those. "I am free to come up here?"

"You are free to go anywhere, Dick. You could go to your boat right now and sail away. But where would you go?"

For that I had no answer.

Twenty-two

"Our name of High Fay is a bit of mistranslation," stated Var. "It makes us sound as if we think we're better than the rest! Which may or may not be so."

Kess had to interject a soft snort at this point. The elf ignored her and continued. "Be that as it may, the words mean something more along the lines of 'tall' or even 'large.' We are indeed the tallest of our sort, that is, elves. Ogres get bigger, to be sure."

"Ogres are fay?" I might as well ask and continue this lunacy.

"Strictly speaking, yes; that is, they are of Faerie. But they are of the goblin kindred, having parted from our lineage in the distant past."

"How did the goblins get here, anyway? Did they sail?" I had seen none go anywhere near the water. Some were here on this open grass, hurrying about whatever errands they might have.

"We are uncertain. They are not sure how they got here themselves. There are no gates on this isle," said Kess.

"It is possible someone brought them by sea. Their ancestors might even have come by air."

What? Flying goblins? "How?"

"Goblins and kobolds sometimes ride upon wyverns—what you heard named lalun in the Arus."

"Griffins, too," Var added. "But not dragons."

Kess actually snickered. "Var came here on a dragon. He likes to mention it now and again."

"I was attacked by a lalun." Both knew this; I had given my full tale once I spoke the Heldun language well enough. They insisted we use no other tongue.

"Yes, the wyvern. I wonder about that. It could have been sent but I don't know by whom."

"It would take great skill," felt Var. "And there may be reasons a sorcerer might wish to harm you."

"Or Maranua. I am still uncertain."

My companions exchanged a glance. I was sure they believed I was the target. "I have spoken with the Woman of the Moon," said

Kess. "She promises to send her priestess dreams telling her you are well."

Spoken? I did not say this aloud yet she sensed the question.

"Another sorcerous art. Speaking from afar. Even to gods, if they are willing."

I could guess this also involved sending part of oneself else-where. I was interested in other questions. "So you sent the sea snake, Kess. How did you know of me?"

"I knew one was to come. That was seen. When, I did not know. Marahina herself told me of you, when she saw your destiny entwined with that of Maranua. And so I spied on you a little."

"Did you send the dream of jewels to me? Of stones?"

Another meaningful exchange between the two. Meaningful to them. "We think one greater than either of us sent that dream to you," spoke Var.

"Possibly Banat," Kess said, "but I believe the stones themselves have called to you."

Var scowled at that but said nothing.

"What of the great shark I saw?"

"A shark? I would think that just random, though one never knows. The same with your eagle that came from another world with you. But—prophecy said one would come with such a companion. That aroused interest in you."

"Some watch for what may come through the gates."

"As best they can. It is possible to watch from afar for their opening but one can not see what comes through them. That takes spies in this world."

"Snakes?"

This earned a smile from Kess. "And human snakes. I would not doubt there are sorcerers among the Aruans who might have spoken of you to someone."

"Goblins, too," said Var. "They all have the ability."

Kess had told me his kind had such powers. Apparently, that meant all fay. It hadn't occurred to me that included the little folk.

"They do gossip, at least with others of their people. News will find its way to mortal sorcerers." We walked on a few steps more before she continued. "I spoke with Teshum last night."

Var shook his head. "A madman. Too dangerous for me."

"But he knows nothing of the Stones. He only senses there is power here and is curious."

"Few know they exist and those are unlikely to share the secret."

I wished these two would get around to sharing this secret with me. "Who's Teshum?" I asked.

"One of the great wizards of the Valley of Visions. Hurasu's realm."

"A grandson of Hurasu, I understand," said Var.

"And one who wishes to throw him down and make himself lord of their valley. He will fail when he tries to test the Vision Lord at last, as have all others before him."

"Most likely," agreed the elf.

A goblin ran up and jabbered something. Var shook his head when he was done.

"It seems another wayward mortal found his way here," spoke Kess. "An adventurer? A sorcerer? Who can say? Perhaps no more than a lost sailor. The spiders have him now."

The goddess seemed nonchalant, disinterested. I could see the news troubled Var. "How much more trouble could the jewels bring if they went out into the world?" he asked.

"Yet they must go. Your duty here nears its end, Guardian."

"I know it must sometime. Is this that time? How can I be certain? How can I know when my task is fulfilled?"

"Neither of us can be certain. In the end, we must both have faith." Kesarra stopped and turned to me. "As must Dick. He should learn soon of the task he will be taking up."

"If he chooses."

"Yes. If he chooses."

Twenty-three

From here I could see much of the isle. Not all; even from the highest peak I wasn't sure I could make out its entire perimeter. That was no climb I desired to make. I was not sure it was a climb I could make, for it was all steep rock above where I now stood.

"I went to the top when first I arrived, just to do it," Kess told me. "Nothing much lies above us here but the nests of the eagles."

I could readily believe her. I had come to recognize the demigoddess had greater strength and greater stamina than I. She also possessed a prodigious appetite. Filling it was no problem; the not-quite-human denizens of the isle, the goblins, the merfolk, held the Hand in awe and strove to keep her well fed. Crabs and fish and huge clams came from the sea. Greens, as well, for there were tasty seaweeds. Var told me no seaweed was poisonous; a good thing to know in an emergency. The elf was full of such knowledge.

The goblins farmed and gathered, and their offerings too found their way to our table. Much of the fare was not greatly different from what I had consumed in the Arus, but there were no pigs or chickens. Many pigeons were to be found, some half-domesticated.

"The goblins didn't dig those tunnels in which we live, did they?" I asked, as I surveyed what lay below us.

"For the most part, no. I put them to work adding a bit here and there but the network precedes them. In part, the caves are natural but some agency shaped them in the distant past. Not humans, I suspect, nor any of their relatives."

I was not sure what she meant. "Animals?"

"Demons. Or not. You understand there are no demons native to this world."

I did not understand at all. "But gods are?"

Kess's eyes seemed fixed on the horizon. "Exura has no gods, strictly speaking. I am not a god of this world. Neither are those the Aruans worship or any others you might encounter. We have our own universes and need not come here at all, nor ever leave our homes. But there are those here who revere or worship us and that keeps us connected."

"Strictly speaking, you say?" I wasn't going to let that slip by.

"Yes. That fact plays a part in the task before you. Before us, for I think I shall still have my role." She laughed softly, saying, "Var can finally retire."

"Will you retire someday to the world of Banat?"

"I suppose. I don't know what I would do with myself. I get bored enough here! I am unlike the greater gods of my universe, each perfectly suited to their role and desiring nothing more. Perhaps I shall wander the worlds. Others have."

"I think I would if I had the power, just as I have wandered the seas. Are gods inclined to do so?"

"Some are, some are not. The gods of the Mora dislike manifesting in other worlds. Other pantheons love to travel about and visit. Banat himself at least comes to this universe from time to time." She read the look I gave her then, the thought that had arisen in my mind. "Yes, and my mother."

"But she lives in your world of the gods? Banat's world?"

"That is so. Gods have no problem visiting other worlds. Mortals can not, not fully, unless they come through a gate, as did you. Any mortal taken to another world would eventually be pulled back to their place of origin." Kess might have actually smirked. That was new. "Every part of them, including their seed if a male coupled with someone. Or their substance if they were devoured. That would feel most unpleasant to the one who ate them."

"So her lovers would have to come through a gate."

"Even so. There are no gates directly between this world—which Hurasu named Exura, by the way—and that of Banat. A visitor would have to travel roundabout through several gates and several worlds. Rarely, Dekata would bring lovers back to her cave. Not always human ones. Most never left; some lingered a while, others she devoured as soon as they mated. But, yes, my mother also wanders this world at times. Maybe other worlds too; I don't know."

Wherever she wandered, I hoped I didn't run into her.

"Through what you call sorcery you can see or reach into other worlds. Do I have that right?"

"You do. Allowing such as this—" Kess reached out a hand and a sword appeared in it, a sword of a bluish metal. It smoked a bit.

"Not from a world quite compatible with ours, it seems. It will return on its own in time." She tossed it aside. "So is it with metals from my world. Understand that the very elements are different there and objects brought from it might lose their integrity. It would seem a very strange universe to you; others are much more like this one or that from which you came. And others are wholly different. There are, of course, an infinite number of each."

"Infinite?"

"Yes. Infinite universes exist in infinite being." She breezed past that. I might need to ponder it for some time. "You carry a metal knife. May I see it?"

I handed it over. The sword, I could see, had dissolved somewhat before disappearing completely.

"Steel. That is the English word for this? I know the word but that does not mean I know anything about it. Only that I can recognize it."

"Steel it is. Iron that has been, um, transmuted into something stronger."

"Iron, I know." Kess handed the blade back. "No one uses it in this world. They make things of bronze in the Valley of Visions. Copper and gold too are known in some places."

"I have seen gold here." The implements Ruheyo had mentioned might have been of bronze.

"Var and I carry knives of stone. The goblins make them and they do quite fine work." She pulled out her polished obsidian blade. It was truly fine craftsmanship. Artistry, even.

But I thought I would stick with steel.

Twenty-four

"Kesarra has remained celibate. I believe she fears becoming like her mother."

Var was most definitely not celibate. His trysts with goblin women were no secret. I suspected trysts with goblin men, as well. As for the mermaids—I was willing to accept Kess's word with regard to them.

I had seen no evidence of half-elf goblin children, however. Best I not inquire into that, I felt. Nor did I think it wise to accept the propositions of goblin women myself. Not that they were unattractive, though perhaps they looked a little too much like children. It was the judgment of Kess that held me back.

Why it should matter to me, I did not know. The goddess had her own reasons to distance herself from emotion. I could not figure out my motives for anything. I dallied on this isle, waiting for something to happen. More than once I considered going to my boat and sailing away. Where? Any direction. Even back to Maranua, maybe.

"As I told you," continued Var, "I avoided the goblin folk when first I came here. I did not trust them and still do not, completely. That did not prevent the occasional, ah, contact with them."

"They don't like the sunlight, do they? I rarely see them outdoors during the midday."

"They do not. The goblins are cave dwellers by nature. My own folk prefer the light of the stars to that of the sun."

I had found the goblins mostly dwelt in caves further up the slopes. Visiting them was another thing I had avoided. I did not wish to become too involved with anything here. Not as long as I remained ignorant of what was expected of me. Like Kess, I was distancing myself.

"Are we ready?" came the goddess' voice from behind us. We had been standing by the enclosed lagoon, waiting for her. Why, I had not been told.

"Yes. Which door are we using?" asked Var.

Kess pointed across the water. "The best way this time, I think." She turned to me. "We will avoid the spiders."

Var amended that to, "Most of them." I was uncertain how serious the fay was.

So instead of asking about it, I noted that a canoe had been added to our little fleet. A crude dugout it was, with double outriggers.

"Left by our latest visitor. Var went and retrieved it."

"From among the spiders?"

"I have walked through them before."

"Many times," said Kess. "Most of the defenses here were the Guardian's doing. It was to him the Jewels were entrusted, not me."

"Yet that does not seem to matter now," said Var.

We paddled across in the largest of the three canoes. It might well have voyaged from the Aru Islands. What had become of they who sailed it here? Another substantial door lay opposite that I had been using. The bar here was on the outside, heavy and high up. Perhaps to keep curious goblins out. Perhaps to keep spiders in! I did not like the idea that someone might bar it behind us, although my guides apparently knew other paths and other door-ways.

"That which we guard here is far down," Kess told me, as we entered. Each held a torch. I wished that I also held my spear; had I known what this pair had planned, I would surely have carried it.

Labyrinth? Maze? Perhaps neither, in truth, but I could easily have become lost in those tunnels. I saw only small spiders. Relatively small. They were still larger than I would prefer.

But then, there would be little for them to eat in the barren caves we traversed. We sloshed through shallow water. Not stale water that had pooled here, dripping from somewhere above; it smelled of the sea. These passages must connect to open water.

"Whatever you guard is well hidden," I commented.

"But not well enough," countered Kess. "Not anymore. And they will be hidden from you no longer."

Var stopped and looked fully into my face. "They may remain hidden from you, if you wish. Say if you would prefer to turn back and forget all this."

"It is time Dick learned of them," was all Kess had to say.

She was right. I had come here seeking answers and whatever

they guarded was a part of that, part of what I needed to understand. "I must go on," I told him. I told them.

I told myself, most of all. "I would think more than spiders
guard these stones you treasure so highly," I said. "And mermaids."

"To be sure," replied Var. "The goblins, of course, if anyone
found their way up to them. The snakes, in general, are not much
use but they are intimidating."

"They certainly could make one nervous," I commented.

"And therefor more vulnerable. I have my magic and have set
many wards and alarms and even a few traps down here. Kess
eschews such things." He perhaps didn't approve.

"You do it well, Guardian. Why should I interfere?"

"Maybe so, Hand. I was at it long before you joined me. We
shall come upon some physical guardians shortly, following this
way."

The roof lowered some. I stooped, passed through a narrow
way to find a large chamber—larger than I could make out by
torch light—before us, its floor covered by water. Something
moved in that water.

"The Cave of Crabs," announced Var.

"Don't be silly," Kess admonished him. "Cave of Crabs indeed!
But admittedly it is a cave and there are crabs. The water is
shallow here, Dick, no more than knee deep."

"Then we wade across?" I was quite sure I did not like that idea.

"Only if you wish to be torn apart by giant crabs. That would be
somewhat more painful than spiders."

"But quicker," Var said. "One lingers paralyzed in the webs of
the spiders."

"We follow the ledge. Be careful of your footing. It is narrow
and damp." Kess started forward. Maybe this was when I should
take Var's advice and turn back. But I advanced in her wake. The
rock ledge was indeed narrow and indeed damp. Moreover, it was
not that far above the level of the water. I could see creatures
moving towards us through that water.

Yes, crabs. Giant? That is relative, I suppose. Their shells
appeared to span two or three feet. I would not greatly fear one
such crab but en masse? Those powerful claws would make quick

work of one who had the misfortune of being in the water with them.

One claw now slipped over the edge of our path, probing. "Can they climb up here?" I asked.

"They can and they will," Var told me, "if we allow them. A bit of smoke, Kesarra?"

"Yes." Immediately, acrid smoke began to billow into the cave, from somewhere in our own vicinity. Had these two somehow lit a fire? Whatever they did, the crabs drew back a short way, splashing and hissing in the dark water, their protruding eye stalks turned toward us.

Instead of the obvious question, I queried, "Are they good to eat?"

Var laughed uproariously. "Indeed they are. We'll send you down sometime to fetch a couple for dinner."

"They do venture out of this cavern to feed," Kess added to this. "It opens to the sea on the other side. The merfolk sometimes catch one or two and bring them to us. Ah, and we are past them."

"So, what did you two just do?"

"We brought smoke from another world," Var explained. "Two different worlds. It is a fairly minor magic, though holding the way open long is fatiguing."

More so for the elf than Kes, I suspected. "Ah. As when you brought that sword, Kess."

"Just so. Smoke will work with the spiders too."

"Better than with crabs. They can't get underwater to escape it," said Var. "I have had moments of danger down here, moments when I thought I might not leave again. I do not think the Hand needs to concern herself with such matters."

The goddess' answer came flat and unemotional. "As far as I know, the spiders could not kill me but only hurt me badly. I am and remain immortal. If damaged badly, I would most likely be pulled back to the world of the gods. Banat's world."

"Where you would heal?" he asked.

"So I assume. I have heard of gods regrowing missing parts. Not just limbs but practically their entire being."

"This is something I did not know. I thank you for the knowledge, Kesarra."

"Var wants to know everything," said Kess. "So here we are." We had entered another larger cavern. "That way," she pointed, "lies the lagoon of the spiders. One will occasionally find its way in here. The snakes usually eat them."

"One knowledgeable can use that door."

One with magical smoke can, I thought to say. But what lay before me took my attention. One massive rock rose in the middle of a dark pool. That the water was deep, I knew without needing to ask. A narrow bridge, a natural arch of rock connected it to where we stood.

From the pool rose the largest sea snake I had yet seen. This was not the one Kesarra had set to watch me. It lifted its sleek, deadly head above the water and regarded us, eyes glittering, before disappearing again into the depths. Did it recognize my companions? Did Kess somehow speak to it, as she had that other snake? I did not now then. I do not know now.

I followed her across the span. In a hollow in the rock lay a stone jar. She lifted its lid to reveal the four gems that had appeared in my dream. Red and blue, gold and green they were, a little smaller than hens' eggs, and seemed almost to have a light within them. I know not how long I stood transfixed, staring at them.

"These are, if you will, the gods of this world."

Twenty-five

The stones remained where I had see them. Both Kess and Var felt it best. But they expected me to carry them away somewhere. When, they did not or could not say.

We sat on the grass above the cliffs, as day faded. "Var must give you the history of the jewels now," stated Kess. "You should know what they are."

"What they are?" asked Var. "Neither of us really can say. A manifestation of the protean beings that shaped this universe would be as good a description as any. They are the Jewels of the Elements and they possess great latent power. A skilled wizard could turn that power to their use, for good or for evil."

"Though I believe they are innately good," interjected Kess. "As is any creative power. Evil destroys."

"Maybe so. Whether those primeval beings consciously shaped the universe about them or whether a world simply manifested in their image, none can honestly say. Not that everyone doesn't have an opinion. From what I have heard, I might suspect a similar demiurge shaped your world, Dick."

"Stick to the story," advised Kess.

"Yes. Thousands of years ago, when men were few, before Hurasu came, even before I was born, the jewels were located by my people. In the mountains near what is now named the Valley of Visions, demons delved deep into rock to free them. All one stone they were then, one colorless raw jewel, but we fay cut them into the four gems you saw and the color of each appeared. Each holds the power of one of the elements.

"We dwelt then near the Great Rift, for there are many gates there, opening to many worlds, including those of our people and kindred. There we kept and guarded the stones, using them infrequently. I fear none of the fay have the gifts needed to truly harness their power." He glanced toward Kess.

"Nor do I," she said. "Not in this world."

"And they can be taken to no other. It was found they would not pass through a gate to another world for, in a sense, they *are* this world. But in time, great human sorcerers arose who could use them and who coveted them."

"This Hurasu you mention from time to time?" I asked.

"Not he. The Lord of Visions undoubtedly knows of their existence but has evinced no interest in them. He prefers to keep himself apart in his valley."

"He seems to have little interest in actually wielding power, save for his own amusement. It is said he sees his realm more as a sort of experiment than aught else."

"Said by whom?" queried the elf.

"Rumors and gossip among the gods," she answered. "Curious deities have visited his valley from time to time. There are a great many sorcerers living there, you know, all Hurasu's descendants."

"His descendants are what caused our problems. Many High Fay dwelt here once but the presence of these powerful human sorcerers made us ever more uneasy. One established her power in the Rift, styling herself the Wizard-Lord. Other Wizard-Lords succeeded her, increasing their realm. These were evil men and women, for the most part, exiled from Hurasu's valley. They pressed us, desiring not only the Jewels but all we possessed. Our knowledge—some fay were enslaved for that purpose. For other purposes, as well, purposes better not spoken of.

"So it was that most of my people departed Exura, entering the gates to other worlds and never returning. But the stones we guarded could not leave, nor would we leave them to be misused. We have our faults, we fay, but most would not permit that."

Kess might have smiled, after a fashion. "If you happened to think of it."

"Yes. We dream too much and forget everyday things, the practicalities of life. You know of that, being immortal. Nothing seems important."

That brought me to ask, "You fay are immortal?"

"Only very long lived. We do age and we may be killed. Unlike, apparently, Kesarra and her fellow gods."

"I am still a very young goddess," Kess told him. "I am actually younger than you, Guardian, yet I have known the ennui of eternal life."

"Not truly eternal."

"No. We will end when our world ends, it is believed. Our universe is finite, and so is time, which is part of its fabric."

"As it is here. But the Jewels—it was decided they would be hidden, taken to a place of safety and guarded. This was debated endlessly but never acted on. Not until the Wizard-Lord of the time brought an army to the gates of our last city. That was when I was chosen to carry them away. I called a dragon to me, for we were friendly with that folk."

"Friendly?" Kess sounded at least a bit incredulous. "Are dragons friendly with anyone?"

"I suppose not. Not even with other dragons. But they feared the might of this sorcerer as much as we, and would not see him possessing the stones. To the loftiest white tower one came, and bore me south and east, across land and wide sea, to this isle we had chosen. Here I have been since."

"As well as the Jewels."

"What became of your city?" I asked. "Your people?"

"The last I glimpsed of them they were ringed about by an army. Not all human was that army, for goblins and other beings also served the Wizard-Lord. For a century or more, I feared seeking answers from others through speaking from afar, and kept myself closed off here. I have learned since it fell, sacked, its towers thrown down and most of those who remained to defend it either dying or escaping through a gate at the last moment. It was built about a gate, a gate that has been well-warded. None could follow them." Var's thoughts might have followed them for a few silent seconds. "I doubt I shall see my people again."

What would be left for Var if his precious stones were carried away? If he were no longer their guardian? He had a purpose as long as they remained here. I could see his reluctance to part with them, with his duty, whatever he felt about the wisdom of removing them.

"Now it is time for your part of the story," he told Kess.

"I think," she began, "Banat always planned this for me. Maybe even before I was born. He sees the twisted possibilities of the future. In his house, I learned, and in time he spoke to me of the Jewels, of what they were, of what must be done about them. Banat may have foreseen an emergency where the stones would be needed or he may have simply thought it was time they go to his people, taking a long view of what is to come."

"His people?" If Var hadn't asked it, I would have.

Kess addressed me. "Banat wishes you to take the jewels to his people—our people, I could say, the mortals of this world who know and reverence us. All I know of them is that they live on the mainland to the west, in high mountain valleys. The road to those valleys we must find."

"We? Then you will leave me too?" asked the elf.

"I am the Hand of Banat. I must act to fulfill his will."

Who was I to be involved in any of this? "But you think I am the one to carry them."

"Each of us has a role. As do the stones; they must leave here to play it."

And so, apparently, must I.

Twenty-six

There seemed no hurry to be off. I suspected both of these powerful individuals were prone to procrastination. A side effect of living immeasurable ages, perhaps. I, on the other hand, was now eager to be away. Eager to be away from this stone in the sea, whether or not I had a mission, whether or not I carried the Jewels of the Elements.

"I should have a spare sail," I told Kess. "At least one for that which brought me here." Such things were on my mind. I was thinking of provisioning, of all that went into again voyaging into the unknown.

She pinched a fold of her garment. "Of this material?"

"Possibly. Of what is it woven?" I had seen the goblins wear clothes made of it too, though more commonly they used the bark cloth, or even banana or coconut fiber. When they didn't go nude, which was fairly common.

"The silk of the spiders." She noted my expression and assured me, "No, we don't go down into the caves to gather it. The goblins raise smaller ones in their own warrens."

I was somewhat relieved to hear that. A quantity of the precious cloth was brought to me. I had no doubt of its strength nor its ability to stand up to weather. Now I and a pair of goblin helpers needed to fashion the fairly simple sail. If cloth enough was available, perhaps two, and some small auxiliary rags if the need arose for them. I knew something of the art of sail-making. Of what could I fashion the grommets? More of the spider silk would work, to be sure, but I would prefer a more rigid material. Bamboo, perhaps, woven. It was plentiful.

If naught else, this relieved my boredom for a time. There was little to take my interest on this Isle of the Stones. Tramping about went only so far. There were no books, and had there been, I couldn't have read them! I could understand why Var amused himself with goblin women.

I could also understand why both he and Kess sometimes 'spoke from afar.' This I was able to recognize now. They sat gazing off into some unknown distance, sending part of themselves elsewhere to converse with a distant wizard. "We meet in another world," Kess explained to me. "There are many little worlds in the infinite suited to this."

"Infinite little worlds?"

She answered that quite seriously—far more seriously than I had asked it. "Indeed so, Dick."

Kess had told me that, being a goddess, she could go to those worlds, any worlds, in the entirety of her being. Only her sense of duty kept her from, so to speak, walking away.

Mixed with that sense of duty, I conjectured, was one of gratitude toward the god who had taken her in. But what did I know of gods? I would not have believed they existed a few months ago. Even now, I must accept that she and Var spoke truthfully to me of them.

Ultimately, these gods were still physical beings, were they not? More powerful than men but not differing so much otherwise. Banat was not the god I had left behind, well before I entered this world.

A little hut, built with the aid of the goblins, stood on the meadow. It was of simple post and beam construction, largely of bamboo. There I slept and worked now, leaving Var again in sole possession of his own chamber. Goblins came and went, both to work and simply to visit. I had picked up a little of their language. Var and Kess both spoke it to them and, much of the time, to each other.

Kess sat watching me stitch with a bone needle, before my home. "Var," said she, of a sudden. She rose without another word and hurried away. I followed, leaving my task. To the elf's chamber we went, through the stone house, down the flight of stairs. There he sat, trembling, breathing deeply in and out, as if trying to steady himself.

"I felt your distress," stated Kess. "An attack?"

"Yes. An immensely powerful wizard, attempting to take my knowledge from me." He looked up at her, saying, "I have allowed myself to be too open. I have trusted too much."

"It did not matter in the past," the goddess told him. "All has changed. We must act soon."

His retort came harsh, almost as a challenge to her words. "Or guard ourselves all the more carefully."

"Certainly, for now." As usual with her, Kess kept an even, unemotional tone, not acknowledging the shaken elf's implication. "Do you know who it was?"

"They remained hidden. I have not the power to make them reveal themselves."

"But enough to escape them."

"This time."

"Possibly the Wizard-Lord. He may be seeking the Jewels."

"Or sensed some power here. We are far from the Rift and there are other sorcerers in the world, Kesarra."

"I do not doubt he would send someone from the other side of the world to take the stones, if he knew they were here. And where here is."

"Do you think he is the one who sent the lalun after me?" I asked.

"He would have no reason," said Kess.

Var nodded his concurrence. "Whoever wished to destroy you has some other goal in mind."

"To prevent his mission. They would be guided by the prophecies, which are decidedly nebulous."

"The Jewels are not named in them," said Var. "But your god is."

"A follower of Asak? Still, undoubtedly a wizard also."

This was new information to me. "So there are two or three powerful sorcerers out to get me?"

"Oh, probably more than that," Kess assured me.

I went back to my sails and my preparations. According to the sun, it was winter. That meant little this close to the equator. Whether I would remain close to the equator when I voyaged away, neither Kess nor Var knew. There were no maps and were there, they did not know where my destination lay. West. That was it.

"Banat will guide us," Kess had assured me. I didn't know why this Banat didn't come and carry the jewels off himself.

I could only assume he didn't know how to sail.

Twenty-seven

"More than one goblin has reported spying a wyvern," Var informed us. "Or wyverns. Possibly with a rider."

"Other goblins?" I wondered.

"Of their breed, most likely. The goblins who live here are on the large size for a wyvern to carry far."

"Maybe kobolds," suggested Kess, "if these riders aren't altogether imaginary. It is too far for them to fly all the way from the Rift, isn't it?"

"Also too cold for them to live there. The reptiles may be flying from the southern Arus, where they do nest."

Or the mainland to the west. I had no idea how far that might be. As far away as the Aru Islands lay in the other direction? I was to learn it was quite a bit closer, in time. As close as the Arus were to the lands east of them.

"In truth," Kess admitted, "I know little of this world. I have been nowhere but this isle."

"That makes two of us," I told her.

"I know more," said Var. "Though not a great traveler I learned from those who were. Yet you are the ones who wish to carry the stones away, not knowing where."

"The Eyes themselves want to go and have called Dick to them. Called since he entered this world."

"Eyes?" That was a new one.

"Some among the Heldu name them the Eyes, whether the Eyes of Banat or the Eyes of the Wind. They certainly do aid in seeing," said Kess.

"They are a great aid to prophecy. That is perhaps their most desirable aspect—the reason most wish to possess and use them."

That was interesting; better than the nebulous 'powers' of which they had spoken previously. Of no practical to use to me, to be sure. "Have either of you tried looking at things with them?" I asked. That *was* practical.

"I never attempted to use them in any fashion," spoke Var. "Nor has Kess, as far as I know. We would not draw attention to them."

"We wouldn't have to actually go down into the caverns to use the Jewels, I think, if one of us became attuned to them. But I too have avoided them. I fear even to touch the stones." Kess then told me, "I expect you to be the one to carry them with you." She sounded quite adamant about this.

Var seemed to agree that was a good idea. "They won't bother one without powers of sorcery."

"But those who want them would readily kill me," I reminded them.

"Then we avoid them!"

Var smiled at this, whether the goddess meant it as a jest or not. "It is common rumor that some power exists on this isle but I believe none suspect it is the Jewels of the Elements. Most have even forgotten they existed. In the Rift, it would be remembered they were carried away, but even the Wizard-Lord is unlikely to have any notion of where they ended up."

At that point, a goblin ran up, jabbering quickly and excitedly. I could make out only part of what she reported but caught that canoes approached the isle. Two of them?

"I've never known more than one at a time," remarked Var.

"Attention has been drawn to us and that we guard," Kess said. "We can hide no longer."

I did not believe the elf was yet convinced of this. We walked to a vantage point above the cliffs. A group of goblins was already gathered there, pointing and gesticulating and babbling. Yes, two craft could be spied, well out, with square sails. No more than that could be told of them.

"If they draw in closer," I noted, "chances are they will spy us." Maybe not our little companions.

Var shrugged. "Not that it would help them any."

"They will seek a landing place. It might give them a clue as to where that lies." Best they find the spiders rather than our hidden beach. There were other beaches here and there about the island, but approach was nearly impossible through the rocky reefs. It might be chanced in a small canoe. Not in those vessels out there. Moreover, the cliffs rose high behind them.

I lay down to make myself less conspicuous. The boats sailed on by. Yes, boats, not canoes. I could see that as they passed.

Broader, squarer, than anything carved from a log. As to how many men each carried, I could not even guess.

"They may sail all the way around," said Kess.

"As I did, before attempting to land." A bit chagrined, I admitted, "And missed your front door entirely."

"But found our other door. Let us hope these do so as well."

I would not wish death among the spiders on anyone. Nor would it matter so much if they found their way into our concealed lagoon. It was a readily defensible spot, if things came to that, with its cliffs rising all about it. Missiles and rocks might be rained down before they could approach the entry to our tunnels. Or that to the other caves, those leading down to the stones.

There was no more to see, The boats sailed on, beyond our sight. The goblins would keep an eye on them. Would those goblins fight intruders? They might have been warlike, once upon a time, but had lived peacefully here for centuries, with almost no contact with outsiders.

I almost wished I had not thrown away my shark-tooth sword. Only almost.

Twenty-eight

"There is a sorcerer among our visitors," announced Var, "and one of the goblins has been speaking with him."

Kess did not seem surprised. "You have heard them?"

"No, I have not found where they meet. He was turned in by his fellows."

The goblins could speak from afar. I hadn't thought about that. Not as much as I should have. "Do they know what you guard here?" I asked.

"They do not," replied the fay. "It would not have stayed a secret long if they did."

"They are terrible gossips," Kess added. "As to this sorcerer, he is looking at the isle from a different perspective than the goblins. He may or may not be able to locate a way in from any description he was given."

"But he will know there is one," I pointed out.

"Yes," agreed Var. "Whether he might be capable of sensing the Jewels and their location, there is no telling. Ah, here we are."

'We' was a group of goblins. Though the others made no effort to restrain him, the culprit was obvious. Nervousness, guilt, were to be read in his heart-shaped face, his very bearing. I wondered what motivated the goblin. A grudge against Kess or Var? A promise of rewards? Perhaps nothing more than curiosity. He'd done no actual damage.

I could catch some of the words but not enough to follow the conversation—or interrogation—that followed. At last, Kess said, "So he has been speaking with the sorceress Ez. Very dangerous for a little goblin."

"I think he is more frightened of her than of us."

"He does not know what I am capable of. No matter. What does matter is that she has not come herself but sent a lesser wizard along with her men. I suppose all that has happened with you, Dick, aroused her curiosity."

"She would be aware of the prophecies."

I asked, "Is she the one who sent the wyvern?" Or wyverns, as more had been spotted.

"I would doubt it," felt Var. "It would be useful to see as they do and watch these men, wouldn't it? I don't suppose you could see through an eagle's eyes, Kess."

"Too intelligent to impose my will on. I might have a snake take a look, but there really isn't much point."

"The one you had follow me?" I asked her.

"Or the one that guards the stones. We must depend on such guardians, those that lurk in the caves."

"And the goblins," added Var, "not that I put much reliance on them. The defenses I have placed here are primarily to prevent the use of magic by others. Other sorcerers have come in the past."

Kess nodded. "Those with powers are more likely to seek this place."

"Such as this Ez," I said. "Who is she?"

"Certainly one of the most powerful sorcerers alive," Var told me. "She is a power on the isle of Nagi."

"And the coasts north of it. An evil woman."

"Evil? I suppose so. Perhaps mad, as well. Magic has driven more than one sorcerer to insanity."

"Seeing the infinite worlds is too much for some," said Kess. "They are unable to keep them out of their minds."

There was nothing to be seen from there on the cliffs. We headed inland, skirting the hidden lagoon. Goblins buzzed about, excited, though there was little for them to do. Piles of rocks had long since been gathered along the clifftops there, ready to hurtle down on any who found their way in. Some were bringing spears of a sort, more like long arrows, fletched for surer flight and with heavy stone heads. Meant to be dropped as much as thrown.

"Can the mermaids speak from afar?" This had not occurred to me before. They would certainly be useful if they could.

Kess shook her head. "None that dwell in the seas about here. It is a gift that sometime appears, as it does among mortal humans."

"Or trolls and dwarfs, for that matter."

"I understand Ez rules over trolls."

"And troll-men. Such mongrels may be among those sailing around our coasts."

Whoever might sail them, we saw the boats no more that day. The goblins kept an eye on their circumnavigation, as long as daylight lasted, reporting their position to Var. Kess disappeared.

Var had no more idea what she was up to than I. "Seeking among the worlds, maybe," he conjectured.

"To learn more of this Ez?"

"Maybe so. Or finding resources for our defense. Or—" He hesitated, thoughtful for a moment. "She may only be preparing herself. Working on her self-discipline. Kess fears the passions within her. She fears becoming like her mother."

Or even mad like Ez? I knew nothing of wizards. I would not have believed they existed not so long ago.

The next morning, the boats landed, one at the way that led through the spiders, the other at our hidden beach. They knew where it was, sailing directly to it, having completed their scouting of the Stone's coasts.

Kess called our goblin traitor to her. Maybe traitor is too strong a word; he owed nothing to any of us. "Can you speak to the wizard down there?" she asked him.

An affirmative. "Then call him and I shall follow you."

Both were elsewhere for a couple minutes. "Very well," spoke the goddess, on returning. "I can find the man myself now and speak to him as I will. If he wills. His power is no match for my own but he could ward himself."

Var gave her a long and, perhaps, fearful look. "You wouldn't think of blasting his mind, would you?"

"I am not sure I have that much power. Nor would I use it if I did." She sounded quite sure of that. "He had little to say. Only that he was sent to find what is here."

Var sighed. "He will find death."

Twenty-nine

Fewer than a dozen men cautiously rowed their way into the lagoon. It could be assumed the other boat held a similar number. Enough to force their way past the spiders? Those below us were our concern now. I understood, with no one saying it, that they could not be allowed to leave. Not having found the way in.

But this distant Ez knew the way, didn't she? It no longer mattered. What did matter was that they not carry away the Jewels of the Elements. Best they not reach them at all and learn what they were. So rocks were pushed over the edge. Not such large rocks, unfortunately, for they were of a size for goblins to use, and the few that struck their target did little damage.

The boat made immediately for the door that led to the stones, opposite our own way in. This too, Ez had apparently been told. The goblins began hurtling—or dropping, more accurately—their feathered spears on the boat and the men, now they had come to a halt. One man, perhaps struck, perhaps only startled, stumbled back into the water. A mermaid took him under.

"The wizard is having trouble with my bindings on the door," noted Var. "I suppose he will figure them out in time."

"Then let us use that time," Kess stated. At once, a glowing rain of cinders and ash began to fall on the intruders,.

"Drawn from a volcano? Very nice," said the elf. It certainly distracted the men below, and discomfited them. How much actual damage it did to them I couldn't say, but I did see another fall to a dart.

It also started a fire in their boat. A pair rushed back to it, seeking to extinguish the flames. I saw an arm reach from the water, snag one by the ankle, pull him into the embrace of more arms. He disappeared beneath the dark surface. The other bolted back to the door.

Which the wizard had puzzled out and opened. All disappeared into the darkness of the tunnel. "I count eight," said Kess. "We must take the battle to them now. Will any of you come?" she asked the goblins around us.

They did not seem eager. One reported that a contingent had

waited outside the back door for any who fled the spiders. "All dead now," he said.

"All dead who are not enmeshed in the webs," commented Var.

"Perhaps so," Kess agreed. "But it is possible some fought past and are on their way to the stones."

"Is their hiding place far from the spiders?" I asked.

"Quite close, actually," Var said. "But there are other dangers between."

"The snakes, mostly. Let's get down there and follow them."

I was for giving the crabs and spiders and snakes plenty of time to deal with the invaders before running after them. Yet I followed Kess down and we crossed the lagoon in a pair of canoes, with Var and several goblins. These refused to enter the caves but posted themselves outside the door. Sensible little fellows.

They also busied themselves putting out the fire on the boat, which I could see was of a wooden framework covered with some sort of hide. Not a vessel I would trust on the deep ocean! The goblins worked without fear of merfolk. There was an understanding between their peoples or, more precisely, between Kesarra and both peoples. She enforced a peace.

Into the tunnel we plunged. I carried my spear, my knife. I felt woefully under-equipped for any encounter. Yet Kess and Var had no better arms; perhaps they would reach into other worlds for weapons, when needed. "Don't trip over the body," hissed Var.

"What happened to him?" I wondered, holding my torch high. The rather bestial face was set in a grimace.

"Sea snake bite," explained Kess, and moved on.

"A troll-man, I think," said Var. "Never have I seen one in the flesh."

"Nor I," admitted the goddess. "Is this Ez part troll?"

"Not that I have heard. Ez is a descendant of Hurasu, of course, but not from his valley. He spent many years on Nagi when first he arrived in this world. Ah, the crabs have been feeding."

"But will gladly feed more if we allow them. Ware there, Dick."

How many intruders had fallen to the crustaceans I could not guess. All, I hoped. The water was shallow enough to make out three or four partially consumed bodies. More might lie beyond our light. Kess proved impatient, too impatient to bother with smoke. Steaming water poured into the pool, driving back the approaching crabs. Perhaps cooking a few.

The stench suggested worse than crabs were being boiled. We hurried along our ledge path to safety. Comparative safety.

Lights ahead. Our torches were not the only ones in these caves. We entered the chamber of the stones, with its pool and rock, to spy four men. No five—one was crossing the bridge. These all looked like fairly normal humans, armed much as were we. We stood facing each other, neither attacking, while the wizard—so I assumed he was—clambered up the great rock. He found the stones at once, lifting the lid of their container and staring into it.

Kess seemed to be somewhere else, staring also, staring into nothingness. The giant sea snake rose from the water and grasped the hapless sorcerer in its jaws, dragging him into the depths. The goddess gasped. "He told Ez what he had discovered before I could summon the snake. She knows now of the Eyes."

"Then they must leave the isle," said Var. "I will argue it no longer. What of these?"

The four men stood, uncertain, watching us. They must have known they had no safe way out of here. Kess regarded them for a few seconds before addressing them in a language I had not heard before. Nor, I think, had Var.

One replied in the same tongue.

"I have promised them safe passage," she informed us and smiled faintly. "As far as the sunlight."

Thirty

"Once we are gone, it might be as well to release our guests," Kess told the fay. "Neither the merfolk nor the goblins will harm them so long as I am here, but I do not think they will obey you."

"Will Var be safe?" I asked.

"It was never quite safe to be around the mermaids," he said, "but the goblin folk have long accepted me. There is no other place for me in this world."

"You can always make one," I told him.

To this Kess added, "Or seek other of your people. They still visit Exura."

He nodded, somewhat distractedly. "As do the Dark Elves. I have spoken with some of them."

I suspected Var could pass for a mortal human if he wished. At least until someone noticed he wasn't aging.

"You are now the guardians of the Jewels," he went on. "This duty has weighed on me for centuries. It may be centuries more before I seek anything but rest."

"No rest for us. We must be off at once," decided Kesarra.

"To some place in the west. What if we sailed some other way? Would it make any difference?" The stones could be hidden anywhere, couldn't they? They could even be dropped into the depths of the ocean and bother nobody for a very long time.

The more I thought of that, the better it seemed to me. Lose the jewels. Sail back to the Arus. Forget gods and prophecies and wizards. Kess probably knew what I was mulling over.

"They will be needed to hold back the evil in this world. They were guarded not so much for fear of their misuse but so they would be ready when the time came."

"I did not realize that when I first fled with them," Var said. "I sought only to keep them safe. Now I understand that was but a part of something much greater."

Oh well, the merfolk would probably find them if they went overboard. "We can leave in the morning," I said. "All we need is already being stowed on my boat."

"Ah, then you were prepared to go."

"Go somewhere," I mumbled.

"Right now we must go down and retrieve the jewels. They will be in your keeping then, Dick."

Why couldn't we have picked them up earlier? Someone should have thought of it. Maybe me. "Past the crabs once again?"

"Unless you prefer the spiders. I can cow them and need not resort to smoke or other such tricks. But it is out of our way."

"And I shall come along," said Var. "The last time, maybe, I ever need go into those caves."

The journey to the chamber of the stones was almost disappointingly uneventful. The crabs seemed sluggish; the few that climbed to us, Kess knocked away with a stick. No sign of any snakes when we reached the pool. I wondered if the big boy had eaten the sorcerer. Not a typical item in its diet, I would think. We crossed to the rocky island.

"You don't need this heavy jar," Kess said, lifting it from its niche and holding it out to me. "Just scoop out the stones and put them in a bag or something of that sort."

She did not want to touch them, did she? She hadn't when we looked at them before. I picked them out of their container, one by one, and tucked them into my belt pouch. "I—thought I felt something when I touched the green one," I said. My imagination?

"The Sea Stone. It may speak to a sailor."

"I doubt you will ever feel more than a faint tingle," Var said.

And I never did. But that night, the Jewels of the Elements were in my dreams. The Jewels and a voice I somehow knew was that of Banat. I could not remember what words he spoke. I only knew when I awoke that I must carry these stones of prophecy west.

I said nothing of it to Kesarra.

PART III. CURRENTS

Thirty-one

Something large, high up. Another lalun? It was possible; whoever sent them before might yet be keeping an eye on us. Or on me. They might or might not know what I carried. Now this Ez was aware of the stones, could the secret be kept from others?

"I heard her minion before he met his end," Kess told me, "but I had already spoken with him and knew where to, ah, listen. Only I and Ez might have heard his report."

Her 'might' did imply others could have, didn't it? There was naught I could do about that. What I could do was sail west.

That is, I could attempt to sail west. The winds were not with us. Not completely; we did trend in a westerly direction, yes, but we were also driven ever further south. Storm after storm carried us from my intended course.

"Only the storms of spring," my shipmate assured me. "No wizard can control the weather. Nor any god, at least in this world." She then smiled faintly. "One of us could, however, open a way to another world and bring through a more favorable wind. Briefly."

Considering the abilities she and Var had shown before, I could believe it. "In an emergency, maybe," I answered. Kess but nodded to this.

So we sailed on. I was not overly worried about our course. We kept moving and that was good. Better than being becalmed or fighting a headwind. And, after all, we did not truly know our destination.

"I have spoken with Var," she reported on a clear, cool morning, a morning that gave me hope for our voyage. "He tells me two of the Ez's men sailed away in a canoe, and two remained and have joined the goblins."

"Can we expect half-human children?" I had wondered about Var producing offspring. Now I wondered about this.

"It could happen. The fay do not breed quickly, at least in Exura." She might have intended to leave it at that but Kess guessed the question in my mind, one I did not intend to voice. "We gods can most certainly breed with humans. I am evidence of that. However, we can choose whether or not to have offspring. Assuming all else is favorable, of course."

"Then I take it fay and humans are mutually fertile. And gods too? There would seem a vast difference."

"Oh, we can have sex with anything and, yes, produce children of one sort or another. We, ah, are able to adapt our forms to enable this. And no, I have no offspring." She sat thinking a moment before going on. "Nor have I ever coupled. But I am not cut out to be a virgin goddess, as are some. That is their nature. Perhaps I shall be like my grandmother Khabata, who has not engaged in sexual relations since the dawn of time. She was raped in an immeasurably distant past by her brother." That brought another slight smile, a shrug nearly as slight. "Or so it is said. I think neither remembers it happening; it is simply part of their respective myths."

"And that led to the birth of your mother?"

"It did. Of Dekata and of her twin sister Arimanata, the goddess of the full moon and my mother's opposite in all things."

I felt it unwise to delve deeper right then. Perhaps someday Kesarra would wish to say more; that was her business, not mine. "Whales." I pointed toward several dark forms breaching the blue surface, where long rolling swells rose and fell. "Migrating, maybe. At this season they might be seeking a place to calve."

She gazed in their direction for some time before nodding. "Yes, most of them are pregnant."

That suggested we might be near a coast. "You touched their minds?"

"So to speak. They are far too intelligent for me to do more than see the surface, but giving birth very much fills their thoughts at the moment."

"I knew those who hunted the whale, in the world from which I came."

"They should have been ashamed of themselves," was the goddess' curt response. Her eyes again lingered on the great whales. "Maybe I will feel as they do someday. Maybe I will be filled with the thought of birth and children." Kess sighed deeply. "I have tried to cut myself off from emotion. I dread awakening the sort of madness that fills my mother. The greater gods are ever serene but that is their nature. I can only emulate them in this."

"Then you must follow your own nature," I offered.

"I know not what that nature might prove to be. I fear learning the truth of me."

Don't we all? I did not say that aloud. I did wonder if Kess could now speak the language of the whales. I might have asked her of it but at that moment I spied a distant dark line lying on the horizon.

"Land," I reported, nodding in its direction. "What land I do not know but we are somewhere."

"I suppose we are," Kess agreed.

Thirty-two

It was not high land. No dim blue mountains rose in the distance; just that low line that proved to be unbroken cliffs as we drew nearer.

"We could follow the whales south along this coast," I said, "but I think our course lies the other way."

"I trust you to set that course." Kess had even less idea of where we were than I did. I, at least, knew of navigation, ignorant though I was of this world. "This land was closer than we thought, wasn't it?"

"It is. I've no idea whether it is the mainland or another island." If island it was, it was a large one. We paralleled the dark cliffs northward, slowly, sailing often close-hauled to the wind. Frequent rain swept across us, cold rain. We were far from the tropics where we had begun our voyage. A spider-silk tent—a spare sail—kept us drier than we might otherwise have been.

We glimpsed no more wyverns but did not doubt they yet sought us. The clouds might have hidden us from them—or their riders—as well. "Another whale?" asked Kess, gazing toward a solitary creature breaking the water.

It looked somehow different. An orca, maybe? No. I could see that as it moved directly toward us. "I think it means us harm," I commented. "Or means to make us lunch."

This was no whale of any sort, though shaped somewhat like one. The head was reptilian, with massive toothy jaws. "Hold on!" I brought us about abruptly; the wind filled my sail and I sped away from the beast. As I had suspected, it was not built for quick pursuit. An ambush hunter, perhaps. But it had come very close and I had no doubt it could have rushed upon us at the last moment.

"I would not be surprised if it preyed on the whale calves," I told the goddess. "It might be wise to maintain more distance from the shore for a while." I brought us back around, again beating into the wind. We had not lost much.

"I won't need this, then," she said, and tossed a massive harpoon overboard, a weapon grabbed from some other world.

Maybe Kess could have used it successfully. I did not truly know her limits. "I think I will speak with Var."

She sat a few minutes, her mind elsewhere. Not all of her mind. Kess was able to keep an eye open to this world while visiting another. "There may be little reason to do that again," she said, on returning. "The elf thinks that land over there is Nagi. It is a very large island and one of the gates from your world opens on it."

"Nagi." I undoubtedly frowned. "Isn't that where this Ez lives?"

"On the west coast. Or at least she holds sway over some who live there. Var also thinks that was an itza that wanted to eat us. The lurker in the deep it is named by those who live here."

It was nice to give it a name. I hoped I'd never have to use it. The coast had been trending ever so slightly eastward as we moved north. Now we rounded a great cape. The cliffs continued unbroken, save for a deep fjord here and there. Those, I would not enter. Who might know whether the itza lurked in their depths? There would be no escape in those narrow places. Past a broad bay and another cape, and the coast curved back to the south and west. Sailing should prove easier now.

Though the winds lightened, becoming more fitful. The rains let up, the sun came out. I sniffed the breeze coming off the land. "I smell—pines?" It certainly seemed to carry their scent. We were too far away to see anything of that sort.

"Pine trees." Kess seemed to search for a moment. "Hmm. The word does not mean much to me, as is true of many of the words I took from you. I need to see one but I understand a little more from having smelled them now. It is not a scent I have come across before." Her gaze swept the distant cliffs. "Many sorcerers dwell here. I can tell this. Not powerful ones."

"You could speak to one of them, couldn't you?"

"It is likely. There is no point." She looked to the sky. "The wyverns have found us again."

We were more vulnerable now, being close to land. Close to Ez, even if she was not the one who sent the winged reptiles to watch us. "If this is an island, we must be off its northern shore. Perhaps we should turn north, seeking a continent."

"Perhaps. I am certain the Heldu do not dwell on Nagi." Kesarra gazed northward. "But certain of little else."

"A high mountain valley on the mainland. That is what you told me."

"And so Banat told me. He seemed to think that directions enough."

I wondered if maybe this chief god felt it would be dangerous for the youngster—relatively speaking—to know too much. "You are related to Banat, right?"

"My great-grandfather. The eldest of all the gods. So most of us believe. He may have, ah, some equivalence to the stones in our universe. An aspect of the creative force that shaped all things." She frowned, seemingly not quite happy with her explanation. "A manifestation. But not exactly that force himself."

Might not everything in a universe be an aspect of that creative force? I wasn't about to pose that question aloud. "It wouldn't hurt to stop here and replenish our supplies."

"Yes. I eat an awful lot, don't I? I could, you realize, walk away from this world and go find a meal elsewhere. Alas, I could not bring anything back for you."

"Too bad you can't take me along," I said.

"Oh, but I could. And anything you ate elsewhere would stay with you but you yourself would, sooner or later, be pulled back to this world. To exactly the same spot." She snickered. "Your boat would be likely to have moved while you were gone."

That wouldn't be so good. If we ever attempted it, we'd best be on solid ground. "Would you be able to find your way back to the boat if you, um, walked away?"

"Hmm, maybe not. I'm not going to try it, anyway. We need to find a port, right?"

"That seems like a good plan," I allowed.

"Then maybe those fellows can tell us where one is," the goddess said, pointing toward a sail bobbing in the distance. We were quickly overtaking it.

I had my spear in my hand at once. The boat looked just a little too akin to those Ez's minions had sailed to the Isle of the Stones, a hide-covered frame, a simple square sail. No warriors manned it, though, only a young couple, dark haired and clad in sheep-skin vests. As to their ancestry, your guess is likely to be as good as mine. You might have told me they were Finns, when I dwelt in another world, and I would have accepted it.

Kesarra had their language at once. I wouldn't need it. I might never encounter another who spoke it. Yet there were familiar words here and there. These were the descendants of people from my world, I reminded myself. People who had come through a gateway, as had I, but a different one. I wondered where it lay.

It makes no difference, Dick Brown. You'll not be going back to that world. I didn't think I would choose to, even if I could.

"Traders," Kess informed me. "Traveling along this bit of coast." She jabbered at them. They jabbered back. "It's easier to carry goods by boat, they claim. They are heading home now, to a place they name Akmem. We are invited."

It would be slow sailing, keeping to the pace of their clumsy boat. I hoped this Akmem was not too far away.

Thirty-three

Our new friends' boat was stuffed with woolen cloth, traded for at some port just to our east, a port we had sailed past unknowingly. Akmem proved to be a fair distance but we reached it on our third day, well into the afternoon. A fine, deep harbor it was.

Or I could say it was two harbors, divided by a broad rocky promontory. Much of the town was located on that spit of high land, with dockage on either side. Not only was it a convenient spot to sail from but one that could be readily defended, if need arise. There was, however, little in the way of fortification. I could spy other villages around the shores of the twin bays. Tall were the docks set here and there; the tides must rise and fall greatly on this coast. That was something to be aware of when I tied up.

It is needless to say that my boat attracted much attention, as we docked beside that of the traders. I was more interested in what they would be unloading from their vessel. Surely there were other goods beneath those bundles of cloth. "I wonder what they traded for this," I commented to Kess.

"I could ask. It is not something I would think of." A few words were exchanged. "Fish. They catch and dry many fish here. And wine. The grape does not grow well further south."

I doubted not there were other items involved but all this was good to know. Interesting, anyway, to one whose life had been spent carrying out just such trade. Whether I would ever return to that life, here in this world, I had no idea. "Antlers?" They had been uncovered as the cloth came onto the dock.

Again, the goddess made inquiries. "Reindeer are herded in the far south. There isn't much trade with those who live there but some items do come north." A few other trade goods appeared, nothing as unusual. Stone tools. This was apparently yet another people who did not know or use metal.

Yet metal must sometimes come through the gate that supposedly lay on this island. I would not pester the goddess with questions now; I could learn more if we remained a few days. We both could use some time ashore.

"We are to meet the headman here." She frowned, reconsidered. "No, headwoman. They used a feminine form of the word. Everything is male or female in their language."

"I have known such languages," I replied.

"Yes, the Español I saw in your mind. I did not bother to take it for myself but caught some of its flavor. Gender is not so important in your English." Kess spoke, as oft she did, in a matter of fact manner, giving no clue as to her feelings on the subject. "I know languages where it does not even exist."

"I suppose it isn't truly necessary."

"And sometimes inaccurate. They're ready to go." We followed our guides, with curious townsfolk making a procession behind us, up a stone-paved way from the docks, sometimes more stair than walkway. There was much stone in Akmem. Many of the buildings were completely of it, in the beehive fashion. Others had stone walls with thatched roofs. Wood, maybe, was not so plentiful. Few trees were to be seen.

I did not look too different from these people. Some looked European, some more Asian; none resembled Kesarra. None was so dark, none had hair so red nor eyes so green.

None was so striking. Kess was tall for a woman, but not ostentatiously so. I wondered if she had some control over this, remembering how she seemed to grow when I first encountered her among the spiders. That her nature as a god had come to the forefront then, I now recognized. How much of it showed in her everyday form, I had no idea.

Nor did I know whether these Akmemians could see the goddess in her, as did I. Surely they sensed something more than a normal woman, though Kess was good to look at as simply that and nothing more. There were certainly more eyes turned toward her than me.

A woman of middle age stood before one of the larger stone houses, wearing mud-colored woolen trousers and tunic. This was Perra, the headwoman, the leader of at least this town. How far her authority extended, I could only guess—and it would be wise not to. Two men flanked her, one squat and broad, the other taller, leaner, and somewhat older, his scant beard graying.

The shorter man spoke rather loudly to the headwoman, loud

enough for all in attendance to hear. Perra, in turn, exchanged words with Kess. "That is the headwoman's husband, Ivan," Kess informed me. "He recognized the language we use with each other as that of the Heldu, for he has traded in the north. None here speak it."

"We could speak to each other in English and confuse them further," I suggested, not very seriously.

But Kess did take it seriously. "If we have need of secrecy, we shall. Best not to make anyone suspicious right now." She then carried on a longer conversation, one in which the older man played more part. Ivan, apparently, had used up everything he knew. Some sort of conclusion was eventually reached. Perra went indoors; the older man ambled over to us.

"We shall lodge in the house of Valado," said Kess. "He is a shaman. A sorcerer. I thought it best they know I also have powers."

But not that she was a goddess, I surmised. We followed the shaman, and a few of the curious yet followed us, though our novelty was wearing off.

"They at first thought maybe I was Ba'esu. That is a nation that lives on the coasts north of Nagi, on the mainland. Sometimes they trade with them. Aside from the color of my skin, I do not seem to resemble them much. Nor do I have any of their language."

"Yet," I said.

"Yet," agreed the goddess. "It is likely we shall travel to their land."

On our journey to the Heldu. At last we had some idea where that people dwelt. That they actually existed, for that matter.

As an afterthought, perhaps, she added, "I think the last visitor to the island, before Ez's men, was of the Ba'esu. Others before him, too."

There was nothing to say about that. Moreover, we had arrived at the home of Valado. It was a narrow place, as were most of Akmem's houses. This, I figured, allowed their roofs to be framed with shorter lengths of timber. What it lacked in width it made up in length. The length was needed for the extended family that dwelt within. Each room opened into the next, with no hallways.

Do not ask me to name any of those children and grandchildren of the shaman, though I undoubtedly was told who they were.

Otherwise, I was thoroughly left out, understanding nothing that was said. I instead turned my attention to the plentiful food. Mutton and fish predominated, with vegetables that were likely to have been stored since the fall, carrots, something that might have been turnips. Barley appeared in more than one dish, and as dark bread. I wondered if they brewed beer of it, but the wine flowed plentifully so it did not matter much at the moment.

For a short time, nothing seemed to matter much. It was good to put aside my cares, to be among more or less ordinary people again. Only for a short time and then I must think again of our mission. Kess spoke of it, as a young woman showed us to our sleeping place. "Valado and I are going to have a serious discussion in the morning. He knows nothing of what we carry, but understands it is important and must be kept safe." She looked about the room we had entered. I would estimate it no more than a dozen feet wide—as all the others in the house of Valado. A doorway—with a heavy woolen curtain, not a door—opened at each end. More curtains provided privacy for the sleeping space along one wall. Perhaps people passed through here all night. "I believe they think we are a couple and will share our bed."

"It is probably as well they think us together. It will simplify our interactions."

Kess nodded slowly. "I see this. But what if you like one of Valado's pretty granddaughters?"

I could not tell how serious a question it might be. Nor would I say aught about the handsome young men of Akmem. "We won't be here that long. Ah, wool blankets."

We had huddled together on our cold, rainy voyage from the Stone. We could huddle now, slumber in this warm, hospitable place. Did I truly need to go any further than Akmem? I asked myself as I drifted into sleep. What was this mission of Kesarra and her god to me? And Valado did have pretty granddaughters.

Thirty-four

Butter! I had not tasted butter in more than a year. Maybe two. There might be cheese here, as well. I must investigate. First, though, I slathered my black bread thickly.

Kess cautiously sniffed at it and directed an inquiry to a boy seated across from us. He was shy about speaking to her but eventually stuttered out the information she wanted. "Made from milk. Sheep's milk. It seems an odd thing to eat," she commented.

Sheep? I supposed that made no difference. I wondered if they even had cattle here. "While you confer with our host, I should go down to the boat and check everything over," I told her. I was not completely happy about having left it unattended overnight. Akmem could be full of thieves, for all I knew.

Again, Kess spoke to the lad. He nodded agreement to something. "Tashi will go with you, to keep you from getting into trouble," she told me. "The boy is a promising shaman, one of his grandfather's best apprentices."

"So if I get out of hand he can call to you from afar?"

"Even so, Dick."

I suspected the boy would be sensible and speak to his grandfather instead. A chill, foggy morn greeted us as we stepped from Valado's house. Such were likely to be common here, I felt. The climate seemed akin to that of northern Europe. But we were past the spring equinox, weren't we? There should be at least some warm weather, in time.

And Kesarra and I would be traveling north, into more temperate climes. I could see much of the town, the shapes of roofs emerging from the mists, for the the shaman's home was built on high ground, well above the water. The boat—somewhere that direction.

There were no shadows on a morning like this. I did not know what hovered above us until I heard the flap of a leathery wing. Tashi looked up even as I did and cried out. I think he at once called to his grandfather.

A wyvern. No, not one but two of them. I tensed, ready for an attack. As quickly, I realized there had been far better opportunities for that when we were at sea. These were scouts, keeping an eye on me for someone. The low skies, the fog, had brought them down for a closer look. The two creatures circled; as one banked I could make out a tiny rider on its back, only as a shape.

The wyverns swooped, circled, rose, disappearing into the gray clouds. I could only shrug and set off again for the boat. I had no reason to do anything else. The boy gave me a curious look and followed.

All was as I had left it but I made a show of checking it over, examining the sail, tying things down more securely. There were many boats, most of the same hide construction, launching. The craft of fishermen and women, they seemed to be for the most past. One stood out, a dugout canoe with double outriggers. "Ba'ezu," Tashi informed me as I looked it over.

None of that folk seemed to be around at the moment. I would encounter them in time. I allowed the boy to lead me back to his home. On my own, I'd soon have become lost in the warren of winding ways and houses all of the same gray stone that made up Akmem.

Word of what had occurred had preceded me. This in no way prevented Tashi from launching into a long account of the incident. Then there was discussion by all there. All but me.

"So," spoke Kess, when they came to a pause, "the wyverns are still with us."

"There was some sort of rider. Quite small." Smaller than the goblins I knew from the Isle of the Stones.

"Tashi says it was a kobold. Some live on Nagi, but these surely came from further north, for the wyvern does not nest here."

North, where we were headed. "You and Valado had your talk?"

"I told him some of our mission and we spoke from afar with a few other shamans of Nagi. No one seemed to know much about what Ez or any other sorcerer might be up to." She and Valado exchanged more words. "We may want to reach out again now."

"Can they help?" And will they help?

"Their knowledge may be useful. They were curious about you. Valado was not surprised to learn you came from another world and told me what he knows of the gate here. The way lies in the far south of the island, the shaman says, where the reindeer herders live. He has never met anyone who came through it but others claim to have. They say those who pass now come from a nation they name Russia."

"I know Russia. It would be on the other side of the world from where I entered."

"Opposite poles, perhaps? As they seem to be in this world." She seemed to muse on that for a moment. "No matter. The gate has played its role, bringing you here."

Here. Here to this world, here to the Arus, to the Stone, to Nagi. "We travel further. Your prophecy."

"Not mine. Some of these shamans have heard of it, though it is a tradition of the Heldu."

We could guess the sender of the wyverns—and of their riders—knew of it as well. Only a guess would it be. He or she might have some completely different reason for being interested in me. At least they were no longer attempting to kill me. For now.

"We could use some provisions before setting forth again." I would not ask when that would be. "We have little with which to buy anything."

Kess smirked. "I could pull trade items from another world. They would disappear in a while, of course." A sudden scowl. "No, I should not think of such evil things nor take pleasure in the thoughts. I should not allow myself to be tempted."

"It's only human to do so," I told her. "That struggle is part of our lives. The free will you claim as your heritage."

"I am not human only. I think these folk of Akmem will give us food to carry on our journey, if Valado tells them to. Certainly water. That we need the most, no?"

I nodded. We could go weeks without replenishing our other supplies. Were there weeks yet to travel? Months? I needed some way to ask these people about distances. Maybe that Ba'esu visitor whose canoe I had seen.

"I could use some more food myself, right now," I said. "Then maybe we can see about our supplies."

Kess conferred again with the shaman, who in turn conferred with his grandson. "Very well," she told me. "Tashi will take you to the, ah—" The proper Heldun word seemed to be missing from her vocabulary so she substituted an English one. "Cistern, where you may replenish our water. Volado will see about getting some food for us."

The boy and I set out after an early lunch. A tiffin, I might have called it, for I did intend to have another lunch when we returned. I enjoyed this solid, plain food of Akmem, food that reminded me of a home I would not see again. First, down to the boat to gather all our water containers in a wheelbarrow Tashi had pushed along. The first such I had seen in this world; the first wheels of any sort, in fact. The cistern collected the plentiful rainwater that fell here. We would deprive no one with the little we needed.

I wheeled the heavy, precarious load back down the slippery rock and mud ways of Akmem, thinking perhaps I should have made two trips. Without Tashi there to help me balance the barrow, it would surely have overturned. Indeed, we came close to doing so at one steep spot when a large, dark man stepped up and steadied the load.

A bulky fellow he was, thick, and broad of shoulder. Quite black, too, but otherwise not so like the negro back in the States. This was the sort of islander I had expected to find when I still thought I sailed the Pacific of my own world, and undoubtedly the Ba'esu voyager whose canoe was moored at the docks. He squinted at me from beneath heavy brows, stroking his curling beard, before speaking in Heldun.

"I heard there were travelers," he said, "and that they have a mission from the gods."

I nodded. "Travelers we are," I admitted. I did not intend to address the mission he mentioned.

"Yes. And I have come to guide you. But first, let us get your water safely down to your boat, rather than spilling it all on the streets of Akmem!"

Thirty-five

"He told me to call him Sharki," I said. "It sounds like a name from English."

"So it does. But I know nothing of the Ba'esu language."

"Until you meet Sharki."

"Yes, I must meet him," Kess agreed. "I also know nothing of anyone sent to guide us. He might serve one who covets the stones."

That had certainly occurred to me. "You and the shaman spoke from afar again?"

"Yes, and others, to whom we had not spoken before, joined us. A powerful young shaman of the trolls. Zup. He and Valado do not share a language but I was able to take his troll tongue. A difficult one it is!" Almost as an afterthought, Kess added, "Zup at once recognized me as a god."

My mind went to the troll-men among those who invaded the Isle of the Stones. "A troll? Aren't they, um, evil?" It wasn't quite the word I wanted. Hostile maybe would have been closer.

"No more so than men, I suspect, though admittedly I'd never met a troll before. Be that as it may, Valado and the other human shamans much respect this Zup's abilities."

I scraped up the last of my stew with a wooden spoon and pondered refilling the bowl. Nothing more than mutton and barley and root vegetables it was, hardly elegant fare, yet I savored it. When we sailed from here I might not see such again. "Did the troll have anything to say?"

"Zup agrees the sorceress Ez would be unlikely to employ either wyverns or kobolds. He suspects the priests of Asak. This makes sense to me."

"You have suggested it before." As well as mentioning the possibility of other wizards being interested.

One of Valado's granddaughters entered and spoke to Kess. I wondered if she could make a decent stew. Ah, but this was idle thought. I would not remain in Akmem, no matter how many pretty girls might reside here, no matter how well they might cook. The goddess informed me, "Your Ba'esu is here. Shall we invite him in?"

I set my empty bowl aside. "I think it best we meet him outside." For safety, for privacy, and primarily from respect for Valado's hospitality. We need not bring strangers into the shaman's home. This was something I think Kess did not quite grasp. She had never lived in the society of men and women.

Sharki seemed clad rather scantily for this clime, even if the day had cleared and become almost warm. A kilt of bark cloth was belted at his midsection; a leather vest hung open. Several necklaces, of the teeth of some large animal, hung about his thick neck. He greeted us in Heldun.

Kesarra stared at him, seemingly perplexed. He turned to me and winked. "She can not find my language," he confided, his voice a stage whisper.

Hands on hips, head tilted, she stated, "Either an extraordinarily strong sorcerer or a god. I would guess the latter."

"You would guess correctly, little goddess." I did not quite like the way he looked her up and down. "You look like my niece Dasemenca when she is in her woodpecker form. Black and white with a great red crest."

"Ah. You are a god of the Ba'esu, are you not? I have heard they can take an animal form."

"We do not take it. It is a part of who we are." He sounded just the slightest offended, but his statement was followed by a deep chuckle. "So the name I gave to your sailor."

The shark. Many questions rose up in my mind but the two deities had moved on to other topics. "I know none of your pantheon," said Kesarra, "and have heard only of Xido, who is said to wander this world at times."

"Yes, Dasemenca's husband. He should stay home with her more. Ha! Yet here am I meddling with mortals myself."

"None of the local gods seem interested, according to the troll Zup. He speaks with some of them."

"Trolls claim to be atheists. That is, they reverence none of the known gods, considering them no better than mortals."

"Which may be true," replied Kess.

"They do honor their ancestors, despite having no belief in an afterlife." What slight serious note had tinged his speech disappeared as he added, "In that lack of belief, they are not so different from some gods."

I could not read the goddess' opinion on that. "Why do you meddle with mortals, Sharki?" she asked. "And should we still call you Sharki?"

"As good a name as any, for now. I am here protecting my own people."

He offered no further explanation nor was I inclined to ask for one. I did ask, "You know the course we must follow?"

"I know you journey to the Heldu. I know what you carry and the importance of keeping them safe."

Kess was at once on guard. As was I. God or not, there was no reason Sharki should know of the stones. "I have long been aware the Eyes were hidden on your island. It wasn't hard to figure out they are now on the move." Sharki peered at me from below craggy brows. "This one carries them. I can feel their power and it makes me uncomfortable!"

As it did Kess. "How could you know this?"

"I was curious and went and peeped at them once. Your guardians were no impediment, even in this form. The stones are of no use to me, of course. I would prefer not be near them, much less touch them."

"Then why get involved?" I asked.

"I recognize the danger they pose, should they fall into the wrong hands. Why anyone thinks they are better off with the Heldu, I do not comprehend, but so be it. I am not a particularly smart god, you know."

I didn't know. I hadn't thought about it, either, assuming any deity would be more intelligent than mortals. "I was curious about you, too, Dick," he went on. "I have watched you from time to time since you came to this world."

"You're not the only one, it seems." I swatted at a mosquito. They were thick in Akmem. Another reason to be on our way.

Thirty-six

The sailors of Nagi had charts of a sort. Their accuracy was suspect; more so as the distance from Akmem increased. The northern coasts were shown but the rest of Nagi was blank. I was told it was shaped like a crescent, with a great bay bordering its western coasts, but none had sailed south to verify this.

"A comma, I think, is the word in your English," Kess told me. "I'm not quite sure what a comma is but that is the shape."

"You are unlikely to ever encounter one," I replied, "nor any of the fabled beasts known as punctuation."

The goddess looked baffled by the remark but moved on. Moved on northward, pointing out the islands marked north of Nagi. "And beyond these, the mainland. A great, um, peninsula." I doubted she grasped the meaning of that word, either, or not completely.

Beyond the southern coasts of the peninsula, little was marked. Akmemians rarely voyaged further. But further lay the home of the Ba'esu and that of the Heldu beyond.

Sharki squinted at the parchment. "Most," he said, "follow the chain of islands to the mainland beyond, steering near to the coast. Better you sail directly north and avoid most of that. The coasts are rocky and inhospitable along much of the peninsula, but sail further and you will reach a wide shallow bay—maybe a gulf, one should call it—and a large river flowing into it. This is the heart of the Ba'esu lands." His thick finger moved to a largely blank spot on the map. "From there, my people can show you the way into the mountains and to the home of the Heldu."

"The river leads to them?" Kess asked.

"No, the Uparhna does not flow from any of their valleys. Those lie beyond the divide of the mountains, and rivers there run the other way." There was nothing at all to point out now. "It is a high path but not so difficult to cross."

For gods maybe. It was for me to raise the sensible question. "Can't we come to them from the other direction?"

"One could sail up the western coast of the peninsula and not cross the mountains at all, though it is still a climb to the homeland of the Heldu. Those coasts are dangerous, for the stronghold of Ez lies there."

Kess nodded agreement. "So have I been told by the traders here."

Less practical, then. It would be best to heed this god's advice—in that it jibed with what the Akmemians said. But I had to comment, "It might be safer with two gods as companions."

"One only," announced Sharki. "And you know we are not worth much more than mortals when we enter your world."

"Enough to make a difference, maybe. So you do not accompany us?" asked Kess.

"I've other business I must be about. This is truly not so important an affair to me and my relatives. We do not take it as seriously as you and Banat, little woodpecker."

"They are a danger to this world."

"But they can not destroy it." The big god pondered that a moment. "I do not think they can. Most who desire to possess them would only use the jewels to bolster their own gifts and skills."

"Then why are you here at all?" I asked.

"Amusement. Curiosity. And I'm pretty much the only god looking out for my people here." I wasn't sure how seriously I took his explanations. Sharki continued. "Perhaps I'll sail with you some of the way. Perhaps I'll meet you in the lands of the Ba'esu. Be all that as it may, I will try to keep an eye on you." He did turn both eyes toward me. "As I have from the time you came to this world."

"The ni'inoe? I thought maybe he was sent by Wanga." Or even was Wanga. I knew very little of gods. That was not surprising in that I would not have believed they existed, not so very long ago.

"That was no minion of Wanga you encountered but one of mine. I would not myself take shark form in Exura unless it were absolutely needed—I would truly become the shark, forgetting who I was." He gave me a toothy grin. "Though an unusually large shark. Larger than ni'inoe."

The next morning, we learned Sharki had sailed away without us. Kess only shrugged on hearing this. "A few days ago, we expected to travel on by ourselves."

That we did, departing before the mid-morn. I was not certain of the wisdom of leaving Akmem at all. Yes, with those jewels I carried, I carried also some sort of obligation, though I was also not certain why I had taken any of it on. Ah, but I would undoubtedly have sailed on anyway, sooner or later. The sailor I am would have yearned for other ports.

"There are spies watching us," remarked Kess as I rounded the point dividing the twin harbors. "So I have been assured."

"Flying ones?" The wind filling our sail quartered out of the northeast. I could work with that.

"And ones on the ground."

There was no point to commenting on that. Many came and went at Akmem, and it was sensible to assume some might be in someone's pay. For that matter, it could be true of some who dwelt there. Instead, I said, "We have a considerable swell rolling." The sea was rough and gray around us, the sky clouded. I had lost sight of land, which was perhaps as well. Straight north I should set our course, according to Sharki, and stay clear of all coasts.

But straight north we did not sail, for the winds pushed us westward, despite my best efforts. Not that far westward, but westward enough! Toward dusk, Kesarra spied land to our port side. Her eyes were better than mine but I could make it out once she pointed west. Could that be the Crane's Foot, the point—or three points, actually—that marked the northern tip of Nagi?

No, surely we were beyond it by now. It must be part of the chain north of the island. Whatever land it was, I wanted to keep it at a safe distance in these wild seas. More so as the skies darkened.

Thirty-seven

It was not only the coming of night that darkened those skies, but the coming of storm. "Were it lighter, I would attempt to get into the lee of that land over there," I informed Kess. "Better I try to get away from the coast now."

The goddess considered this. "Hmm. I could pull in a favorable wind from another world, maybe." She shook her head almost as soon as she said it. "But no, not with so strong a gale already blowing here. Better to let one who is knowledgeable of such things deal with it."

I was quite in agreement. "You have no, um, control over the weather."

"None whatsoever. No wizard nor even a god can do that."

So had I understood. "If necessary, I'll turn us back the way we came. Better to lose some time than to wreck on unseen rocks." I turned us into the wind, tacking as best I could to work us away from the land. Soon, that land could not be seen.

This was nothing like the cyclone that had brought me to this world, but a storm front working its way south. Spring weather. Bands of rain and wind came and went; I steered as best I could without compass to guide me. Kess busied herself with bailing, occasionally pulling a bit of light from somewhere to aid her in the task. Sometime in the night, the storm lessened, rain became drizzle, wind became a warm breeze, the warmest I had felt in weeks.

A gray dawn crept in from the east, from the direction of the Arus. All my mornings might be calm, all my breezes warm, had I remained there—remained with Maranua in her valley. Ah, I would be no more than a memory to her now. She should be no more than that to me, should she? Other places, other duties, demanded my attention.

"No telling where we are," I informed my shipmate. "I shall take a northwesterly bearing and we'll end up somewhere."

And we did, before noon. "I strongly suspect," I told Kess, "that shore over there is the same one we saw last evening." I thought it unlikely any other island would be near, if I could trust the maps we had seen. "The first large isle north of the Crane's Foot. We should set a course due north from here, I think."

"Any course would take us somewhere, would it not? Better you choose it than I."

I agreed. "And from somewhere we can always go somewhere else."

Kess only smiled at this. "So it is to be hoped."

We paralleled the coast to our left and soon sailed past its northernmost point. People lived over there somewhere, didn't they? So I understood. Seasonal fishermen, at least. As we pulled into open water, shapes appeared in the distance. Three? No, four. Four boats bobbing in the swell, their square sails appearing and disappearing. I did not think it a good idea to let them get nearer.

They did not seem to agree. No matter; I should be able to easily out-sail them, even with this modest breeze. I doubted they could even sail close reach, quartering into the wind, as I was. Certainly not with any efficiency or speed.

It did not matter. "They are full of men," said Kess.

And all had paddles. Neither fishermen nor traders were they, but warriors—men seeking us. The familiar skin-covered boats grew inexorably closer as they steadily paddled on. They chanted as they stroked, deep, harsh voices, the sound growing ever louder. I tried to make the best of the fickle winds but could see it would be no use.

Kesarra reached out to some other world and retrieved a bow, recurved in the Turkish fashion, and a quiver of long, red-fletched arrows. One by one, she released them toward our pursuers. It was a far longer shot than any man could make, I was certain. Some arrows struck enemies; some sailed over them or stuck into the sides of the boats. I had looked at the hide-covered boats of Akmem and knew they had at least two layers of skins and often three. It was unlikely even arrows driven by Kess would cause much damage there.

"Some are troll-men," she commented, lowering her weapon and then dropping it to clatter on the bottom of our boat. "Certainly the minions of Ez." There came a deep sigh. "I must leave. Best if you don't look," she warned. Not knowing what she meant, I did look, as she dissolved into a whirlwind of disjointed images before disappearing completely. I stood there, bewildered, for a moment, as cries of astonishment, and perhaps of fear, arose from the boats. That did not prevent many hands from grasping my gunwales shortly after. Then they grasped me.

I had no time to think about Kesarra's abrupt departure. A broadly built fellow, a head shorter than me, stepped aboard my boat. Dark eyes glittered in a pale face framed by a great black beard. He addressed me in a language I felt sure was that spoken in Akmem.

"I don't know that tongue," I responded in Heldun.

He gave me a doubtful look before answering in the same language. "You are not of the Heldu," he stated, and then shrugged. "Not that it matters. I am Oatza. I lead here."

The individual at his side was surely a troll, of pure blood, not a troll-man as were many here. He stood no higher than my waist and had a grayish cast to his skin. Seeing him beside Oatza allowed me to recognize the troll heritage in that man, though I doubted it was strong.

"What do you wish of me?" I asked.

"What you carry." He spoke to the troll, who nodded and came over to relieve me of the bag containing the jewels. This he handed to Oatza. The man did not bother to look at them, only weighed the pouch a moment in his hand, before tucking it away in a broad sash about his waist. "We will take you along, though my warriors would as soon eat you as deliver you to the nedre."

"Nedre?" It was the obvious question.

"The lady, it means. Our queen, Ez. It would be best if you address me as awn."

"Means lord in tongue ours," added the troll.

Oatza—the awn—seemed amused. "An older tongue than ours, in truth, spoken by some of the first to live on Nagi. So I have been told by the Nedre Ez."

"I have heard of Ez."

"I am not surprised." He gave my boat a brief perusal. "Your craft interests me. We will bring it too." He barked orders to his followers. Shortly, a line was attached and the hide boats paddled southward, with me in tow.

I remained unbound but two men had come aboard as guards. I did not like the hungry looks they gave me.

Thirty-eight

Down the western shore of the forested island they paddled and into open sea. Headed back to Nagi, I guessed. I did not attempt to ask anything of my guards. It was unlikely we shared a language.

Kesarra—I knew she had gone to another world, another universe. Briefly, perhaps. I knew too that the gems I had carried could not pass from this world. Leaving me was the logical move for the goddess. Whether she intended to return, whether she intended to continue her mission, I could not even guess.

More land, off to port. This surely was the Crane's Foot, most likely the middle 'toe.' The boats angled more westerly from there, across the mouth of a wide bay bounded at the south by the third point at Nagi's northern end. Those of Akmem never voyaged beyond it; nothing lay there but dangerous savages, they said, and definitely no profits were to be made. Rounding the third toe, the boats turned in toward a rocky, forbidding coast.

The troll-men's hide boats were soon being pulled onto a narrow beach of gray sand. My vessel was not cooperative, with its deeper draft. Those who strained at its ropes seemed baffled. I only hoped they had done no damage to its bottom, though I saw little hope of sailing it away from here. A curt order from their leader had them tie it off where it lay. My guards jerked me to my feet and waded me ashore.

Up a narrow valley, a gorge, we marched, to reach a rudimentary fence of piled rocks—it would be an exaggeration to call it a wall—and at a hail from Oatza, a notched log was slid over the top to serve as a ladder. The narrow crevice beyond gave way to a wider, hidden valley, walled all about by cliffs. A long, sod-roofed house of timber and rock, half sunk into the ground, lay there. Naught else was to be seen save a few huts and heaps of refuse.

And my captors, who ranged from pure trolls to pure men. Assuming either truly exists; maybe we are all mongrels of some sort. Not all were male, either. Those who were trolls, or troll-like, were stocky, barrel-bodied creatures, many with quite huge noses. The gray complexions I had noted before were perhaps more a faint purplish-blue, made more noticeable by the pallor of most. This was not a latitude where one got much sun.

We followed Oatza into a dimly-lit single room. Figures were to be made out, some seated in the gloom around the walls, and more apparently standing above a smoking fire-pit at the far end of the space. As we drew nearer I could see these were dried bodies, posed on a rough stone ledge.

"Trophies?" I asked.

The awn's little troll aide answered. It is unlikely any of the others knew the language I had spoken. "Guards. Warriors who protect hall." He chuckled in a quite unpleasant manner. "Enemies we eat!"

"Not that Gub here actually believes that," said Oatza. "Some of the others might. You should talk to our mistress now," he told the troll.

So the little fellow was a shaman or wizard, this captain's means of communication with Ez. He went into some sort of trance. This was no longer very interesting to me and my eyes went back to the mummies. Guardians—there were men of my world with similar practices, who set such tasks for the spirits of the dead. Religion of some sort seems universal.

I myself had long been something of a skeptic, disillusioned by religion in general and Christianity in particular. Now I had met gods—or powerful beings who named themselves gods—but was no closer to knowing whether there was one god over all, a creator. Were there truly infinite worlds? Such boundless existence should perhaps be named God. Naught else would qualify.

As far as life after death, it seemed the gods were as much in the dark as mortals. Perhaps in those infinite worlds we lived again. Infinite heavens and infinite hells might await!

Gub returned and exchanged words in their own tongue with Oatza. He, in turn, informed me, "The nedre says she will come to us. That is unexpected nor do I understand the reason, but we do her will."

The sorceress dwelt in the north, not on Nagi, or so Sharki had said. Ez would have to sail south to take possession of the stones. I could understand why she would prefer they remain safe here, now that her followers held them. If Oatza knew their power, he too would have recognized this. He was not lacking in brains.

The troll-man gave me a long look. "You would be safer in the caves. I do not trust these–" He nodded toward his warriors. "Not to molest you."

"More if take *zor*," added Gub.

My ignorance must have been evident. "A drug," said Oatza. "Many are dependent."

"And all like!"

I thought maybe Gub was included in that. The captain assigned two men to escort me. "Do not wander out once they take you there," he warned. "It would not be safe and I am not overly concerned about keeping you alive for Ez. It is these she cares about." He patted the pouch holding the jewels.

I suspected he was right. Ez might not care about keeping me alive at all, once she came and took possession of the stones. Out I was led, and upward. The valley narrowed above the house, becoming a grotto and then a cave. I could see it was used as storage, though much that had been stored appeared to have been neglected, forgotten. My guards shoved me toward a spot they deemed acceptable, and left at once. Maybe they wished to make sure of getting their share of the zor.

Food and water? I could only hope someone remembered to bring some. I would most certainly take Oatza's advice and not stray from here. At least it felt no colder than outside and there were hides of some sort stored in one unruly stack. Reindeer would have been my guess. I wrapped one of them around me, despite its mold and must, and explored as best I could, as far as the light from the entrance permitted. The tunnel seemed to extend far beyond that.

Maybe I could find a lamp or torch somewhere in here. First, though, I slept.

Thirty-nine

Only the faintest of light shone at the opening when I awoke. Night? Down in a hole as the troll-men's fort was, it would grow dark before sunset. I could go as far as the cave mouth to take a look and to relieve myself.

"Awake at last."

"Kesarra. I didn't know if you could find me." She was somewhere near but I couldn't make her out.

"It was easier to locate the Eyes. I knew you would be near." A pause. "If you were alive." Her form emerged from the gloom. "I am sorry to have left you like that but it was the logical course."

"Even if I had been slain."

"Getting the jewels to safety was more important. It still is."

Which was why she was here now. I was incidental. "So where did you go?" I asked.

"My own world, first. It is far easier to go there and then back to this one, than to move from one place to another here. Not that I can't, but I have ties to my home, lines of less resistance. And it gave me a moment to catch my breath, so to speak. Then I popped back. Not to Akmem. That would raise too many questions, as none there know I am a god."

"Save your troll friend Zup."

"And it is to him I have been speaking. His people are going to help me. Help us. They told me of this place."

"Ez is on her way, with more followers. We'd better act before she arrives." We stood now at the opening to the cave, peering out into the dark ravine. I could see stars above, those stars that still seemed strange when I chose to scan the skies. The stars of another world, reminding me I was alone here, on an errand I did not understand.

"Zup tells me this cave has other entrances. A troll could come and show you the way out."

"I wouldn't be much better off lost in these mountains. And you still need to reclaim the gems." As I would prefer to reclaim my boat.

"But you would be alive, Dick."

Yes, I would. Perhaps I could find my way back to Akmem. Perhaps I could forget all this, live there in peace, be no more than the sailor I was once. "We should have two or three days before Ez comes," I said. Depending on how far away her headquarters lay, how the winds blew, and many other things. "Maybe more."

Kess nodded. "So I shall tell Zup. He has trolls on the way already." She peered out into the darkness for a moment. "They understand how important this is. Ah, I shall cloak myself when I leave this time and not dazzle you." With that, darkness seemed to thicken about her, indeed, to cloak her, and the goddess Kesarra disappeared.

We would have to steal the stones. Kess could handle them, I knew, if need be, but it would be better I or one of those promised trolls do it. Then, if possible, I could make my way to my boat, attempt to launch it and sail away. There would most likely be pursuit. Maybe the cave was a better escape route.

Someone approached. The path was somewhat steep here, just before the cave. It might be a dangerous way at a time of heavy rainfall. The figure was nearly upon me before I recognized Oatza himself.

"I bring you food and water, um—I know not what to name you."

"Dick will do."

"Dick. None of my warriors are capable of performing such a task at the moment, nor would I trust them if they were, so I bring it myself." The man handed me a stone crock and some dried meat. Despite these people being cannibals, I suspected it was safe enough.

"The woman who was with you. She was not mortal, was she?"

"A goddess," I told him, tearing a piece of meat off and attempting to chew it. "A goddess of the Heldu."

He only nodded. "I would have had Gub speak to the Nedre Ez of it but he, too, is incapacitated."

"The zor."

"Yes. It makes one fierce and active for a time but that wears off and a stupor follows. It is a way of controlling them." He eyed me for a few seconds. "Men such as you are more useful. You are not born of this world, are you?"

I managed to choke down the wad of meat in my mouth and replied, "No."

Oatza nodded. "Others I have met who came through the gate. Think on this before Ez arrives. She might listen if I recommend taking you on." A grim smile. "Or she might give you to the men to torture. One never knows."

Attempting to escape through the cave became more attractive. I thought on it some and slept again.

Forty

"I spent much of the day sitting atop the cliffs, watching. I was there when you were brought to this cave, too, having already followed the Eyes."

"That sounds nearly as uninteresting as my day." Which had consisted of sitting in the cave. I had crept back a short distance into the dark but was cautious of going too far. Soon, being cautious might no longer be a good idea.

"Oh, but I was speaking from afar with others. Zup, mostly. Some of his friends are already here, including one who is a shaman." I am not sure whether the pause that followed was true hesitation or only for effect. "We also spoke to Barad."

I was not going to ask of the unfamiliar name. Kess recognized this, adding, "The Wizard-Lord, in his far-off realm."

"What you and Var called the Rift."

"Yes, the Great Rift, or Tul Sunac as it is known in the language spoken there. The Broken Place, it means. He, too, is concerned about the jewels ending up in the wrong hands."

"Would he consider his own to be the right hands?"

"Undoubtedly, but he is too distant to do anything about it. Oh, you joked, didn't you?" she asked, seeing my smile at her so-serious reply. "Even when you seem drained, you do this."

I did feel drained. No more food or water had been brought, though I had found little puddles back in the cave, where bitter water dripped from the roof. Worrying about being tortured by troll-men didn't help things. "What did you do when you disappeared yesterday? That darkness that hid you. I've been wondering about it."

"I drew shadow from another world. It is a fairly good way to conceal oneself but doesn't last very long." Kess allowed herself a small smile. "I suspect there are mortal wizards who can do that sort of thing better than I."

"Could one hide in them long enough to steal the Eyes?"

She shook her head. "Maybe for a minute or two, if we could get close enough first. Fog would be more effective and lingers much longer, but it would obscure our vision too. Shadow doesn't do that when you are within it."

Fog—what else could she draw from another world? "Smoke?"

"We would have to breathe it in, as well as being blinded."

"Blinded," I said, and no more.

"You have an idea, Dick."

"What about, ah, light? Could you draw a blinding light from somewhere? We could cover our eyes."

"Maybe." I would let her think about it. It was her area of knowledge, not mine. Something moved deep in the cave.

"One of our friendly trolls," spoke Kess, raising a hand in greeting and beginning a conversation in a language I was certain I had never before heard. When they concluded, she informed me, "Bumug here could guide you out and into the mountains. You would be safe enough with the trolls."

I shook my head at this tempting offer. "If need be, but not now."

The goddess seemed pleased, not that one could always tell. "He also offers to go scout the camp. It is unlikely he would be noticed."

"That, too," I said, "is something to be done only if we need it."

"Agreed." She and Bumug spoke further before he retreated into the depths of the tunnel. Trolls must see better in the dark than I can.

"Bumug has half a dozen trolls with him. That number should double in a few hours."

"And then?"

"Then would be as good a time as any to act."

We would still be greatly outnumbered, five or more to one. Before I could point this out, Kess hissed, "Someone comes. I'll back off into the shadows and bring in some of my own." Within a few seconds, the goddess had vanished and Oatza, with his troll wizard at his side, had appeared.

Gub sniffed the air, his head and huge nose turning back and forth. "Smell troll."

"One was up here looking at me," I offered. The statement was true, if misleading.

"If I knew which, he'd look at nothing again," spoke the awn. "They probably all look the same to you."

I had to agree that was so, though I might have been able to recognize Gub.

Oatza went on. "Gub says Ez is a day away. Do you have an answer for me?"

"I think I will receive no better offers."

That brought a laugh. Gub only looked from one of us to the other, puzzled. "Probably not," the troll-man told me. "It will be up to the Nedre Ez, to be sure. She might even wish you in her service and take you away from me."

The wizard now gave me another looking over. "Nedre like young mans."

"Indeed she does," agreed Oatza, "but you would be safer with me. We must keep you in this hole until she arrives."

"As you think best, Awn Oatza," I replied. I thought it as well to say nothing of not having been fed again. We did not need someone intruding on us to bring food.

But I was exceptionally hungry. Maybe Bumug and his buddies had something to eat with them. Kess stepped out of her shadows when my visitors left. "Oatza, eh? That means 'Wolf' in their language. I would guess he chose the name himself."

So would I. The troll-man leader seemed truly interested only in himself, his own image, his own power. Everyone and everything else would be seen as a tool. Perhaps even Ez herself.

How Ez saw Oatza was undoubtedly quite another matter. "We must act before this sorceress arrives," I said, "and be well on our way. Wherever that may lie."

"That," she said, "must be decided now."

Forty-one

An uproar arose from below us. "They revel tonight," Kess announced. "Bumug says zor has been taken." The troll had slipped down at dusk to look over the camp.

"That is good unless they take it into their heads to come up here and add me to their feast."

"Let them. The trolls would like nothing better than to ambush some of them here." She turned and exchanged a few words with Bumug, who laughed rather uproariously. "This could be their chance to remove this evil folk from their borders."

Now they had overcome whatever inertia had kept them from it before. I had become the catalyst that started it all in action. I and Kesarra and Zup and the jewels—and everything else in the world, maybe! "I would hazard Oatza allowed this orgy so his followers would be more tractable when his mistress arrives."

"Perhaps so, Dick. You are wiser in such things than I."

Wiser? I suppose I did know men—and apparently trolls—better than the goddess. But wisdom means making good decisions. I was not so sure of my abilities there.

"I thought on your idea of blinding light," Kess went on. "It might prove useful as an emergency measure. I do not believe it would work to get us into the camp and to the jewels."

"I would assume Oatza no longer carries them," I said. If the troll-man captain did, she would have noted them, felt their presence. Indeed, she and her troll allies could have slain him and Gub, and made their escape. Our escape.

"Bumug tells me there are always guards at the entrance to their hall. I would think the Eyes are within."

It made sense. "Can we trust those guards to also indulge in zor, this night?"

She shrugged. Again, I knew more of such things. "If a friendly troll offered them some, I think they might," I continued.

"Ah! Yes, Dick." She thought only a moment on this. "It should be done immediately." She gazed into space for a few seconds, speaking from afar with someone. It seemed likely to be the shaman who accompanied our friendly trolls.

"They are ready to infiltrate the camp, anyway," she reported on returning. "Some will be near the boats to help us there."

"We may not be able to escape that way," I warned.

"But we must sail on, Dick," was her answer.

I did not believe I 'must' do anything. It would, however, be nice to recover my boat. My boat—again, I name it so. Even if its owner in another world lived, I had done him no great harm. Though I have never believed the end justifies the means, there had been little choice but to steal—yes, steal was the word—the vessel. It was the least of a number of evils. That there would be more evils to choose among in my future, I had little doubt.

We had moved as far as we dared toward the end of the grotto before the cave, to a point where we could see what was going on in the camp. There were no guards to be spied; were it not for the Eyes, I believe I could have easily slipped away. Yes, I considered it, and decided abandoning them—and Kess—would be too great an evil for me to choose right then. Maybe later. Circumstances do change.

The troll-men caroused below, clapping and stamping out a rhythm for their tuneless chanting. "They will dance until they collapse, I am told, but they would be very dangerous right now. Zor makes its user quite focused for a short time."

"So we wait."

Kess nodded, the movement barely discernible in the gloom. "As long as necessary. They will fall into a stupor eventually."

I could only hope all had indulged in their drug, Oatza and his wizard included. As an hour passed and another progressed, they grew more subdued. Dancing became akin to staggering. Was their orgy fueled only by zor or did these bestial raiders indulge in alcohol as well? I suspected the two would not mix well. Even from this distance, I could see some of their debauchery was of a sexual nature. Which genders were involved I could not tell and would as soon not be able to.

But no fighting. I might have expected some. "Soon, I think," I remarked to Kesarra. The goddess had stood silently beside me through this time, though I am sure she spoke from afar once or twice.

"Yes." She stared toward the encampment. Little movement

was to be seen; the fires, small to begin with, were become no more than glowing coals in the night. "I did not know men could be so—so twisted," she said. "They are like the creatures of my mother."

"We are all what we choose to be. Are we ready?" I addressed this to a handful of trolls who had emerged from the cave, though they could not understand my words.

They did understand my meaning, I am sure. A quick confer-ence with Kess, who nodded in my direction a couple times. The trolls gave me a looking over. Most had not seen me until that moment. One gnarled fellow with a beard falling below his belt came over and handed me a club. A weapon—that I could appre-ciate and I attempted to make my gratitude obvious.

More words with the goddess before she informed me, "They expect you to help them kill many troll-men."

"Tell them I'll do my best."

She did so, to their apparent approval, and then told me they asked if I needed anything more.

"A drink. I am parched!"

That was forthcoming at once. I was surprised the skin I was offered held not water but rather good beer. I should spend more time with trolls, maybe. Not too much of it right now. I needed my wits for the business at hand. We crept forward, into the night.

Forty-two

There was to be no killing—unless necessary—until Kess and I had the stones. "Keep low," I warned her. "We don't want to stick up any higher than the trolls."

She would be more likely to stand out than me—Kess looked nothing like any of Oatza's minions. Crouching, we crept into the camp, not as a group but spread out. If any sluggish troll-men noticed us, they must have dismissed us as some of their fellows. The guards before the hall's entrance were glassy-eyed but one did stagger to his feet. Flint knives in the hands of our troll companions swiftly silenced both.

No one seemed to be inside the rough structure, save the dead guardians above the fire pit. Kess cocked her head at them. She hadn't been in here before. "Harmless," she decided. "The Eyes are over there."

'Over there' meant a dark wooden chest. It had no lock, only pins to hold the lid in place. I had seen no locks and very little metal since coming to this world. Kess reached and pulled her hand back. "Gub has put an alarm on them," she said. "He would know if we tried to open it."

"If he is conscious."

She made no answer. Kess seemed to be concentrating on something. It was much as if she were speaking to someone from afar yet seemed different. Then a relaxing, a release of held breath. "There. I reached around through another world and undid his work." She smiled slightly as she slid the pins out. "It wasn't really all that well done."

I was the one to reach in and retrieve the Eyes. A quick glance into the familiar pouch—my pouch—assured me all four were there. I was pleased to see my steel knife had been also been kept in the chest. I held it there in my hand a moment, feeling the familiar weight, before fastening it at my waist. "What now?"

"We head for our boat. The trolls will let us get some distance before they attack here."

"Is that wise? There aren't all that many of them, even if their enemies aren't in the best of shape."

"This they know. They will kill what number they can and then run for the mountains. It is to be hoped the troll-men will run after them while we are going the other direction."

The little guys looked eager to get at their business when we emerged. One accompanied us as we crept down into the narrower canyon. I was fairly sure it was he who had served as our liaison from the start. We had reached the stone wall at its mouth when an uproar arose behind us. "No more caution," I said. "Time to hurry!"

I hoped no sentry was posted at the fence. Then I stumbled over the body of one who had undoubtedly had that duty. The trolls had thought further ahead than I. The log-ladder was already in place for us.

Our troll companion jabbered something. Kess turned her head back the way we had come. "Yes, we are being followed. Not by many, I think."

"Then let's get down and take the ladder with us."

Not that removing it would do much to slow pursuit. Two more trolls awaited us when we burst onto the narrow beach. Younger trolls, I thought. They seemed rather pleased with themselves as they reported to our guide.

"They have made holes in all the boats so we may not be pursued," Kess informed me.

It might have been better had they waited to see if we were able to launch our own. We might have had need of one of those hide-covered craft! There was no assurance we could budge our boat from where Oatza's men had run it aground. Nothing to do but try.

It did not appear the troll-men had touched the boat since leaving it here, tied with a single line to a post driven into the sand. I looked up at the waning moon, near its zenith. That was a good sign. The tide might be high enough to float us without too much effort. Or at least we could see what we were doing.

I waded out to the boat. Damn, the water was frigid! Ah, it was not stuck at all but floated free. The tides at Akmem rose and fell considerably; perhaps it was not so different on this side of Nagi.

A shout rang from the darkness above the beach. Oatza appeared, perhaps a half-dozen bewildered warriors trailing. Gub was not with them. I could only guess where the troll wizard might be. Maybe sleeping off a zor binge. Maybe speaking to Ez. Our three trolls had promptly disappeared. I did not blame them at all.

The awn held a great ax. The moon glinted on its polished stone head as he held it aloft, shook it toward us, bellowed orders to his followers. They half-heartedly charged—or plodded—in our direction, spears in hands. Oatza himself seemed as ever. He must not be one to indulge in zor but where he was while his men did, I had no idea.

"Get aboard," I said. "Our best chance is to get beyond their reach." Little wind disturbed the sea. We would have to row.

"Cover your eyes," ordered Kess. It was not enough to completely shut out the blinding flash that came seconds later. "I've been wanting to try that ever since you suggested it. I went and found just the perfect world from which to pull the light." She came out and helped me nudge the boat into motion before we both clambered aboard. The last I heard as we moved away from the shore was Oatza's curses in some language I did not know.

"He is going to do terrible things to both of us." Kess giggled. "But his imagination really isn't all that good. Can we use the sail?"

"We can try." The sail was somewhat in disarray, our captors having had no idea of the proper way to stow it. No tears. It was looking a bit frayed here and there. I might need to try out our spider silk spare soon. I got the canvas up and we soon were gliding northward. What course now? Ez was out there some-where, and quite possibly told of our escape by now. Did she have a fleet? Would she be able to find us?

Best we swing wide one way or another? Or head north as rapidly as we could, hoping to elude and outrun any pursuit? I must decide. This was indeed outside Kess's expertise. I decided it would depend on the winds; if they blew strong and favorable I would make a run for it. We came around the Crane's third toe before dawn.

"We could return to Akmem and make another try in a few days," I suggested.

"But won't that give Ez and Oatza more time to be ready for us?"

"I suppose so. Do you think Ez knows about us now?"

"She does. Both Barad and I have managed to listen in to some of what is going on. Ez has strong wards against that but Gub not so much. We know he told her what happened. She can guess where we are heading."

"But can't know exactly where we are."

"Unless we are spotted from above. The wyverns and their riders are still about, and though they do not serve Ez, Barad thinks there may be some alliance." Kess paused but a moment before saying, "We know Ez speaks to another somewhere but he or she remains hidden."

I could only nod to this. A good breeze came up by mid-morn, fresh and crisp out of the southwest, and we sped before it.

Forty-three

Land could be spied to our right, lying low and distant. I was certain it was the island where we had encountered Oatza but we were passing up its western coast this time. It soon faded from view, only open water remaining. At least we'd made it a little further north this time, a little closer to our destination.

The only thing to be seen flying were seabirds, gulls, the great petrels, others I could not recognize or name. I would have liked to see my eagle again, but he had found a home in this new world, a home in the Arus, while I still searched for my place. I did not know whether it lay ahead, in the lands to which I journeyed, or somewhere further. I did not know if I belonged here at all.

"It might be best to trend a little east of north now," I told the goddess. "Not too greatly. I haven't much trust in the maps we were shown."

"Would that distance us more from Ez?"

"It might. Heading east into the great ocean would work even better. We could always turn back toward land later."

Kess frowned. "I think, Dick, we should go as straight and as quickly as we can. I am tired of sailing."

There was no way I could not laugh at that. In a few seconds, she joined me. "You could happily sail forever," she stated. Though it was not quite true, I did feel more at home minding the tiller and sail than on any land I had walked in this world. Here, I had at least the illusion of control.

So I kept to the north-northeast course I had set. And so, Ez found us, late that day. Whether we had been spied out, we had no way of telling, but it seemed likely. "Three boats," I reported, scanning the seas to our west. "I believe they do not so much pursue us as they hope to intercept us."

They did have a good chance of cutting us off. Despite their clumsy sails, the wind was favorable. "There are not many paddlers," said Kesarra, gazing in their direction. Her eyes again were proving better than mine. "Nor many men at all."

The sorceress led no raiding party. She would have wanted to travel quickly, with only a guard. "It is going to be close." If the winds shifted, the advantage might shift our way as well. If they grew lighter, for that matter. Or I could veer out into the ocean right now, and trust that Ez and her boats could not catch up.

Kess was standing, reaching out to—somewhere. She seemed taller, more god-like, but, once more, that might have just been in my mind. Something seemed to rain on the other boats, something that briefly glowed. The goddess shrugged. "Too far away, though the wind was good."

"Was that volcanic ash again?" I recalled her use of it on the island.

"It was. At least yon wizardess knows she has someone to contend with now."

"Do you think she can retaliate in kind?"

"She would not want to sink us and lose the Eyes."

That was not exactly an answer to my question. Turning hard to starboard seemed the better choice than ever, yet I hesitated. If we could just slip by, I was fairly certain we could outrun the wallowing hide-boats. The approach of night could help there, though the nights were somewhat brief at this time of year, and twilight lingered.

"I believe she is pulling in a wind to help her," said Kess. "No, not her but the lead boat. She is directing it toward its sail. Two can do that."

The goddess brought almost too strong a wind to bear on our sail, drawn from some unknown—but decidedly cold—world. The canvas strained and snapped, before our boat leapt forward. I should warn her sometime against drawing such a gale. Now my task was to make the most of it.

That one boat, sped ahead of the others, was in our path. There was no going around it without losing speed, without letting the others come closer. I could see bows in the hands of the warriors that manned them. "Hold on!" I called out to Kess and plowed directly into the skin-covered craft, solid oak meeting its fragile framework. Then we sailed on, leaving Ez and the other boat behind. I wondered if they stopped to pick up the crew of the smashed vessel. Somehow, I doubted it.

I did veer more easterly now, broad reached, the brisk south-westerly breeze still prevailing. The boats of Ez, if they followed, would not be as efficient as we on this course. But there was another concern now. "I will have to stop and repair the sail," I informed Kess. "Your wind has torn it." It might well have split top to bottom had it blown a few seconds more. It might still.

"You will use one we made for you?"

"Yes, for now. I might be able to patch this canvas when we are on land again."

As soon as darkness fell—as did the wind—I lowered the sail that had caught the breezes of two worlds and lifted that woven of spider silk. It worked well when I turned us back toward land in the morning. A day later, we saw that land, rising mountainous before us, and followed the rugged coast north.

Forty-four

"A wyvern," stated Kess, gazing toward the peaks. "They spy on us yet."

We were beyond the reach of Ez; of that I was fairly sure. Those lalun and their riders reported to another, unknown adversary. "The kobolds speak to someone from afar, don't they?" I asked. "Can you listen to them?"

"I could search forever through the infinite worlds for the place they meet. Longer than forever, for even time is finite."

"Best you don't try, then," I advised, none too seriously.

Her eyes were still turned toward the mountains, the great mass of clouds rising behind them. "Yet it is tempting to do just that, to wander there eternally, forgetting my world and this world both. Ah, not yet, Dick. Not yet." She sat down on one of the benches, facing me where I minded the tiller. "I listen, none the less. I have left an infinitesimal part of my being here and there, watching those of whom we already know, ready to follow them if they go to speak with someone. I watch Gub; that is easy as his warding is weak. Ez is far more difficult. I must be careful not to reveal myself and am not sure I could follow her without doing so."

"She is powerful."

"Yes. Barad is more powerful, I think, though not greatly so. He, too, watches."

I did not know whether that was a good thing. "Your power is of a different sort."

"Yet not so very different when it comes to, um, magic in this world. I do not match up to either of them as a sorcerer." She sighed, staring now at the gray, rolling seas. "I easily outstrip our Var, of course. He is not even the equal of Gub, save for having far more experience. I should talk to him sometime and see how he is doing."

"When our task is done, maybe," I offered.

"Yes. Then." I had my doubts she ever would. Her world—all the world, perhaps—had changed, and Var was no longer part of it.

"A boat." I motioned toward it with my head. Kess turned to peer at the distant sail.

"It avoids us," she commented. Yes, it had veered toward the open sea, eastward away from us. Traders, maybe even from Akmem, and wary of unknown craft they might encounter. Particularly one with our unfamiliar silhouette.

The spider-silk sail was working well enough. Would it continue to do so? I had no idea of its durability or strength, but did suspect it was less susceptible to damage from moisture than the canvas it replaced, even without any coating. With the proper tools, heavy needles, strong cord, I could perhaps repair the old sail, but I had no such with me. I did not know if they even existed in this world.

Nor did I know if I would ever voyage beyond the land of the Ba'esu. A wide bay, Sharki had told us, and a river. That was what we sought now, but it was not our destination. That lay in the mountains, somewhere in those mountains that rose to the west. They were higher now but not so close to the rocky and rugged shore.

We saw another vessel that day, a canoe I thought, that passed at some distance, seemingly uninterested. It was the next morning the bay lay before us. Maybe a gulf, as Sharki had said. Wide beaches rose to forested slopes. This was still a temperate land but certainly closer to the tropical clime I had known on the Stone or in the Aru Islands. More canoes passed by us, their occupants on their own business. Sometimes there was a wave of greeting.

"We might be expected," I told Kess.

The dugouts we saw looked much like that Sharki had sailed, fitted with double outriggers. Villages stood here and there along the shore; more were undoubtedly in the hills beyond. Streams flowed into the sea, none large. Certainly the river we were meant to find was further along.

"Lagoon. Is that the word?" asked Kess, as we passed another village nestled among coconut palms, canoes drawn onto the beach.

"Yes, the English word. I've no idea what it would be called in Heldun, though I could give you several different names in the language of the Arus. A stream comes down to it over there, see?" I pointed. "There are no reefs here. Only sand bars."

"I might like to rest in such a place, Dick."

So might I. We sailed on and into the next day.

Forty-five

"I thought it best to be here when you arrived." Sharki grabbed the line I tossed him and made it fast to the bamboo dock. "My people are welcoming enough of strangers but they would be unlikely to do you any favors."

Kess and I shipped the oars; it was good to have another pair of strong—quite strong—arms for rowing.

"I am known here as Toh, another trader who plies these coasts," the big god continued. "I have heard your voyage was eventful."

Who told him, I couldn't guess. Maybe Zup, maybe some other wizard. I suspected they all gossiped a bit. "*Your* people, you say?" He had claimed something of the sort before.

"The Ba'esu." We climbed up to stand beside him, surveying the sizable town at the river mouth. "They name themselves for Ba'es, a great hero and leader who brought them together as a nation. It is said he was a demigod, the son of Arco."

Kess gave him a knowing smile. "Your son."

Toh—or Sharki or, apparently, Arco—roared with laughter. "Yes, wise little godling, Ba'es was my son, and indeed a demigod, though ultimately mortal. This is why I consider the Ba'esu particularly *my* people, more so than any others of my pantheon, though they honor us all, in their lackadaisical fashion."

"Arco." I said it as much as a question as a statement.

"Arco the Shark, brother of Krat, who shaped our world from chaos. I advised him against it! Come along now."

We started across the dock when Kesarra suddenly held up a hand. "Hmm, she has gone elsewhere," said Arco, giving her a long look. "I won't butt in."

"But you could."

"To be sure but my clumsiness might cause her problems. It's good manners not to go where uninvited, too."

I doubted the god cared overly much about the latter reason. He seemed the sort who went wherever he wished.

"Well," said Kess, abruptly returning. "I learned some things but

I am afraid Ez did too. I could not remain hidden from her. We'll talk of it later." She frowned. "I should talk to Barad as well."

"Do not trust him," advised Arco.

As in Akmem, Kesarra's appearance aroused much interest. I assume I was dismissed as simply another trader from Nagi. A crowd followed us into the town. This was built on stilts, at least that part close to the water, and much of the construction was of bamboo. It did not differ greatly from what I had found in the Aru Islands, the same sort of post and beam houses, roofs thatched with palm fronds.

"There is an hereditary ruler here," the god informed us. "A prince, maybe, in your language, Dick. I don't know an equivalent title in Heldun."

"Some speak Heldun here, do they not?" asked Kess.

"A few. The Ba'esu are a people who are willing to travel far and learn new things." There might have been a bit of pride in his voice. "And then, the occasional Heldu come down from the mountains to trade. Perhaps we can find one to guide you."

I guessed Arco intended to abandon us again. It would do no good to speak of it. We approached the largest house in the town, rising on a low hill. The crowd following us had grown. "The prince would be one of my descendants," the god told us, "but maybe not in direct male lineage from Ba'esu as he believes."

"Many a man holds such mistaken beliefs," I observed. Then I held my tongue for the prince, a little fellow who looked nothing at all like his ancestor, rose languidly from a mat on his porch and spoke to us in the language of the Ba'esu.

The man remained above us, maintaining an advantage of height. I understood that; I had addressed sailors from a quarter deck's elevation more than once. As I comprehended not a word, I could study the man himself. Slight but not soft was this prince of the Ba'esu. Lean and hard, rather, and in the prime of life. His eyes rested on me for a moment before he made a comment.

"Budong has heard one much like you escaped the clutches of Ez," Arco informed me. "He does not wish to know whether you are that man so he need not lie to the sorceress about you being here."

"Surely he is not a friend of Ez."

"He is not but he prefers not to make an enemy of her either."

I was again left out of the conversation after that. The influence of Ez was unlikely to reach this far, I felt, but that might not prevent Oatza or some other henchman from seeking me and the stones I carried.

Ez—I had glimpsed her only from a distance during our encounter at sea. I could not say if she were young or old nor, truly, even that she was female. I did make out her long dark hair flying in the wind.

Both my companions abruptly turned away from the prince's house. The interview must be over; I turned as well and hurried to catch up for a few steps. Not so easy with a pair of long-legged gods! "Where now?"

"I have a house." Arco grinned. "The house of my woman here, I should say. She will put up with a couple guests, if you remain not too long."

"We will use the time to prepare for our journey into the mountains," added Kess.

"I will see about finding a guide or two. Or Budong will. He promised to ask around. Traders do travel upriver though most not all the way to the home of the Heldu."

The sooner we left, the better, I felt. "Are we safe here?" I asked.

"Safe enough," said Arco. "Here we are." We had halted before a low, rambling, thatched-roof place, nearly hidden among trees hung with fragrant golden flowers. "None would dare attack you, but we can be sure there are individuals with wizard-gifts in the town or nearby. That any serve Ez is not so likely but gossip is likely to reach those who do."

"But Budong will deny we are here? Does he fear Ez?" asked Kess.

"He will deny knowing you are here. The prince is a renowned fighting man but also a prudent leader." He called out to the house and vaulted onto the bamboo porch. "I have told Cha'ana we have guests!"

Forty-six

"I followed the troll to his meeting with Ez, and their ally was there. He was a man, and of the Heldu. This I could see at once, but the sorceress recognized my presence almost as quickly. She spoke to me, telling me she had intended to blast me until she recognized I was a goddess and could not truly be harmed in that manner. She laughed and then she blocked me. That Ez could do."

Arco nodded knowingly, perhaps intending—and largely failing —to appear wise. "We can not match the powers of the greatest mortal sorcerers." He glanced toward his Ba'esu lover, saying, "Cha'ana knows I am something more than an ordinary mortal but not that I am one of her gods. Call me Toh when you are around her and my people." We conversed in Heldun, which the woman understood not at all.

"Does not your failure to grow old bring questions?" wondered Kesarra.

"If I remained, it would. Here, have some more of the mangoes, Dick."

I did, as well as yams and what seemed some sort of ginger root. "What are these greens, Toh?"

"A fern, gathered wild in the forests. They are a considered a delicacy but I am a meat-eater myself!" He gave Cha'ana a long and rather fond look before continuing. "I am gone from this place for years sometimes, even decades. As the rest of my family, I tend to be forgetful of this world when I return to my own. But I make certain those I leave behind have wealth enough to live well and find another man. Not as good a one!"

"We would have to ask them about that," commented Kess. I would not have had the nerve.

The big god only chuckled. Big—I wondered if he was bigger in his own world of the gods, if he even looked like a man. Arco had called himself the Shark, after all. His woman was big too, as mortals go. Cha'ana stood as tall as Kesarra, but was gaunt and raw-boned, with a great shock of curling hair. Somehow, she seemed right for her mate and he apparently agreed.

"I will attempt to speak to Barad later," spoke Kess. "Food and rest first."

"Sensible," agreed Arco, refilling his bowl.

The sleeping space to which Cha'ana showed me later was obviously a storeroom, at most times. Stacks of odds and ends had been shoved to one side, a mat unrolled on the floor. At least there was a window for ventilation on what was proving a somewhat muggy night. This was a very different clime from that of Nagi.

The air was heavy, carrying both the sweet scent of flowers and the less pleasant odors of the harbor. It was not a bad little rivermouth port; someday, there might be sufficient trade along these coasts to make it important. I wouldn't be here. Sleep came slowly, fitfully. There was much on my mind, thoughts of the future, thoughts of the past. Thoughts of gods and mortals, wizards and mystic baubles.

Perhaps those baubles were what disturbed my dreams. It was something else that made me come suddenly and fully awake. The slightest of sounds? A subtle change in the starlight at the window? I am not sure, but I could see a shadow at that window, someone stealthily slipping through. That was surprising as it was not at all a large opening. I had no time to think on that.

Rather, my thoughts went at once to whether that shadow might be carrying a weapon. My own knife was close, somewhere, but best not to grope for it in the dark and give the intruder warning. Closer. Whoever it was reached forward, slowly, feeling their way, probing the few belongings I'd left lying beside my mat. A thief then, not an assassin. Probably.

Now. I scrambled to my feet, grabbed the thief about the waist, lifting them from the floor. The individual was surprisingly slight—but loud. Shrill invective filled the darkness, some of it recognizable as Heldun, as she struggled in my grasp. Yes, I could now tell my guest was female.

Arco was the first to arrive, holding a lamp unlike any I had seen here. Borrowed from another world, undoubtedly. "Emat?" he wondered, holding the light high. "What do you here, girl?"

He spoke in Heldun and she replied in the same tongue. "Only visiting my old friend, Toh," she claimed. Kess and Cha'ana now crowded into the room behind him.

"And burglarizing his house while you're at it," I said, releasing her. "Don't think of trying to make it back out the window, young lady."

"Ah, she knows of what you carry." Arco frowned at the girl. "How?"

She looked from one to another of us, and sighed. I'm not certain it was a sincere sigh. "I was, um, hired to find some jewels. There was to be a reward." Emat now grinned. "But I might have kept them myself."

"And they would bring a good price, even if one did not know what they were," remarked the god. "They have far more value than you might suspect, Emat. Now—just who put you up to this?"

She became reticent. "It wouldn't be right to tattle, would it?"

"You mean it would get out and ruin your reputation," I said. I didn't put much faith in the honor among thieves fable.

"And I can make you talk if you won't volunteer the information," warned Kesarra. The goddess looked decidedly threatening.

Our host held up a broad hand in admonishment. "None of that," said he. I'm not sure but it was a bit of play-acting between the two. They could, I realized, be communicating with each other in another world even as they spoke in this room. "Emat will tell us where this man—it is a man, isn't it?" The girl nodded. "She will tell us where this man may be found. She knows that is wisdom."

Emat apparently decided he was right. She swallowed, a bit ostentatiously, and blurted, "It was Hogak. He awaits me at his house."

Arco allowed himself a fleeting smile before resuming his grave manner. "A local wizard. Or witch doctor might be a better name for him." He gave both Cha'ana and Emat orders in Ba'esun, before turning to Kess and me. "The girl will stay here. Let's go visit Hogak in this little thief's place."

Forty-seven

"I'll admit to being relieved to learn it was no one more formidable than Hogak," admitted the god. Three of us ventured through the dark. This town of Prince Budong might not have advanced far enough for streetlights, but more than a few of its folk were out on business of their own on this warm night, and fires and lamps burnt here and there. We headed away from the river, into higher ground where houses and huts began to give way to scrub forest.

"The girl is not Ba'esu, is she?" I asked. She was dark but did not look that much like the folk here otherwise.

"Her mother was. Her father is a Heldu trader, one of those few who come down the Uparhna from time to time. The girl traveled with him sometimes after her mother died but mostly has been on her own."

"Just a thief, then, who knows nothing of the Stones," mused Kess.

"So it seems. She probably thought it little more than a lark. Here we are." The barking of several dogs announced our arrival.

"Watch out for my garden," came a querulous voice from within, speaking Heldun. "Visitors are forever trampling through it." A bald and wizened black man in a loincloth came out, looking about as if he had expected someone else to show up. Someone to whom he could speak in a language other than Ba'esun.

Three dogs came sniffing at us. I could not keep myself from crouching and making friends with them. I hoped the folk here did not eat dogs, as did those in the Arus. "I've missed having a dog," I admitted, rising. Not since before my last voyage in the world of my birth had I enjoyed ones companionship.

As for cats, I had seen none in this world. Hogak looked at us with dawning realization that his plans of thievery had gone awry. Had he been younger, I believe he would have bolted.

"This is the wizard?" asked Kess. She sounded doubtful.

"It is. He is not one who would have gone after the gems on his own. Who set you to it, Hogak? Has Ez been speaking to you?"

"Ez? By the Scorpion, no!" That name seemed to scare him even more than Arco and Kesarra, and they looked pretty scary. "A sorcerer of the Heldu spoke to me and told me, ah, that there were precious jewels he would like to possess. Jewels that might show up here."

"And he offered a generous reward," said Arco.

"More than generous, sir. His name was Dyges. He's a priest of some sort, up in the mountains." The man nodded in their general direction.

"Hmm. I suppose that is all you know. I won't report you to Budong, though I probably should." The god turned to us, saying, "The old witch doctor actually does a bit of good for the folk here, from time to time. But," he said, glaring at Hogak, "I warn you to have no further dealings of this sort with the girl. She is under my protection."

Hogak nodded eagerly. "Understood, sir. Thank you, sir." He was backing slowly toward his hut.

"One more thing," spoke Kess. "We wish to speak with this Dyges. You will take us to him."

The old Ba'esu deflated. He'd thought himself clear. "You are a sorcerer, my lady?"

"As am I," stated Arco. "And it is best no one learn of that. Do you understand this as well?"

"Yes, well. Very well. Shall I call the priest right now?"

Any sensible wizard should be asleep but we followed Hogak into his disheveled abode, and they began at once. I remained by the door—in the company of the dogs—as the three settled onto mats.

For no more that two or three minutes did they stay put. Hogak looked unhappy on their return; the other two looked thoughtful and not completely satisfied. "Maybe I should have called another to join us," said Kess. I knew she meant Barad and knew why she would not mention his name in front of this wizard.

"The less he knows, the better," felt Arco. "Let's get home." I think we both knew she would tell the far-off Wizard-Lord at least some of what had occurred. "And you had best block yourself against this Dyges in the future," he told Hogak. "He seems the sort that might try to pay you back."

"Indeed, my lord." Lord? Arco might have revealed a little too much of his true nature. Kess, too—the wizard looked at both with a fair amount of awe. I never saw nor heard of him again so I'll say no more of Hogak.

"A thoroughly unpleasant man," spoke Arco, as we retraced our way. The town was a little darker, a little quieter now, but many were still awake. The night was a good time for activity when the days grew hot.

"Hogak?" I thought him inoffensive—weak, not evil.

"No, this Dyges. A devotee of Asak." He spat and then laughed. "A thoroughly unpleasant god!"

Kess made no response to this comment about her grandfather. She might well have agreed with it. Cha'ana and Emat sat chatting and eating when we returned. The girl was small indeed—not terribly short but quite slender, with almost a starved look to her. And young. Certainly still in her teen years.

"Now what shall we do about you?" asked Arco, taking a place on the mat and helping himself to a chunk of dried fish.

Emat immediately went on defense. She might have been rehearsing arguments ever since we left. "It's not like I tried to steal from you, Toh. I'd never do that!" I think she was sincere.

"But Dick was a guest in my house. You have offended against me and my hospitality." He gave me a wink. "And you have offended against him. He might not be so ready to forgive."

"He'll do what you and the woman tell him," she declared. "I can see that."

'The woman' snickered. "My name is Kesarra. And in truth, I think I serve Dick."

I shook my head. "No, we both serve these." I opened my pouch and let the gems spill onto the mat. "These are what you meant to steal."

Both gods recoiled just slightly from the Stones. I've no doubt Emat noted it. "Pretty," she said, and then shrugged. "But where would one sell them?"

"There are those who would risk kingdoms to possess them. They are to be given to the Heldu to be kept safe," Arco told her. He pondered Kess and me, and seemed to come to a decision. "I wish you to guide this pair on their journey into the mountains."

The girl was probably every bit as surprised as we were but managed to remain nonchalant. "I'm getting tired of this town anyway. How much are you going to pay me?" Her eyes went from one to another of us. She wondered which was the paymaster, perhaps.

"That can be worked out. And other things." Arco's own eyes lingered on his woman for a few moments. "I think it is time I said goodbye to Cha'ana and left this place."

Emat would have had no idea what he meant by that. "If we're to be among my father's people," she said, "we should use my Heldu name. Phraata."

I repeated it. "Frata."

"No, no. *Phraata.*"

"Oh, of course."

"He'll never get it quite right," Kess informed her. "Now let's get a little sleep before the night is all gone. We have plans to make tomorrow."

I scooped up the Eyes and headed toward my chamber.

Forty-eight

"I went to speak with Barad as soon as I arose." None of us chose to comment on this so Kess went on. "We agree this Dyges is the one who has been sending the wyverns to spy on us."

"It would seem plausible," Arco allowed.

"Yes. Is this some kind of melon? I like it." She proceeded to converse with Cha'ana in Ba'esun, probably about melons. "Anyway," said Kess, switching back to us and Heldun, "he wouldn't have known about the Stones, only about the prophecy. Dick's arrival in possible fulfillment of that prophecy would perturb any priest of Asak."

Things fell together. "Hence, the attack on me. This Dyges was responsible. But he has learned of the gems, hasn't he?"

"So it seems, after he and Ez were forced to collaborate. She wouldn't have known where we were and Dyges doesn't have the resources to come after us. At some point, he must have figured it out or Ez simply told him."

"Then they may no longer be working together," felt Arco.

"I would doubt it. He will want the Eyes for himself and his cult. Dyges does not have the abilities of Ez but he does have a god to help him." She hesitated, briefly, and added, "My mother might be involved, too."

Arco said only, "Asak is exceptionally powerful."

"But not actively evil. He is too detached for that, too deeply nihilistic to care."

"Your Banat is also an extraordinarily powerful god, far more powerful than me when we are in our own worlds. Here, we both are diminished and might be on a more equal footing."

"Hope you never have to test that," Kess told him.

Emat—or Phraata now, I supposed—was taking this all in without saying anything. I suspected she understood more than she was letting us know.

It was time we began our preparations. "Will I have to leave my boat here," I asked, "or could it travel upriver?"

"There are many treacherous bars where one might go

aground or tear the bottom out of a boat like yours. It might be safer to leave it in the prince's care. I'll talk to him about it."

"Then we need a canoe."

"I'll find you one," volunteered Phraata. "No, I'll find *us* one!"

Arco approved. "You go with her, Dick. You might want to transfer anything you need from your boat."

I followed the girl's lead toward the river. "It looks like it will rain early today," I observed. It might well rain here every day in this season.

Phraata peered at the darkening sky. "The Ba'esu say the clouds were created to hold up the sky and separate it from the earth."

"But you don't believe that, do you?"

"I do not believe many things both the Ba'esu and Heldu priests tell me." She gave me a sidelong look before adding, "But I have heard strange things today."

"I have been hearing strange things for some time. I travel with strange companions."

"You're a bit unusual yourself, Dick. I should call you Dick, shouldn't I?" She barely waited for my nod. "Kesarra. Is she a sorceress?"

"No, she is a god."

The girl took that in stride. "And so is Toh? Which one? Xido? I've heard he often walks among mortals."

I did not think there would be any harm in telling. "He is Arco."

"Wow. I think I believe you, Dick! I won't let on I know. Here we are. We won't need a very big canoe with just the three of us. Nothing like Toh's big outrigger!"

Most of the speech from that point was in Ba'esun, so I under-stood little as Phraata asked questions and haggled. The Uparhna was quite a large river here. A broad river. I suspected it was shallow. "Are there, um, beasts that live in the river?" I asked the young woman. I didn't know a word for crocodile but that was what I meant.

"Oh, many, Dick, and they would all like to eat you!" I could see she was not going to be a good source of information today, not in her current mood. Maybe she'd settle down once we started our journey.

Which would be on the morrow, or so it was decided when we

returned to the house of Toh. I might have liked to linger and rest a little longer. I might even have liked to stay. I have said that of other places.

We feasted that night, not only we five but various friends and neighbors of Cha'ana and Toh, before their house. The rain had ended, the sky had cleared and stars appeared one by one. A pig had been roasted. There was laughter, and singing, soft and tuneful.

I might have fallen asleep but Arco began speaking to me, his voice subdued. It took me a few seconds to realize he did so in English. "It is unlikely you will ever see me again, Dick," he told me. "Few mortals do and fewer know who I am. To be sure, with all eternity to do so, it is possible that Kesarra and I shall meet sometime."

I was likely to be long dead. "You return to your own world."

"Yes, soon. I've had enough of messing about in the affairs of mortals for a time. I'll check back someday." There came a deep, rumbling chuckle. "If I remember."

"You will," I said, turning my eyes to his guests. "These are your people."

PART IV. HEIGHTS

Forty-nine

"One more day," said Phraata. "Then we must leave the canoe and travel on foot."

The journey had not been difficult, so far, paddling against the sluggish current. Sluggish for the most part—rapids of a sort had appeared as we entered these upper reaches, requiring more effort but no portaging. It seemed the way would become impass-able soon.

There had been no crocodiles in the Uparhna but there were crocodile-like reptiles. They reminded me more of the itza we had spied off Nagi's coast than any crocodile I had seen in my world. That they were dangerous, I had no doubt. This did not prevent travel on the river nor the Ba'esu from living in villages on its banks. In some of these we stopped, mainly so Phraata might gossip and hear the latest news of what happened along the river, but also to barter for fresh food. Arco had provided us with enough of what we needed for this, his parting gift.

How soon might he say goodbye to Cha'ana, to his life among his people? He had not seemed in a hurry but I suspected he would be gone by the time we found our way again to the sea. I found my way, I should say. Kesarra would no longer have a reason to travel with me. There must have been many farewells for the god, over the eons, as the mortal world went its way and he, his own. Now Kess would be facing such losses too, no longer insu-lated on her island.

Or maybe she would return to her world of gods, to never leave. I was not going to ask; chances were, she would have no answer yet.

We had been traversing a great sweeping bend in the Uparhna, with the land rising ever more rugged on either side. "It runs quite straight, further up," Phratta informed us, "but also quite swift, down a long gorge."

"We will still follow it?"

"For a little while. That would be the shortest way to the valleys of the Heldu, but the passes further south are easier to traverse." She shook her head and scowled. "I'll have to wear a top when we reach the Heldu homeland. No more getting by with just a loin-cloth!"

"It is already becoming a bit cool to dress so," I said.

"Oh, but you like seeing me this way, Dick," she asserted. I had no answer but busied myself with my paddling.

By that evening, another village came up on the left hand. "Here's where we stop," said our guide. "We can leave the canoe if we pull it up out of the way. No one will bother it."

This we did, removing all our belongings, and turning it bottom-side up. Kess scanned the darkening skies as we finished the chore and shouldered our packs. "I have seen no wyverns," she remarked.

Nor had I. We had both been checking the skies from time to time. "I do not think they would recognize us from the heights. We would look like any other travelers." Further on, where there would be less traffic, that might not be so. Dyges surely knew the lands of the Heldu were our destination. He might or might not have let Ez in on it.

"Wyverns?" asked Phraata.

"With riders to spy on us. Toh did tell you there would be danger, didn't he?"

"Oh, I guess he said something. I didn't much attention. People are always telling me to be careful!"

"With good reason, I am sure," Kess said. I could not have put it better.

"Well, safety in numbers, right? We can attach ourselves to a group of traders here. I hope."

I asked, "You have made this journey frequently?"

"Um, well, twice."

"Twice more than we have," stated Kess. "Now where can we sleep?"

"There's a campground. We can ask around there if anyone's heading west."

I gazed across the river. It was still fairly wide here. "A village lies on the other bank." It looked smaller.

"Those who trade further up the river travel the other side. We who intend to cross the mountains mostly stay on this side and cut away within a couple days. Ardysa!"

A stout Heldu woman—I could recognize Heldu by now—came and embraced her. "You go to see your father, Phraata?"

The girl made a face. "His wife doesn't want me around. I'm guiding these two." She swept an arm in our direction. "Are you traveling our way?"

"Down river. Otherwise I'd go with you and give Dursilis a piece of my mind!"

"That's all right," asserted Phraata. "I can take care of myself these days. Why I've been turning down marriage proposals right and left! Maybe I'll keep turning them down and be a trader like you."

"Hmmph. You like the boys too much to be always traveling. There were some traders gathering here to cross together. And a priest—he's been waiting for someone to arrive." The woman gave Kess and me a suspicious look.

"A priest of Banat?" asked Kess.

"So it is. You expected him?"

"No, but I am not surprised. We should find him," she told Phraata.

"Might as well. I'll see you later, Ardy!" As we moved on, the girl confided, "It is true that more than one wealthy man has offered to marry me back in the river town, but it was only as a second or third wife. That's no good."

"Definitely not," I agreed. I think Phraata expected Kess to be the one to comment, but the goddess seemed oblivious.

"How will we recognize this priest?" asked Kess. "Does he wear vestments?"

"Not when he has to travel over mountains, I would think. But one never knows with priests!"

"Then perhaps this is he hurrying toward us," I commented. The man was definitely not in vestments; he looked much like the other Heldu travelers here, a belted loose blouse hanging over his kilt. A young man, certainly younger than I, despite his flowing beard.

He seemed tongue-tied once he reached us. Perhaps Kess

intimidated him. She would intimidate many a man, and more so one who knew she was a goddess. This young fellow was unmistakably aware of that fact. "Um, my lady?" he began, bobbing his head toward her once or twice. "I, uh, we had word—"

An impatient Phraata broke in. "Oh, speak up, boy! Did they send you to escort us?"

The priest only glanced in her direction, but he did straighten up and spoke with more authority. Some more, anyway. He still seemed somewhat awestruck. "My lady, I am Xardes, a priest of Banat. I have indeed—" Another quick glance toward the girl. "Been dispatched to accompany you to our temple."

At once, Phraata wanted to know, "Is there a party we can travel with?"

The young priest shook his head. "Those who had gathered took off this morning, feeling they were enough and there was no point in waiting longer." He sounded more apologetic than he had reason to be.

"We shall leave tomorrow morning," Kess decided, "whether there be any to accompany us or not."

Phraata's squint suggested she did not quite approve of this but the girl kept any objections to herself. "Where are you camped?" she asked the priest. "We'd better settle in so we can make an early start."

"Very well. Follow me—um, but maybe I should first report your arrival. Excuse me a moment." With that he closed his eyes and stood motionless for a minute or so. I knew what he was up to, as did Kesarra. Phraata only cocked her head at the priest, asking no questions. I knew she wanted to.

On his return to us, the goddess, stated, "You have wizard abilities."

"Yes, my lady. That is why I was chosen for this task. Um, one reason."

Phraata snickered. Not for the first time and undoubtedly not for the last. "I can't imagine any of the elder priests hiking across the mountains."

I had to smile, myself. "Being young and healthy helped your cause, I am sure," I commented.

"And willing, my lord." The girl snickered again on hearing this title. "I jumped at the opportunity when it was offered. I know I have no great talent but I am able to speak from afar."

Out to prove himself. Xardes wasn't the first young man to set himself that course; that I knew from experience! "Don't call me lord," I told him. "I'm Dick."

Our divine companion shrugged. "You might as well address me as Kess."

"And don't expect *any* of us to call you Brother," added Phraata.

Somehow, I think he did not.

Fifty

Thatch-roofed, open-sided huts were arrayed around a fire pit. A few travelers huddled about the small blaze, for the night was grown cool. The seasons might not make much difference here but it did become colder as one climbed higher. We would need to don warmer clothes. Even Phraata.

"Here is where I have been sleeping," said Xardes, leading us under one of the roofs. "There should be room for you but there are unoccupied huts if you prefer." He waved an arm toward them. Only an untidy bundle occupied this space at the moment.

"It is safe to leave your belongings unattended?" I asked. Meager though they appeared, I would not trust them to be there when I returned.

"Traders would never steal from each other!" Phraata declared.

"So I was told," said the priest. "However, this I preferred to keep with me." He reached into the loosely-woven satchel slung from his shoulder. "The book of the prophecy, Dick. Your prophecy." What he brought forth and opened was neither a scroll nor a bound book, but a continuous page folded into pleats. Slotted wooden rods protected each crease, the page passing through them and doubling back. "It is a copy, of course," continued Xardes, "and the language is very old and not always completely understood."

It was the first writing I had seen since leaving the Stone, where Var occasionally scribbled on bark paper. Of course, I could make neither head nor tail of it, but I liked the idea of going to visit a folk who wrote and read. "I don't suppose it actually says 'Dick' anywhere in it." I remained at least a little skeptical, despite all I had witnessed since arriving in this world.

Xardes did not even smile at my little jest. "'Creator of prophets,' the poem names you. Or that might be a reference to what you carry. It's not likely to matter. Then, 'from the storm,' yes, yes, and this word we think means 'sea.'" He pointed it out, not that it made any sense to me. "It is long since our people dwelt near the sea. Hmm, 'from another world, comes he promised, the eagle his companion.' We don't understand that one."

"An eagle came from my world with me, brought by the same storm."

"Ah. Then that is straightforward enough. For once! The prophecy is quite long-winded and full of puzzling metaphors. It says the one—that being you, it seems—bears the beginning—or perhaps the word means source—of the world."

"That he does," spoke Kess. "A manifestation of it."

Though obviously curious, Xardes asked no question but plowed on through his manuscript. "Hmm, yes, the salvation, or maybe it is future, of our people. He will show us our path. Or what he carries will." The priest scrutinized me for a few seconds. "Are you a prophet?"

Kess answered for me. "Dick's gifts are of another sort. Put that away, young man, and let's eat."

"There are those who sell meals here," volunteered Phraata. "It would be our last chance to eat something other than Dick's cooking."

"I could enjoy a chunk of fresh meat," said Kess.

Xardes was aghast. "We who serve Lord Banat do not eat flesh! I thought—I understood you were of us."

I believe Phraata struggled as much as I to keep from laughing at his expression. Kess answered quite seriously, "I am Banat's tool but I am not Banat, and do not follow his ways nor have the same nature. Go with Phraata now and get us something to eat, and whatever you prefer for yourself."

"No bartering here, or at least not for anything we carry," said the girl. "I'll need some of your silver, Kess."

The goddess passed a handful of matchstick-sized pieces of tarnished metal over. Far more than needed, I was sure. As Phraata strode away, the priest in her wake, she confided, "I can not read the writing of the Heldu. That I can not take the way I do speech."

"But it can be learned." If I had time, maybe I would myself. "Xardes seems more a scholar than aught else," I went on. "Like Var."

"Oh? I suppose he does."

"I would guess that was another reason he was chosen to greet us."

"He seems like the perfect choice, doesn't he? I hope he can live up to it." Introspection gave way, of a sudden, to a smile. "As have you, to being a hero of prophecy."

"Through no choice of mine."

"That is not true, Dick. You could have turned aside at any time."

"Admittedly so. Still, at times I feel rather like the victim of a press gang."

"Press gang." She weighed the English phrase I had used. "Yes, I think I understand what that means. But your voyage nears its end!"

With no pay awaiting me.

No steaks were among the victuals Phraata and Xardes brought us, but there was plenty of a meaty stew. What meat, I neither knew nor asked. Sated, none of us wanted more than to sleep; none of us travelers, that is. I am sure our priest of Banat was bursting with questions and would have kept us awake with them all night, if encouraged. Our sleeping space felt a little cramped, so I bedded down in a nearby hut. No need to keep a watch, no need to remain together, in this safe, public place. That would change tomorrow.

Perhaps I had dozed, perhaps I was still half-awake, when I sensed another near me. There was enough light to recognize Phraata's slender form. "This is the second time you have disturbed my sleep," I said. "What do you seek to steal now?"

"Nothing you aren't willing to give me, Dick," she whispered, slipping beneath the thin blanket.

Fifty-one

"There were no opportunities while we traveled up the river," said Phraata. "And I thought at first maybe you were Kess's man."

I could have said much about Kess but made light of the suggestion instead. "We'll leave her to Xardes."

The girl giggled. "Yes, he is already in love with her!" A pause, a solemn look I could just make out in the half-light. "None of us will find more opportunities for anything for a while, I think."

"It is a good thing, then, you took advantage of this one."

"Let's take advantage again." We did, and then slept. Phraata was gone when I once more opened my eyes.

Whether our traveling companions had any idea of how we spent the night, I did not know. Nor could I see it mattered. The campground was still and a chilling mist had descended. Ah, there was the young priest. I joined him, the two of us only nodding to each other. The latrine proved to be his destination. Just what I sought myself.

"The Lady Kesarra wished to make an early start," he volunteered on our return trip. "She and the girl roused me from my sleep."

I wondered if maybe Phraata was the one in a hurry. The goddess seemed inclined to let things come when and how they would. "I'll be glad to get going," I told him and that was the truth. "Is your home a pleasant land?"

He shrugged. "So it seems to me. I have traveled little. This is the first time I ever crossed the mountains."

"It is good then we have Phraata as a guide." To that he had no answer. We joined the women and, having partaken of a light breakfast, followed the trail into the mountains, only the four of us. All that day, we paralleled the river, sometimes able to glimpse the Uparhna in its gorge, more often not, and ever climbing.

"We'll turn aside tomorrow," Phraata informed us, in the mid-afternoon, "but now we should stop walking." The spot, shielded some by a tumble of broken rock, seemed to see occasional use as a campsite, but only we occupied it that night. There was no shelter, our roof the sky, our light the stars spread across its black depths. The stars that ever reminded me I had left the world of my birth.

"I do not know the word," I said, gazing up at them. "Constellations it is in my native language. Shapes formed by the stars. Have you names for them here?"

"Some see the forms of gods or heroes," answered Xardes.

"And the Ba'esu see their own gods and heroes," Phraata added to this. "But those three down near the horizon are called the Arrow of Beyana. I don't know who that is."

"A god of the south, I believe," said the priest.

"Goddess," Kess corrected him. "Beyana the Huntress is reverenced on Nagi."

"Ah. I'll have to ask the elder priests if they know of this. All I know is that the stars point to the true south."

"True enough," Phraata said. "Or so Toh says." She turned to me. "We won't see Toh again, will we?"

"It seems unlikely."

"I'll miss him. He watched out for me."

I had to smile at that. "The best sort of god."

"The best sort of man, too. I need to sleep." With that the girl rolled over, wrapping her blanket around her. The rest of us followed her example.

The next morning, when the priest and I went aside, for our privacy and that of the women, he asked, "Who was this Toh the girl spoke of?" He still referred to her as 'the girl' rather than speaking her name.

There was no reason not to tell him. "A Ba'esu god who was living among mortals for a while. Arco is his name."

He nodded. "I have heard of this god. And you met him?"

"I did. He has assisted us in our journey."

Xardes was silent for a moment. "I find it hard to believe I am traveling with a goddess, when I stop to think about it. But already I grow accustomed to her and—and almost forget who she is."

I had done much the same. "She will remind us from time to time," I promised.

We set out again, our course primarily north-northwest. And upward. It was work enough and the sun strong enough that we needn't yet don heavy clothing. Indeed, we found ourselves shucking garments as the day progressed. Xardes, as our ostensible guide, went first, clad as we had first seen him, but now with a wide-brimmed hat shading his eyes. Felt, I thought, though knew not what animal provided the hair. As long as we stayed with this well-traveled road, he should have no problem playing leader. We passed parties heading the other direction twice that day.

And in the early afternoon, we came to the place the path veered away from the Uparhna. A less traveled way continued north but we now headed nearly due west on the main trail. It was not long after that Kess came to an abrupt halt, turning her eyes upward. "There," she spoke, pointing to the sky.

There might be something, very high. "A wyvern?"

Our companions peered up. I don't know if they were able to make it out. "Wyverns are not uncommon in the mountains," said Xardes.

"This one has a rider. I heard him."

It seemed the young priest knew what that meant. "A servant of Asak."

"Yes. Let's move on."

We camped early again. Almost at once, Kess announced, "This route is too well known. We need to take another way."

Though this was directed at Xardes, Phraata spoke before any words could leave his mouth. "I have heard of other paths but never walked them."

"And I know even less," the priest admitted. "Maybe I could, um, ask for directions. Speak afar to someone at the temple."

She agreed at once. "Do so. May I accompany you?"

"Certainly, my lady. I will call to Haatus, the chief among we who have such abilities."

The two left us at once. Phraata gave them a glance and confided, "Lots of those who can do wizard stuff end up in the service of Banat. The good ones, that is."

"And the bad ones go to Asak?"

"Or Dekata. She is supposed to be the goddess of evil sorcery and madness and all of that."

Should I mention she was also Kesarra's mother? It was no secret and I wouldn't be surprised if Xardes were aware of it. No, there was no reason to tell the girl. We sat watching in silence for several minutes.

Immediately on returning to us, Kess said, "Try to get some rest. We will depart this place soon." The priest took a little longer to get his wits about him but nodded in agreement.

We rose in the dark, perhaps three hours later. "There is a turning aside a league or so further up this trail," the goddess told us. "Between Xardes and me, I think we can find our way."

"Haatus had to call a man to him knowledgeable in traversing the mountains," Xardes further explained. "Fortunately, he had thought to keep him close at hand."

"A prudent man. No great talent as a wizard, however."

For the first time, Xardes put aside at least a little of the defer-ence he had shown the goddess. "He has other talents to make up for it, my lady."

I thought at the moment she had missed the edge in his voice. "Indeed. A good leader, I would think."

The priest seemed satisfied with this, and started up the road. As we made our way, Kess leaned in and confided, "I have told you I myself have no great skill nor power as a sorcerer, only an immu-nity to much of the harm a mortal wizard might seek to inflict."

"So I have understood. Yet you are competent enough, aren't you?"

"For most things." She left it at that.

But I knew there was more.

Fifty-two

"It would be best to lay up for at least part of the day," I said. We had hiked through the night and well into the morning, along a narrow, barely to be discerned path. "We can expect the spies up there—" I pointed to the sky. "To know we have left the road by now."

"They'll be circling about, searching for our new direction, won't they?" Kess considered this only for a few seconds. "Concealment would be sensible."

"So would rest," commented Phraata.

"Whatever you feel best, my lady, um, Kess," Xardes said.

"No, whatever Dick says. He is our leader. He bears the Eyes."

She would bring that up. Yes, I was the one who, ultimately, must make the decisions. Which way to go. Whether to go at all. "Let's find a likely spot to camp a few hours. Some food and some sleep would be good for all of us."

A decidedly audible sigh of relief came from Phraata.

"But not too long," I went on. "It would be good to put distance between ourselves and where last we were seen."

As we continued along our path, the priest suddenly halted and held up a hand. "Haatus is calling me."

Kess did not choose to accompany him this time, but waited with the rest of us. No more than a couple minutes later, Xardes announced, "Haatus is sending men to meet us. He says had he known enemies sought the Eyes, he would have done this before."

There was no point in regretting that now. "Then we had best stick with the route he chose."

"Not that we can't inform him if we change it," said Kess.

"There may be no one with abilities among those he sends, my lady," Xardes told her. "It is not so common a gift." He looked down the trail, now gradually falling before us. "He says there will be forest to conceal us part of the way and we should take advantage of that, but eventually we must emerge onto barren rock. There is no choice if we are to cross the mountains."

We would have to worry about that when we got there, with or without an escort. "That looks like a good spot," I said, pointing out a level space beneath towering conifers. "We'll make a stop here."

We settled onto a thick cushion of fallen needles. I think a weary Phraata fell asleep almost at once. Xardes and I both reclined, while Kess sat a little apart, seemingly lost in thought.

"Tell me," I asked the priest, "where did this prophecy about me or the stones or whatever come from anyway?"

"Lord Banat spoke it to a prophetess, long ago. Toward the end, there seems to be a promise of a new prophetess or priestess to lead us. Perhaps a line of them. And the, um, hero of promise was to bring that too." He glanced toward the oblivious Kess. "I wonder if that means the goddess."

I tended to doubt it. "And that is all of it?"

"A final passage seems to speak of bringing peace to a troubled soul. Or maybe to a god. The word *deta* is ambiguous and none are sure just what is meant." He might have smiled beneath his beard. "But many are willing to argue about it."

"And Banat sees the future?"

Kesarra turned toward us. "He sees a host of possible futures. No finite being could see all possibilities, of course. I think he chose us to make real that one possible future he desires."

That might have been the clearest explanation of my part in things I had heard.

Xardes mulled this for a moment. "And the Eyes play a part in this. I understand—well, maybe not understand—but have been taught that infinite worlds have their versions of the Eyes."

"And infinite worlds do not." There was the suggestion of a smirk. "I'm not sure which of those infinities is the larger!"

"Huh? I mean, pardon me, my lady?"

"A jest of gods and mathematicians. But so it is with the stones. Banat himself is a manifestation, one might say, of such objects of power in his world. Or they are a manifestation of him. Either way, he feels an affinity for them. Enough of that. I was just speaking to Barad."

"Will he be of any use to us?" I asked. It seemed unlikely the distant wizard could help, or even be trusted, for that matter.

"He is listening. He might learn something. I will sleep now."

That seemed a good idea, so Xardes and I followed her into slumber. The sun lay low in the sky when we all stirred again.

We should have set watches, shouldn't we? I would not neglect that again. "Are there dangerous beasts in these hills?" That might be more of a concern than men, at the moment.

"Bears," answered Phraata, at once. "And lions and dragons."

"Dragons might be welcome. They would keep the wyverns from flying," said Xardes. "But they are likely to be ranging further south in this season."

Phraata nodded wisely. "Mating season."

"Um, yes, I believe it is. There may be tree crocodiles as we descend toward the river. Best to keep a watch overhead."

The girl snickered. "Someone's been telling you tall tales. They don't get big enough to attack humans."

"What about trolls?" I asked.

"They don't attack them either," she informed me. I ignored her.

"Raiding parties are unlikely to range this far," said the priest. "They dwell mostly along the far coast—" He thrust an arm westerly. "Under the dominion of Ez."

But Ez might well send them after us. About that, I could do nothing. We marched well into night, until the forest around us turned to thick jungle and we were no longer sure of finding our way in the darkness. Tomorrow, we must travel in daylight.

I made certain we stood turns at sentry that night.

Fifty-three

Maybe I would like the land of the Heldu. Phraata had expanded on its attractions at some length as we walked along, she at my side more often than not. Maybe I would like her at my side in the land of the Heldu. Maybe it would be the place I ended my journey through this world.

All journeys do end, and once I handed over the jewels I carried I would have no need to travel further. But Phraata—did she have a place among the Heldu, being of mixed parentage? I did not know if that made a difference and felt it best not to bring it up. A faint sound, a murmur, pushed these thoughts aside. "Is that water I hear?"

"We shouldn't be to the river yet," said Phraata. "I think."

Xardes seemed uncertain about this, as well. The question was answered as we crossed a low ridge and our path descended toward a boisterous stream, bouncing over a series of low, rocky falls. Wide but shallow it seemed. "We can ford that," I said. As, apparently, did anyone else who followed this pathway.

"We will be in the open," commented Kess.

Yes, we must emerge from the concealment of the trees. There was more cover across the valley but it would become progressively more difficult to hide ourselves as we traveled on. Perhaps in more open ground we could return to traveling at night. Were it not early in the day, I might have suggested we wait until dark for this crossing. "Let's make it quick then," I said.

"There is supposed to be a suspension bridge at the Uparhna," spoke Xardes. I wasn't certain why he brought that up.

Kess caught the implication at once. "We will be vulnerable crossing it."

That might well be best done in darkness. We could concern ourselves with it when we reached it. A few minutes later we stood by the stream. "Cold," commented Phraata, dipping a hand.

I gazed toward the opposite bank. It stood as steep as the one down which we had just clambered. "I would assume it is safe." I put a few fingers into the flow myself. Yes, it was chilly. "A good place to fill our water flasks too."

This we hurriedly did, before stripping off shoes and leggings, and stepping into the stream. It would not do to go forward with soggy footwear.

Kess led the way; I brought up the rear. This was the order we had now fallen into on our trek, in unspoken accord. Perhaps it reflected who were—the goddess, the one who pushed ahead, I a man who preferred to see what was happening ahead of him. We were no more than halfway across, the water never deeper than our knees, when Phraata glanced upriver and gasped, "Wagga!"

Wagga? I followed her gaze to see a great, gray-green mass moving through the water, undulating about the rocks. It took me a few seconds to identify it as a giant snake, a larger snake even than those I had seen on the Isle of the Stones. Fully forty feet, maybe, it stretched.

Kess stared at it, concentrating, then shook her head. "I can not control it," she stated. "You must protect the Eyes, Dick!"

The Eyes. There was no time to ponder my best course. I tossed the pouch containing them, the pouch I always kept close at hand, toward Phraata. The girl grabbed them but stood frozen. "Get her to safety," I barked at Xardes. At once, he took her arm and urged her toward the further shore. Kess and I stood with our knives, mine steel, hers stone, and backed away, covering their retreat. Not that we could do much to stop that serpentine monster.

It reared now, its great blunt snout rising above our heads. I doubted there was venom in its fangs. It would smash into its victim, wrap it in its coils. I was not about to wait for that but darted toward it, prepared to thrust with my all too inadequate blade.

It veered away suddenly, seemingly distracted, perhaps confused. Pivoting, I saw Kess—Kess becoming more than Kess, becoming Kesarra the goddess. There had been only glimpses of this before. Taller she grew, taller than any man I had known, and a strange light played about her form. No, she was pulling light into herself, into an unfathomable darkness. The snake hesitated no more than a few seconds before thrusting its battering ram of a head toward her.

To be met with a shower of sparks. I suspected she had done

no more than I had seen her do before, pull fire or cinders from some other world. It startled the great creature sufficiently for the goddess to dart in, grasp its neck in her hands and squeeze. The tables were turned on this constrictor!

For no more than a few seconds. It shook itself loose from her grip and threw a loop of its body around her. By then, I was beside it—though I do not in truth remember moving toward the snake—and hacked at it with my knife. The blade bounced off the monster's scaled hide. Maybe I distracted it for a moment. Maybe it did not notice me at all.

The coils fell from Kess and the snake backed away, uncertain, its head swaying back and forth. She tore a rock from the riverbed, a far larger rock than I could have lifted even as high as my knees, and hurled it. Wisely, at its thick body rather than the more difficult target of the head. It might not have hurt the serpent greatly but it certainly got its attention.

Again, it gathered itself to attack. Kess rushed in, her own blade now in her hand. With the force of her arm behind it, the knife penetrated all the way to its hilt—and snapped off. A hiss like the whistle of a steam launch erupted from the serpent, which turned, to writhe its way back upstream and then up a bank to disappear into the jungle.

Kess deflated, sagged. Her clothes hung in rags. I helped her to the far bank. She seemed surer on her feet even before we reached the shore.

"Are you all right, my lady?" was Xardes's immediate question.

"I am a bit bruised up." She ran a hand along her torso. "One or two broken ribs. Though I heal more rapidly than a mortal it will still take some time."

He appeared relieved to hear this. I was myself. "Why did it release you, my lady?"

"I was too cold for it." She did not offer to explain further.

Nor did I intend to ask her about it then. I had a different question. "You do not think another controlled it, do you?"

Kess seemed a little surprised by the query and pondered it a few seconds. "No, Ez might have the power to set it on us, but she knows not where we are."

Could we be certain of that? I did not think the wyvern riders of Dyges had found us, nor did I think the priest of Asak would share the knowledge if they had. But one with Ez's powers might have other ways, ways of which even Kess might not be knowledgeable.

"Very well. Let's get under cover and then rest a while." All but Phraata turned to the trail. She stood, seemingly dazed, clutching the bag containing the Eyes.

I gently took the pouch from her hands. She roused, shook her head. "I–I felt them. Or something."

By this time, I knew Kess well enough to recognize her surprise. She recovered at once, saying only, "We must learn more of this. Later."

We climbed until we had passed out of that valley and our trail wound downward again, before setting up camp. Though it was early, I felt it a good spot to remain until the morrow. No one objected.

I helped Kess into fresh clothes, and bandaged her ribs with strips from her torn ones. Xardes avoided looking directly at her as I did this. From what Phraata had said, I assumed the Heldu were not comfortable with nudity. Not so long ago, I myself was not.

The goddess did not speak to Phraata until we had eaten and settled in. Dusk, too, was settling in, the sun fallen behind the mountains to our west. "Have you felt the stones before?"

"Um, well, maybe. I've been feeling–uneasy on our trip up the river. I keep thinking I'm seeing things that aren't there. Or *almost* seeing them."

Xardes seemed to be seeing something for the first time as well, as he peered at the girl. "A sorceress?"

"I would hazard Phraata has latent talents. Proximity to the stones awakened them."

"It is unusual for them to manifest at so late an age."

Phraata giggled. "Hey, I'm not that old!"

"No, you are not, but most know their gift by the time they are in their teens. Sometimes earlier. I did."

Kess held up a hand and stared in silence at her for some time, before again speaking. "She has strong wards against magic. Against the intrusion of the other worlds. She has created them unknowingly, to protect herself. That takes considerable innate ability."

"I don't want it!" objected Phraata.

The young priest shrugged. "You could probably go on as you have."

But Kess shook her head. "The sorceress in you has been awakened. I do not think she will sleep again."

"Then she must be trained," said Xardes.

"That she must." Kess again gave Phraata a long look. "I think this too was something Lord Banat foresaw."

Fifty-four

Kesarra, not surprisingly, was stiff in the morning. By noon, one could scarcely tell she had been hurt.

"We should reach the river before dark," Xardes told us, when we stopped for a meal and a few minutes of rest.

"And cross to the path along its other side," said Kess. "Which none of us have traveled."

"I've met those who have. As has Phraata, I am sure," he said, nodding toward the girl. "And Haatus has given us directions."

How useful any of that might be, I had no idea. Still, it was better than knowing nothing. "I think we should cross this bridge after dark," I said. "It is certainly a place an enemy would watch."

Already, there was less concealment. Jungle was giving way to patches of upland scrub, overhanging branches to spindly erect conifers, dark, silent sentinels.

"And return to traveling at night?" Phraata asked.

"If it is practical."

We did reach the Uparhna before sunset. A narrow suspension bridge spanned the gorge, the river rushing far below. Four weary travelers surveyed the crossing from the shadow of an outcropping.

Phraata took a look and shivered. "I don't think I want to go across in the dark."

"You won't be able to see how far down it is then," Xardes told her. "That should make it easier."

"But I'll know!"

"We'll wait," I decided. "An hour or so. Let's rest and eat a little, so we can press on some after we cross."

As we sat or reclined, according to our inclinations, I asked Kess, "You say you were too cold for the snake. The what-did-you-call-it, Phraata?"

"Wagga. It is a Ba'esu name for the great snake."

I nodded and returned my attention to Kess. She sat staring at the ground. "Yes. When in—that form, I pull light and heat into myself. Or I *can* pull them. It is something I have learned to control." She hesitated before adding, "At most times."

Xardes squinted in her direction. "Is this not said to be an attribute of the Evil One?"

"It is. I inherited it from my grandfather, though not to anywhere the same degree. Asak may not truly be seen; all the light around him is devoured, leaving only shadow."

"So you would have felt cold to the wagga. Colder than anything on which it normally preys, I assume." I thought on that a moment. "Or the air around you is cold. Your, um, surface."

She looked at least a little surprised. "Exactly, Dick. I forget that you are knowledgeable of the sciences."

"In other words," chimed in Phraata, "it was like embracing a chunk of ice. I've known men like that!"

An hour more we waited. Some of us dozed; at least our legs were rested. No longer– "It is time to cross," I decided, rising. "I think we must trust its strength and cross together. And quickly."

At least there was little wind. I might not have attempted the bridge at night, had it been swaying. The span was not so long and truly seemed sturdy, supported on thick ropes. Who built and maintained it? That was not a question to ask right now. Best just to get across.

"It looks clear on the other side," said Kess. "Best I go first anyway."

I nodded my agreement. "Not much concealment over there." There was both good and bad to that; neither we nor enemies could hide ourselves. Xardes followed Kess; I brought up the rear. Below our feet, as we trod the dangling boards, I could hear the rush of the hidden Uparhna. How far would our new path parallel it? The priest should have some idea.

Halfway across. We were not as invisible in the starlight as I might have hoped. Another sound rose above that of the river, at first barely discernible as separate. A rhythmic beating of some sort? From the gloom emerged a great winged figure. It swooped close before banking away, allowing me to glimpse the small manlike figure on its back. "Hurry!" I cried out, though it was unnecessary. We all knew what the wyvern meant: Dyges had discovered our route.

The winged reptile circled back toward the span, screeching

once as it fixed a large, glittering eye on us, and then rose into the darkness. We hastened on to solid ground.

Nor did we slow on reaching it. Not until we reached the shelter of a stand of pines did we stop for a breath. "Dyges knows what path we follow. Is there another way we can go?" I asked.

"I have heard there are many trails used by hunters," offered Phraata. She turned to the priest. "Maybe that fellow you talk to knows where they are."

"Perhaps. But," Xardes pointed out, "we must stick to this way if we are to encounter those coming to meet us."

"It would still be wise to speak to Haatus. Better we push on now, though," felt Kess.

Whether a few hours more right now would make any difference, I had no idea. "Agreed. Let's move."

It might have been midnight when we stopped, threw our weary bodies on the ground. I thought to set a guard but dozed off before saying anything of it. No matter; only the sun visited us, a few hours later. I opened my eyes to see Kess and Phraata sitting huddled together.

"Hey!" Phraata spouted, on spying I had awakened. "Kessie is showing me how to do stuff. Wizard stuff."

The goddess favored us with a little smile. "Xardes, I suspect, would be a far better teacher. He has more experience in such things."

"He's still snoring," noted the girl.

"Not much longer," I said. "We need to move on again."

That we did, taking no time to breakfast then but eating as we trudged along. Our path did move away from the river. The terrain also became ever more open, the trees dwindling to the occasional stunted conifer, our only cover the broken rocks. The way climbed steeply for a time, then wound along mountain ledges. The truly high mountains loomed closer now, still to our west.

Relatively high. I suspected they did not rival those of the American West, of which I had only heard tales. They certainly were not the equals of the Andes. Perhaps the Adirondacks I had known were of similar height. By early afternoon we had dropped into another wooded valley. It seemed a good place to call a halt, at least for a little while.

Almost at once, Xardes left us to communicate with his distant superior. His trance lasted longer than any before. On returning, the priest at once informed us, "There are none who can speak afar among the warriors sent to meet us. They travel to the pass we must use, with orders to wait for us if they arrive first."

"Then we must stay on this road," said Kess. Typically, it was difficult to say exactly how she felt about this.

"Not necessarily, my lady. There are other paths to the pass, ways more roundabout. Haatus has told me of one we might take."

Phraata frowned. "That sounds good for now, but ultimately we must walk the road leading up to the pass itself."

"Dyges will know this." I said. But perhaps we could confuse him if we left this route. "Time to move."

Fifty-five

We traveled on well past the setting of the sun. Not one human had we met on the trail, though it apparently saw use. "There are said to be dwarfs in the mountains," Phraata informed us, a little too cheerfully. "Ogres, too. Maybe we'll run into some of them on the road."

Having met both goblins and trolls–not to mention the elf Var– I could not be skeptical of this. "Have you seen either?" I asked her.

She shook her head. "But I know those who claim to trade with them."

I did make certain we took turns at watch, once we stopped, no matter who lived or traveled in these wild lands. We had settled in the darkness beside a little stream that crossed the trail.

"Halt! Who are you? Diiick!"

I woke of a sudden when Phraata cried out. A dim and foggy dawn was struggling toward daylight. I was on my feet at once, as two decidedly large figures loomed from the mist. Human or human-like, but both must have stood over seven feet in height. One was dark, its color seeming to constantly shift from a deep bluish to a stormy gray. The other seemed to shine with some internal light, a pale gold nimbus surrounding it. Him, not it. Both of them. And their faces–they were at once beautiful and terrifying.

Kess strode up to the pair. "Oh, don't stand around in god form. It looks silly in this world."

"It's not really god form," said the golden one. "You know what we look like back home."

"But we'll diminish ourselves anyway. How's that?" asked the other. Both had become somewhat man-sized, though still rather impressive men. Their color remained unique, as well, the one of a light gold, the other a slate-like darkness.

Phraata put her hands on hips and looked the two over. "I figured you were ogres, as big as you are. Were. But I've heard ogres aren't so good looking."

Kess did no more than raise an eyebrow, ever so slightly, at this. "These are my cousins. Oesurat, god of dawn, and Tesut, who likes to style himself lord of storms. Twins, as are many of our pantheon."

Xardes nodded. He probably knew about them. "Cousins?" asked Phraata.

"Yes. First cousins, once removed, right?" Both gods nodded. "Sons of Ditarra, who is sister of Khabata, who is my grandmother. And, as do I, they have a mortal father."

"Had," spoke Tesut.

"Oh, right. Their mom isn't evil like mine. Just impetuous and emotional."

"That's a rather nice way of putting it," felt Oesurat. "We just learned you had left your island."

"Lord Banat ordered us not to bother you while you did his bidding there."

"So now you do bother me."

"We felt you draw on your godhead and came searching."

"Know that I still do Banat's bidding. My work as his Hand is not done."

Both gods looked a bit disappointed. "You know why we sought you," said Tesut.

"To propose yet again." Kess sighed. "I would have thought a few centuries might change that."

"You are destined for me," stated Tesut.

Oesurat objected to this at a once. "No, for me," he said, sounding every bit as sure of it.

Kess might have been amused. She might also have been annoyed. "The very fact that you both make this claim proves it untrue. We are not like the great gods who mate for eternity and seek no other lovers."

The golden god was undeterred. "We are right for each other. You draw light into yourself even as I radiate it, creating a balance."

"But where I am storm, Kesarra is calm," maintained Tesut. "We also balance each other."

"It was your brother who taught me to find that calmness," Kess informed him. The gods had remained standing when the rest of us had settled again on the ground. I suspected these two weren't used to picking up cues from mortals. She turned to us, saying, "It is Oesurat's specialty. He helped me achieve the self-discipline I needed." I suspected the goddess aimed this statement at me. The others knew little of her.

"I am indeed a god of harmony," stated Oesurat, without the slightest self-consciousness.

"He who lives in harmony with himself lives in harmony with the universe," I spouted. I wasn't sure why. Maybe I felt a need to vie with these two.

"That is good," Oesurat allowed. "Did a god of your world say it?" It would seem he knew my origin had been elsewhere.

"A mortal philosopher." There would be no point in saying anything more. They would have no idea who Marcus Aurelius was.

Yes, I had read Aurelius, as I had read the popular poets and novelists of my time. I always made sure to have books with me when I voyaged, even when I was a common sailor. Cooper's novels of the sea might well have started me on the path—or voyage—I followed. I had read Voltaire. I had read Diderot. They had led me to think of things I might not ever have otherwise.

But they never led me to think I might someday find myself in another world, with its own questions. And that I might be carrying on a conversation with gods. Whether either of them intended to continue that conversation, I was not to learn. Tesut had fixed his gaze on Phraata. "This one has power," he said.

Oesurat gave the girl a moment of grave regard. "So she does. I sense not only wizard ancestry but that of the gods. Not any of us, I think."

"No, a god of the Ba'esu perhaps. I almost failed to notice her with those stones burning so brightly. They are part of your mission, Kesarra?"

"They are all of my mission."

"Then we must wait a while longer," spoke Tesut. Oesurat nodded his agreement and each pulled a sort of cloud about himself, one dark, the other aglow, and vanished.

I stared a moment at the empty space where they had stood. "We could have used their help," I ventured.

"They would not even have thought to offer it. Our mission means nothing to them."

The twin gods had come for Kesarra. Nothing else. "Then we had best help ourselves by getting on the move again."

"It should not be much further to where we can turn away," said Xardes.

The sooner, the better, felt I. We shouldered our packs and started up the trail.

Fifty-six

"I have a god among my ancestors?" asked Phraata. She must have been thinking of it as we moved along.

Kess answered. "I would guess our friend Arco. His son Ba'es did father quite a few children."

"I'll have to call him grandpa if I ever see him again! Hmm, it must be interesting to make love to a god. Your cousins certainly look nice."

"I wouldn't know," came Kess's flat reply.

"Nothing wrong with waiting for the right man." Did she give me a quick sidelong glance?

"Here it is," called out Xardes. "This trail should wind back toward the Uparhna a little before turning again to the pass."

Had the priest not pointed out the narrow path to our left, I might not even have noticed it. It could be hoped any pursuers would equally unobservant.

"The traders who spoke with Haatus told him there are dwellers on the upper reaches of the river they sometimes visit. We shouldn't go that far."

"You will know where to turn again?" I asked. The boy nodded, though he didn't look all that confident to me.

Yet Xardes did spy the place to turn to the right, before twilight took us. We traveled a short distance up the new trail before halting for the night. It would not do to attempt these faint and narrow ways in the darkness.

So we ate and rested and talked, none ready yet to sleep. It was the young priest who again brought up our visitors of the morning. "You say, Kess," he began, "the gods would not think to assist us. But what if you asked them? For that matter–" He gulped, hesitated, before rushing on. "What of Lord Banat himself? Why does he not act?"

"He acts through me. I am the Hand of Banat." Our expressions told her that was not sufficient. "Banat can quite literally not handle the Eyes. Maybe if he diminished himself to a near-mortal level–"

"As have you," I said.

"Yes, as have I. And I am uncomfortable touching them." Kess turned her attention to Phraata. "Let us give you another lesson in using your gift," she said. "You come too, Xardes."

Leaving me alone, so to speak. They took quite long. I supposed there was much to teach their novice sorceress.

As ever, Kess was immediately alert upon her return. "Phraata is drawn to the Eyes when we go elsewhere," she said. "Drawn *into* the Eyes, maybe. It is not a place to which I would wish to follow her."

"I believe one of us will need to," said the priest, shaking off his momentary disorientation.

The girl's eyes went from the one to the other before she spoke. "I—I saw someone else there. With Xardes."

"Haatus, maybe?" he hazarded. "I attempt to keep myself open to his call."

She shook her head emphatically. "No. A woman. It was like she was hiding in a corner of your head and listening."

I spoke the name even before Kess. "Ez."

"I would think so. She got past your wards, Xardes, and probably heard all your conversations with Haatus."

The young priest was dismayed. "Then she knows were we are. I am sorry."

"Your master did not notice her either. Nor," admitted Kess, "did I."

"But Phraata did," I pointed out. I had to believe others' assessments of her abilities. And I came to a quick decision. "We can not remain on this path. Up and back the way we came."

No one objected. We returned to where we had earlier turned aside, and went right along that trail, the trail that should carry us toward the Uparhna. A couple hours later, I said, "Far enough. Take the first watch again, Xardes." Tomorrow, we would find another way.

It was well past dawn when we all roused. We needed the rest, though I begrudged it some. "It is not safe for Xardes to ask for directions, I assume," I said to Kess.

"No. You must put up all your wards and allow no one and nothing in," she told him. "But I can speak with Haatus. He knows me now." To Phraata she said, "I think you should come along when I do."

"Later," I said. "Let's get some more distance first."

We again passed through land more open than I would prefer, some of it barren rock. Markers kept us on the right path; one might not have even known it existed without them. They were odd scratchings on rock, for the most part, some sort of symbols. Of course, I could not understand them but thought they looked nothing like the writing in Xardes's book. The sun was overhead when we stopped in the shade of an overhang, a shallow cave.

"I do not recognize the markings either," admitted the priest, when I asked of them.

Phraata made a rather rude noise and shook her head. "Dwarf runes." I did not bother to ask how she knew this. It might be no more than a guess. Or fabrication.

"It is time to contact Haatus," stated Kess. "Follow me, Phraata."

They were gone some minutes before I remarked on how long it was. "Haatus will need to confer with someone on the routes before he can give directions," Xardes informed me. "He does not know the wilds himself."

I had known that, to be sure. I was simply being impatient.

Phraata recovered almost as quickly as Kess when they came back to us. "We know the way now!" she crowed. "I can show you."

"Yes," Kess said. "We explained all to the priest. He suggested Xardes speak to him and the two of them provide false information to Ez, but I do not trust either's ability to fool someone with her power. Only Phraata might match her and she has not the training."

"Could you call on your friend Barad?" I wasn't overly serious with the question.

"I would if I thought there were some way he could help. I wonder also if these fellows can help us." She nodded in the direction of a handful of small, stocky men who had come along the trail.

Phraata looked them over. "Wow, there really *are* dwarfs up here."

Fifty-seven

Kesarra immediately greeted the newcomers in a harsh, guttural language. Taken straight from the dwarfs' minds, I knew. They did not know and were astonished.

The dwarfs were bigger than the trolls I had encountered, or the goblins on the Isle of the Stones. Some rose to chest-high on me. All had heavy brows and deep chests, with long beards of brown or reddish hues. I might have been impressed by the size of their noses had I not seen larger ones on trolls.

And they were light of skin. As light as I would have been were I not so deeply tanned. One stepped forward and addressed us in broken Heldun. "How secret words know?"

"I know many secrets," she replied, likewise in Heldun.

"She's a goddess," Phraata told them. Kess looked rightfully annoyed.

But didn't let it slow her down. "I am an enemy of trolls," Kess went on. "They seek me now, with the aid of the sorceress Ez."

That certainly set up a buzz. "Trolls like not much! Best not into mountains come," said the apparent leader. Or maybe only translator. "No not much like Ez too."

"Ez bad woman," volunteered another dwarf. "Witch!" At least two could speak a sort of Heldun.

"Pay not for flint. Tight-a-wad!"

Oh, ho. So commerce played a part in their dislike of the sorceress. "I understand she intends to send trolls up here to dig for it," I told them.

Phraata caught on immediately and took things a long step further. "They will be hungry. You had best keep your children safe at home."

"Come we kill!" roared the spokesman. This was greeted by uproar and the shaking of clubs and spears by his companions. A half-dozen of them there were, attired in hide loincloths, broad flint knives hanging at their sides. The dwarf looked us over and came to a decision. "With come. Show safe way."

"We might as well," I said in English.

Kess nodded and told our new acquaintances, "We will travel with you, and thank you for your kindness."

As we fell in with the dwarfs, going the direction we had already intended, their leader asked, "Ba-ha-esu god you?"

"No, Heldu, though few know my name where we are going."

"Name?"

"Kesarra, the Hand of Banat."

The dwarf did not look overly impressed by her title. "Look Ba-ha-esu. Trade with sometimes." That the dwarfs traded with Heldu as well seemed likely, as they spoke their language. After a fashion. "Name me call Kagakupa."

"What sort of trade do you carry on with the Ba'esu?" I asked.

"Dig flint. Tools make good! Look." He pulled his hefty stone blade from its sheath, holding it out for inspection but not handing it over.

Not metalworkers then. That skill, as many others, had yet to reach here. But the Ba'esu and the folk of Nagi both used silver and gold for jewelry and for trade. Perhaps that was mined up here as well. I did not intend to pry and raise any suspicions.

"Fine work," I commented. "Kesarra needs a new blade. She broke hers in combat with the wagga."

That probably raised her further in their eyes than any title or claim of deity. "Will sell new," promised Kagakupa. "Good deal give."

Shortly, we turned from our way, where it crossed a rivulet, bouncing down a narrow valley toward the Uparhna. Our path led the other direction, climbing steeply. "Home," announced Kagakupa a couple minutes later.

Home was a cave set in a low cliff. It was a pleasant spot, in fact. A basin stood before the cave, fed by a falling stream of water. More dwarfs were busy about the pool, women and children for the most part. The women dressed much the same as their men.

Cacophony greeted the returning males. "They are asking why we were brought here," Kess informed me. "It is not custom and they do not seem at all happy about it."

Kagakupa got his people—his tribe?—settled down. Kess did not bother to translate whatever explanations he gave them.

The dwarf turned to us. "Stay with dwarf-folk night this," he said. "Lead then through caves and secret ways! From trolls safe. By Great Bear swear Kagakupa!"

I had spent too much time in caves, that of Wanga, those on the Isle of Stones, the one in Oatza's hidden stronghold. This tale had begun in the caves of Juan Fernandez, as a prisoner. Each time I had emerged as a free man, free to follow what path I might choose.

Free to follow a fate already laid out, to fulfill some prophecy. I would have laughed at the idea once, yet there it was. I could not deny it existed. Couldn't I have turned aside at any time, had I chosen? Perhaps in one of those infinite worlds of which Kess spoke, I had.

There would be no turning aside here. We followed the dwarfs into their cavern.

Fifty-eight

"The Eyes are a manifestation of the elemental beings who shaped this world. Var and I said something of that sort to you before, did we not?"

I felt it best to simply nod, and let Kess go on. "Their essence is woven into all that is around us but these stones remain a locus of their power—each powerful on its own but far more so joined. The jewels are a, ah, connection to those protean forces. One could almost say they are a gate, a gate to a world within a world."

Phraata frowned as she took all this in. "So they are of this world and Banat is of another? Why is he concerned with them?"

A good question. I would have asked it myself, had I thought of it.

"He has an affinity for them, it seems. I do not pretend to understand all the mysteries of Banat. I do know, unlike the Eyes, he can travel to other worlds. He is not the source of his universe but the one who shaped it."

"As Krat did Arco's world," I said.

"Even so, from its primal chaos. Lord Banat does not remember this except as a sort of dream, it was so far in the past, but his wife, the goddess Vulata, does, and told me of it."

That would be Kess's great-grandmother, wouldn't it? "Was she part of what he shaped?"

"She was not of his universe. Banat found her in another world, a universe of rigid logic. Much of my relatives' nature is inherited from her; Banat himself, though good, is not quite so simple in his makeup."

Phraata sat with knit brow, puzzling something out. "Banat sees things to come, right?" she asked.

"Things that might come. The many ways forward."

"All right. And these stones—the Eyes you call them?"

"Yes. Some name them the Jewels of the Elements, others the Eyes of the Wind."

"They also see—no, that's not right. Those who use them see."

"The Eyes are indeed an aid to prophecy. That is the source of their name, I would think."

"So that is their link to Banat," said the girl. It surely was not quite so simple but I felt there was truth to her conclusion.

So did Xardes. "They are sacred to Lord Banat then. His priest-hood must guard them."

I could have said they were sacred to this entire world. But if the priest and his fellows wanted to keep watch on the jewels, I was ready to hand them over.

Kagakupa and some of his fellows—those who understood Heldun, most likely—had sat and listened but not taken part in our conversation. We were well-fed on dwarf food. Maybe not Xardes, for the meal was heavy on the meat from which he refrained. These people hunted, in addition to quarrying and crafting flint.

Most of the flint, we had learned, went to the Ba'esu. Kagakupa was altogether willing to go on about their trade and did so at considerable length at the communal meal. Two communal meals, I might say, for males and females sat separately, each in their own circle. It seemed most of the actual trade was with Heldu merchants, who carried the products of the dwarfs on to the coast. The Heldu themselves had their own sources of flint and obsidian, and their own craftsmen, but their work rarely crossed the divide.

It was a meager existence for the dwarfs but it was the life they knew. As all things, it would change someday.

"We'd best try to sleep now," I said. "There is a long way yet to go and we need our rest." Beds of pine boughs had been provided, and furs, for the nights were cool here in the heights. Cooler further on, I assumed, and in the land of the Heldu.

Phraata chose to settle down next to me; indeed, snuggled against me. It was the first public acknowledgment that anything existed between us. I'd begun to doubt it myself. Perhaps, I thought, she felt safer at my side among these strange folk. A few dwarfs yet huddled around the communal fire, silhouetted by its ruddy, flickering light as I drifted into sleep.

Do not think I did not set watches, just as when we were on the trail. I felt inclined to trust these dwarfs, but only within reason. Xardes sat up first, as was our usual practice. He would wake Kess in a while, before I and then Phraata took our turns.

A hand on my shoulder wakened me. Was it time already for

me to stand sentry? "Shh." Kess crouched beside me. "Phraata explores the Eyes," she whispered.

The girl was hunched over the stones, cupped in her hands. She must have lifted the pouch after I fell asleep. "Xardes sat looking outward and didn't see her," the goddess went on. "Not until he came to wake me."

I could see the priest at a short distance, watching. "Is she in danger?"

"That I can not say. We can only wait for her return."

Would she return? I knew nothing, understood nothing. Both Kess and I seemed to wordlessly agree it would be best not to disturb her.

Phraata's eyes flickered open. "Oh," the girl said, realizing she had been discovered. "I borrowed these." She dumped the gems into their bag and handed it to me. "And now I need to sleep before my watch!" With that she lay down and pulled her fur over her.

"I suppose," said Kess, "she will tell us about it in the morning. I'll wake you again in a few hours."

I eyed Phraata's form for a few seconds, wondering if she had chosen to be close to me only to get at the Eyes. I did not think I would ask her.

Fifty-nine

Kess and Kagakupa were haggling at dawn. In Dwarfish, so I could not understand the words, but soon the goddess passed over several little silver rods and took possession of a broad flint blade with a horn handle.

"It is not as pretty as the obsidian knife the goblins made me," she said, "but perhaps more practical."

If she intended to hack at more giant snakes, it certainly would be. I could not fault the craftsmanship; it was as good as any I had seen in this world. "Has Phraata said anything yet?"

"No. She may have much to sort out before she can speak of it."

Not only Phraata. We breakfasted on strips of cold, fatty meat. I don't believe it had been cooked nor was it exactly fresh. The dwarfs apparently relished it.

"Our host may swear by the Great Bear," remarked Phraata, "but he doesn't seem to mind eating his children."

Bear? Maybe. For a moment I envied Xardes, gnawing his chunk of stale bread.

"Follow," ordered Kagakupa when we were done. He and another dwarf led us toward the back of the cave, where the roof became so low even they must stoop. "Others leave," he explained. "Tribe protect." He'd taken Phraata's warning about hungry trolls to heart.

If any of Ez's minions were about, I would have preferred all the dwarfs with us. It did seem unlikely anyone knew our location now. Our exact location; both Ez and Dyges would have an idea of the general area and might have men out searching for us. Or they could still be far away, even on the other side of the mountains.

We passed into a roomier chamber. Dim light filtered into it from somewhere above. "The way out?" asked Kess, looking up.

"Only bat for," said Kagakupa, pointing to ranks of the little winged animals hanging above. He led us into another tight tunnel. Both dwarfs held stone lamps and we proceeded by their flickering illumination.

"Hold onto one another," I whispered to my companions. "It would be too easy to lose one of us in here."

On we wound, climbing, dropping. There were great, stalactite-filled rooms. There were subterranean lakes through which we splashed. Something else splashed in those waters but we did not stop to learn what. The dwarfs did not have to worry, I was sure, of anyone coming in their back door.

They didn't even need spiders to protect it. At last we emerged through a gash in the rock into a narrow grotto, white walls rising high on either side. I reached out to touch one. Marble? These dwarfs probably did not care about it as a building material; they would seek the flint that might lie hidden within.

The sun stood near overhead, making it difficult to judge directions. "Take trail to you," said our guide. "Look we trolls for too!"

Down the ravine we followed. What direction we moved, again, was uncertain. And who could guess what way we had gone underground? For all I knew, we could have moved back toward the Uparhna.

The valley unexpectedly opened onto a wide pathway. "Road mountains to," announced Kagakupa. "Traders go."

"So we're back to the main trail up to the pass?" Xardes wondered.

"Good guess," said Phraata.

He ignored the slight tone of sarcasm. "We should be well away from the river."

"Long far," Kagakupa agreed. His comrade jabbered something in Dwarfish, pointing to the ground. They both perused his discovery for a moment.

We might as well all get a look at it, I thought, and joined them. There in the dirt was a footprint, wide, short, bare. "Troll," stated the dwarf. I did not doubt it.

And headed the opposite direction from that we should follow. "There is no telling how many," I observed. "And it is likely not all are trolls."

"Trolls not?" We had not mentioned this to Kagakupa before.

"Men and troll-men too," Kess told him. "Many serve Ez."

The dwarf nodded knowingly. "True. Hear we this. Come."

I could make out now we were headed nearly due north. "It is likely," said Xardes, as we trotted along, "that these, um, intruders did not pass through the heartland of my people."

Said Phraata, "They would have crossed the mountains further south."

Ez's headquarters lay far south, but where these peaks were best crossed over, I had not the slightest idea. We were definitely higher in them now. The land had grown more barren. "Why, then," I asked, "do her minions travel south?"

"Scouts," supplied Kagakupa. That made sense. The sorceress' troop must be somewhere behind us and had sent these ahead. It was to be hoped the scouting party would report no sign of us and they would search the opposite direction. "Go we back look later. Come when night."

"You will leave us then?" asked Kesarra.

The dwarf chieftain nodded. "Road follow. Good you."

It was near dark and the parting of our ways, when the goddess sniffed the air. "Smoke."

The dwarfs at once lifted their own sizable noses and took a whiff. "Yes. Road off!"

We followed them into the rocks, climbing the low ridge to our right, and then turning again north. It had been a wise decision; a pair of sentries could be spied beside the road below. Kagakupa and the other dwarf exchanged a few words before laughing. "Stupid troll-men. Hide bad."

If they were attempting to conceal themselves at all. "There must be a camp."

"Find." We crept along, remaining on the far side of the ridge. A good commander would have placed at least one sentry up here as well, but none were to be seen.

And there they were, more than twenty individuals, around a couple fires. From our vantage they were only dark shapes, but there was much variety in size. The dwarfs held another conference. "Too many," whispered Kagakupa. "We hide stay." He didn't sound happy about not being able to kill a troll or two.

"That seems a good idea," I answered.

"What is this? More of them?" said Kess.

Definitely too many now. Perhaps a half dozen men came into the camp, from the same direction we had traveled. "The scouting party. They must have been right behind us all the way."

"But not smart enough to read our tracks," Phraata said.

"They probably didn't even look." Their leader had gone directly to the center of the camp and was speaking to a slighter figure, one with a head of long hair. I could make out nothing more but knew it must be Ez. "The sorceress herself has come."

"It is not surprising," felt Kess. "Her desire for the Eyes burns within her."

"Night soon," said Kagakupa. "Go on you then. Return dwarfs to people."

"We thank you for your guidance," spoke Kess. In a few seconds, the dwarfs had melted into the twilight.

We slipped by Ez's warriors in the dark and walked on for several hours.

Sixty

"I was inside them, sort of." Phraata halted, considered. "No, I don't think that's quite right. I was in a room, maybe, filled with their light. And—and there was a doorway but I was afraid to go through it."

"I do not blame you," said Kess.

"I don't think I need to, not to, um, see through the Eyes. But I think maybe I should."

"What *did* you see?" asked Xardes. "Will we return home safely?"

Kess shook her head. "It is a truism that prophets can not glimpse their own future."

"But I did see your home." Phraata frowned. "I think it must now be my home too, if we get there. I saw our people traveling to a new home? Maybe."

"Soon?"

"Hmm, no, not soon." She sat speechless for a moment. "I'm still sorting it out but I think my own descendants were among them."

"That is a great prophecy," said the priest, "and you will be a great prophetess. As was foretold to us." There was an awe in his voice we had not heard before. Certainly not in conjunction with Phraata.

Kess and I turned our eyes to the little girl with whom we had traveled. She, the one in Xardes's book? "He is probably right," the goddess told me. "Another thing Banat saw and guided into being."

Why not? But I had no doubt Phraata would remain a source of annoyance and aggravation. Did I wish her to annoy and aggravate me, if or when we reached the valleys of the Heldu? I could glimpse my own future no more than Phraata could hers.

We had holed up for only a couple hours before continuing our journey. The way turned west now. "The final way up to the pass itself," Xardes informed us, though he knew nothing of it personally. And there on the road, in the light of midday, a wyvern swooped toward us.

"We may have eluded Ez but Dyges has found us," commented Kess.

I wasn't so sure we were safe from Ez's pursuit. "How far yet to safety?" I asked.

"I think about two days to where friends await us at the pass," said Xardes. "I admit to not being certain."

"They would wait on this side, at the entry, if they have any sense," Phraata added.

Kess and I exchanged a brief look. "Best to hurry on," I said.

"Agreed. Hiding might only let one or the other catch up to us."

We were no more than an hour up the road—very much up, for it rose steadily within a wide valley—when Xardes clutched at his head and wordlessly collapsed.

At once, Kess knelt beside his body, seeking the cause, seeking in those places closed to those such as I. "Ez has broken down his warding," she gasped, "and seeks to wrest knowledge of our location from him. I can not stop her." I was certain she was trying, none the less, struggling with the sorceress in some other world.

"No!" cried Phraata. "She will kill him. Give me the Eyes, Dick."

I did as she demanded, not hesitating, not thinking to object. The stones were no longer mine, but Phraata's. She cupped them, two in each hand, and went elsewhere. Into Xardes's head? That is probably all wrong. I know only that I do not know, and never can know, the where and the how of it.

The girl returned surprisingly quickly, and seemingly none the worse. Xardes had come to a seated position but seemed dazed, oblivious, his eyes unfocused. Phraata gave him a glance. "He'll be all right." She sounded sure of it and maybe she was. "I led him into the Eyes. All the way. All the way we could go, anyway. Maybe there is more beyond to someday see. He was safe there. Both of us were. But—I fear Ez took what she wanted from his mind before I could—could release him."

"Then she knows where we are."

"She does." She turned her eyes to Kess. "If you had not held her at bay for for at least a few seconds, I would have been too late."

"Ez battered me pretty badly, trying to get past what obstructions I could erect." Kess released a short, sharp laugh. "I may not be much as a sorceress but I can absorb a lot of punishment. Ah, the boy returns to us."

Xardes sat looking around, still perhaps a bit bewildered. "It was beautiful," he half-mumbled. "Ha, that word is so inadequate. It was beyond anything I have seen or known. I will never be able to understand it or come close to describing it." He squinted at Phraata. "I think—you healed me? Or the Eyes did."

"We might have been one and the same for a little while."

"I take it you went through the door," said Kess.

Phraata nodded. "I believe I am forever linked to the Eyes now. But there is so much yet to learn!"

"Not right now. Can you march, Xardes?" I asked.

"I can." He sprang to his feet. "I feel stronger than I have for days!"

That surely had something to do with the Eyes. I somehow doubted he was linked to them in the same way as Phraata. A residual effect, maybe.

The effect did not last. All of us were soon weary. Even Kess, though she had far greater stamina than we mortals. Maybe the 'battering' she had endured at the hands—I use the word hands in a very loose sense—of Ez had worn her down some. We trudged on until we could no more, throwing ourselves down to rest sometime after sunset. None had the energy to stand guard or even think of it.

Before the sun rose again, we were back at it, ever climbing. The high mountains no longer seemed so hopelessly distant; I knew we were in fact among them. I found myself gasping. "Dick is not used to the thinner air here," observed Kess.

"Panting like a Ba'esu," Phraata stated, ignoring the fact that she was half-Ba'esu herself.

You can make it one more day, Dick Brown, I told myself. A little more than a day, I guessed. Then safety and descent into the lands of the Heldu. An end to my journey.

At least this part of it. I could not think beyond the next few days, of the futures of Phraata and of Xardes, of Kesarra, of myself. That all swirled about and tried to come into focus, like a kaleido-scope through which I had once peered. Where was that? Boston? Boston—that too swirled, to remake itself in new shapes and colors. A world in which I had walked and sailed and known companions, in which I had lived another life, was gone. It had been reassembled here, in new patterns, and I with it.

We rested little. Twilight found us still on the road. We had seen no one, neither enemies nor travelers. A little further, maybe, if we could still see our way, and then we might rest a few hours. There, where a few stars began to shine through a gap in the peaks. That was our destination. It did not seem so far now. We were almost there.

Something blocked those stars, rising out of the darkness. There stood Oatza, the troll wizard Gub at his side, a handful of warriors arrayed behind them.

"Ez told us you were headed this way."

Sixty-one

Could I fight this many opponents? Kess and I, that is—I knew I couldn't myself but if she put on her godhood, it seemed possible.

But there was Phraata to consider. I couldn't take a chance of her being injured. Or Xardes. Where had he gone? The young priest was nowhere to be seen. Spears were leveled at us and Kess showed no inclination to resist.

"Sit," ordered the troll-man captain. "The nedre will be along soon."

Not too soon. She had been a day or more behind us. I took a place on the ground beside Kess. "Where is Xardes?" I asked, my voice low.

"I threw shadow around him and told him to run. He will go to the Heldu at the pass."

It seemed unlikely they could get here soon enough. We would see about that. "It's too bad I couldn't slip him the stones." Those I still carried, would carry into the Heldu realm, whether Phraata was linked to them or not. If possible.

"Are you all right?" I asked the girl, seated beyond Kess. She only nodded in reply. "We might as well sleep then," I said, and laid myself down.

I was too worn not to fall into a deep sleep. Our captors' camp was astir before I again opened my eyes.

So were my two companions, who conversed in low voices. Seeing me sit up, Oatza strode over, his wizard scuttling at his side. "Take back to Nedre Ez now?" Gub asked him.

There was a firm shake of his dark head. "Ez ordered me to wait and wait I shall." Gub shrugged and wandered off. "I was fortunate to survive her wrath when you escaped and will take no chances now." He took a sidelong look at the wizard, talking now to the warriors. "I would have made a run for it but too many had their eyes on me."

"You still could," I suggested.

"To where? I will be back in the nedre's graces now, having taken you." He gave me a looking over. "She orders me not to touch what you carry, nor allow any other. Especially the girl."

Oatza wheeled and returned to his men. His warriors, I should say. I was fairly certain two were women of some breed.

We were not mistreated. Neither were we fed nor given water, but were not prevented from getting our own from our packs. We had to relieve ourselves where we were; Kess and I sat in front of Phraata to shield her from the view of the bestial warriors.

"Can you speak to Xardes?" I asked eventually. "Either of you?"

"Not safely," felt Kess. "He is still vulnerable to Ez and it might be best she have no clue where he is, nor even that he is alive. I have spoken to Haatus and told him of our current situation. He did not seem happy."

I could imagine. The day whiled on, with talk of this and that, of our pasts in one world or another. "So you left a lover on that island?" asked Phraata, when I told of the Arus.

"I did, though I did not wish it. I was called. Maybe by the Eyes."

"But you could have stayed."

"Yes, I could have. I suppose I am only a fond memory now to Maranua." And she to me. A fading memory.

"None of my memories are that good."

"Nor mine," said Kess. "There is a great deal of dreariness and self-denial behind me."

"No lovers?" asked Phraata. "Like those two handsome gods who visited us?"

"I fear to allow myself. Who knows what might happen? I could become like my crazy mother and devour my lover."

So the day wore on and night followed. It was mid-morn of the next day when Ez showed up, with all her followers, bringing the total to nearly forty men, trolls, and troll-men. And, yes, women. I almost forgot that again.

As many I had encountered on Nagi, the sorceress Ez had a vaguely Asian look about her. Her hair lay thick and black about her head, with a fleck of gray here and there. The face was round and somewhat pleasant, but the dark eyes within it glittered with a light that spoke of obsession, of madness, perhaps. She fixed those eyes on us as soon as she arrived.

"Where is the other?" she asked. "The priest."

"He died," fibbed Phraata. "You hurt him too badly."

Ez shrugged at the news. "He was unimportant. Were he still

alive I would have given him to my warriors." For torture and a cannibal feast. I thanked Kess silently for saving the boy.

"As for you three—"

"Best to kill them all now," growled Oatza, "and take what you wanted."

"There are things I wish to learn from them." She stared at Phraata, narrowing those eyes as if attempting to puzzle something out. "This one in particular." Her gaze shifted to Kesarra. "The goddess can not be killed. She could walk away from us right now if she wished, off to some other world." A bit of a smirk appeared. "I suspect she may yet."

"She not use to you, Great Nedre?" asked Gup.

"Not the least. I'd just as soon she was gone. Hmm, but know, goddess, I hold these two hostage against your good behavior if you remain. My followers would love to play with them. Now you," she said, shifting her attention to me, "carry what I want." She gave Oatza a sidelong glance.

"So I assume, Nedre Ez. As you ordered, I did not touch them."

"Good. Perhaps you will redeem yourself yet." To me, she said, "I'd have already had them, had not Oatza been off screwing and let you escape." Gub snickered. "And if my wizard hadn't been in a stupor from indulging in zor." At once, the troll sobered, looking elsewhere. "Yes, my captain, I know you were shacked up in a private hut with some boy who'd caught your fancy. There are eyes enough among your troop to see such things, even when you dole out zor to them."

She turned to me again. "I could trust one such as you, were you willing to swear your loyalty. And it would keep the girl safe."

"He broke his word to me before," hissed Oatza.

"Not so," I replied. "I said only that it seemed the best idea to go along with you."

The captain scratched at his beard and attempted no rebuttal. Subtlety of thought and word was not his strength.

"What I would wish," spoke Ez, "is to take the both of you back to my stronghold. Know this of not great importance to me but give me no trouble and you will arrive there safely. After? That depends on what choices you might make. Right now, your only choice is to hand the stones over to me."

She was right. There was no other choice. I gave her the pouch.

Ez looked into and then tucked it away in her sash, much as Oatza had done weeks earlier. Only the two wore such sashes. Otherwise, they dressed much as the warriors, short, loose trousers and vests. "I'm tired of walking, Oatza. We'll rest here a couple hours."

"As you will, Nedre." He gave me an unfriendly look as the two turned away.

"Oatza does not like you," commented Phraata.

"He sees me as a possible rival. I do not believe there is any deeper animosity." Oatza cared only about his own position and power. Everything and everyone else existed solely as objects to further his career. "Are you going to remain?" I asked Kess.

"For now."

Which could mean an hour or two, or all the way to Ez's fortress. There would be no reason to stay with us; she could not steal back the Eyes. Not on her own, no matter how powerful she might be.

And it would probably mean the death of Phraata and myself if she attempted it. "You could go to the Heldu," I said. "They could be on their way toward us by now." If Xardes had found them.

"So might others," came her enigmatic reply.

Sixty-two

Others, indeed. Before the sun stood directly overhead, a contingent came up the road. "They come from the wrong direction," I whispered to Kess. "Do you think Ez had more warriors hidden somewhere?"

"I suspect it to be Dyges. I have noted the wyverns yesterday and today."

"He's even worse than Ez," Phraata added to this. "The priests of Asak go out of their way to do evil, where she is just ambitious, I think."

"Yes, they believe they serve the will of Asak, though he does not care about any of it. Except when they kill; he does desire death for all things. But Ez—" Kess thought on her words a moment before going on. "She is obsessed with the Eyes and their power. This I can see. She would do anything to hold them, to wield them."

The newcomers were dressed much as the Heldu merchants I had met, kilts and tunics, and numbered nearly as many as Ez's troop. "Are they fighting men?" I asked Phraata.

"I have heard some priests of Asak are trained as assassins," she whispered.

"It is more likely to be the followers of my mother who practice the art of assassination," said Kess. "These Asakians prefer brutal, random murder."

Like the thuggees I had heard of in the India of my world? "I doubt either side wishes to engage in a battle."

"But they will," Kess informed me, sounding quite certain. "Both desire the Jewels and neither will be willing to leave without them."

"And we're stuck in the middle," sighed Phraata. "Great."

Asak's followers—his priests, if they were such—halted at a sensible distance. I would guess their flying spies had told them the size of the force they would face. Or perhaps not; Ez's troop might not have yet arrived when last the reptiles and their riders passed over. A lean fellow with a short beard came forward, raising a hand in greeting. Oatza was sent to meet him.

"That's Dyges, all right," he reported on his return from the brief conference. "He wants those stones every bit as much as you, my nedre. I feel he is a fanatic who would be willing to die in the attempt to possess them."

Ez weighed this. "Then it is likely to come to fighting. Get our warriors into order. And," she told him, "if aught goes wrong, you will cover my escape."

Oatza's sour look could not be hidden but he made no comment. Ez turned to me as he departed to do her bidding. "You should fight for me, Awn Dick. You can expect nothing from yon priests but a slit throat." When Ez had decided to bestow a title on me, I couldn't guess. We glanced at Phraata almost simultaneously. "They may wish to make use of the girl's talents as much as I do. Dyges is unlikely to kill her. Not right away."

I suspected I could say the same of Ez. I would not trust her to keep Phraata alive once she had learned what she could of her. But I didn't really know, did I?

It was Phraata who piped up. "You'd both like me to prophesy for you, huh?"

"They more than I, child. I can find other uses for the Eyes." Almost unconsciously, she patted the slight bulge in her sash, the pouch containing the gems. "I do not truly need you but neither have I any reason to wish you ill." A sly smile appeared. "But I think having you with me will make Dick behave. I am also fairly certain you will not desert the Eyes. If I must retreat, I expect you both to come with me. It would be the sensible course."

I had to admit it would. The two belligerent parties had arrayed themselves for combat, the troll-men jeering at their adversaries, the Asakians remaining silent, faces set and grim. Those in front formed a tight, curved wall of shields. They seemed disciplined. Was it discipline that would survive their first clash?

Phraates whispered to me, "Heldu men all train for combat. I'd bet even Xardes would be able to take a place in that shield wall."

"I thought the priests of Banat were, um, nonviolent."

"Banat himself is not," spoke Kess. "Nor is his great-grand-daughter. Would I had that fine knife of the dwarfs in my hand!"

I would not have minded having my own steel weapon. I was pretty sure Oatza had appropriated it. Ez's warriors now made a feint toward one end of the Heldu line, jabbing with spears from behind their own small round shields. The precision of the priest-soldiers in positioning themselves to repel the attack was admirable. The troll men could in no way match it.

But they were ferocious fighters and there were more of them. I think zor had been handed out, as well. That would make them fearless, if what I had been told was so. Again they came together, with more serious intent, most of Ez's men pushing into the center of the Asakian line, hoping to smash through, while a few warriors attempted to circle around and come at them from the rear. I saw one troll-man who tried this fall to a cast javelin.

A blast of a horn—I know not from which side, but both forces fell back, and stood glaring at each other. "The priests have positioned themselves well in the rocks," I commented. "Ez could draw on her powers, couldn't she?"

"She could," agreed Kess. "As could Dyges. He may be able to call on the power of Asak. I will not risk using mine."

For fear of Ez's retaliation against Phraata and me. I knew it would do no good to assure her we could take care of ourselves. "Something is going on." The combatants were looking past us, looking toward the mountain crests.

"It's Xardes!" crowed Phaatra. "He's brought the good guys!"

That he had, but not as many as I might have hoped, a force no larger than those of Dyges and Ez. They jogged toward us, spears and shields set for action.

Ez's followers at once fell back to a defensive position. Troll-men grabbed Phraata and me, and hauled us along. Damn, had I thought more quickly, the two of us might have rushed to the protection of the newcomers. As for Kess, she could do as she wished and no one would attempt to move her.

So she sat down to wait.

Sixty-three

Three pocket armies now faced off. All against all or should we expect an alliance to form? Ez stood and called out to the newly arrived force, "I have the prophetess. Let us go or I shall surely slay her."

"Go ahead," cried out someone among the Asakians.

"You want her as much as they do, Dyges," she called in return.

Not quite as much, I was fairly certain. Dyges now yelled toward the other Heldu. "Who is in charge over there?"

"I, Tepelus," came the reply. "Captain of the temple guard."

"The temple of Kamat, no? I did not think a Banatian would be willing to come and fight."

"I am!" came Xardes's voice. I couldn't help smiling at it. Nor did I fail to notice Phraata doing the same.

But Dyges probably had no idea who the boy was. "Both of us want the Eyes to be with our nation," he called. "We must take them, whether the girl dies or not."

"Better they be far away than in your hands, Asakian!"

Dyges had no more to say. So there was to be no joining of forces. Yet the Heldu forces made no moves toward each other. Of course not, I told myself. Ez has what both want. There would be no sense in attacking each other—now.

Ez had moved to a defensive position on the rocky hillside. The south side of the road; it might not be so hard to slip away into the wilderness from there when battle erupted. The coming of night would make it eaier. That was surely on her mind. And I would go with her if she did. The stones remained my responsibility. Best though to get Phraata away.

To our right were the men of Dyges. More accurately, they were almost across the road from us. To the left, the west, those who had crossed the mountains to aid us. They too would know Ez must be defeated before darkness fell.

Three hours perhaps. Much could happen in that long a time. I watched the sorceress straighten up, stare into space. Then a noxious, yellowish rain seemed to fall on Dyges's position. Most didn't actually reach it and pools of hissing liquid lay in the road. "Too far," she muttered.

Acid? Something she had drawn from some other world. I suspected that could easily backfire, that she could have rained it on herself if not careful. Maybe even if she was careful.

I could see Kess rise and peer in our direction. Ez's action had caught her attention. She dare not do anything of the same sort; not against Ez, while Phraata and I were with her. Kess surveyed the not-yet battlefield before taking a seat again.

"Will the goddess take part?" wondered Oatza.

"She won't take act against us," Ez assured him. "Not while these two remain my hostages. What is the Asakian up to?"

I could glimpse Dyges standing erect, his arms outstretched. Above him a dark cloud was forming. "The fool is calling on his god. He's liable to get us all killed," she said.

Considering what Kess had told me of the god and his followers, the priest might not care. A sickly green light now surrounded his form. It reminded me of the color I had glimpsed on those spiders, back on the Stone. "This is not something you can fight, is it?" I asked the sorceress.

"I can try." She considered the question again. "Or I can run."

"The goddess is moving toward him," Oatza reported. "Is she strong enough to stand against the Lord of Evil?"

"Dyges can pull but a little bit of Asak's power to himself. He is only a mortal vessel, after all. Hmm." Ez placed a hand on the stones she had hidden away. "With the aid of these, I suspect I could easily enough defeat him myself. If I knew more." She again gazed toward the Asakian. "If need be, I'll call on them anyway."

"I'm not going to teach her," whispered Phraata.

"If we got hold of them you could wield them yourself."

Her smile was just a little too smug. "I don't need to hold them anymore. I am inside the Eyes right now."

Below us, Kess and Dyges joined battle. The goddess had become a shadow. A large shadow. She reached toward the luminescence coalescing about Dyges and pulled it to her, into her. The cloud above the Asakians roiled with unknown winds. For no more than a few seconds all was in stasis; then Dyges collapsed, the cloud dissipated.

"I don't think she killed him," said Phraates. "Oh! Kess is hurt!"

She too had fallen to the ground. "Remember she can't die," I told her.

Ez had overheard us. "She has pulled Asak's essence into her. Who can say what effect that might have?"

"Xardes is running out to her."

The sorceress raised an eyebrow at the girl. "I thought you said I killed him."

"I brought him back."

Ez laughed at that. "I can almost believe it. The Kamatians are carrying her away." She returned her attention to preparation for battle.

Sixty-four

Dyges, seemingly little the worse for wear, was directing his troop forward, as much toward the other Heldu as toward Ez's position. Those other Heldu—the guardsmen from the temple of Kamat—began to move as well. I knew Kess had mentioned Kamat but I could not quite place the god in his pantheon.

"Do you know what relation Kamat is to Kess?" I asked Phraata. She was likely to know. If not, she was just as likely to make something up.

"Some kind of uncle. He's Asak's twin brother."

"Oh. And his opposite, I would guess?" That seemed to be the norm.

"Yep. God of light. Fire too."

Then this Kamatian contingent seemed just the right bunch to oppose the Asakians.

"I'm going to try to reach out to Kess," she whispered. "I don't think Ez will notice." She sat there longer than I expected. Her face contorted more than once. At last, "I couldn't reach Kess. All I saw was darkness. So I spoke to Xardes and he says she remains unconscious." She frowned. "I'll bet the Eyes would help me get through. But not while Ez has hold of them, maybe."

I assumed that was wise but, again, I knew nothing of such things. "I think the two bands are going to ignore each other and attack Ez," I said.

"Tepelus won't trust the Asakians. He knows they worship evil and consider it a badge of honor to break any promises they make."

That, too, could be something she exaggerated, but I'd take her word for it. But it would be to the Asakian's advantage to defeat Ez first and hope to grab the Eyes before the Kamatians. That they would contest for them after was a given.

If they did beat Ez, if they did liberate the jewels. That was in no way certain. We could but sit and watch. One troll-man stood guard over us, but he was not needed. I, at least, was not going to leave the stones.

Ez again called upon other worlds, this time showering the

seemingly tried and true volcanic ash. If some drifted onto her own troops, so be it. The stuff must be hard to direct. The troll-men's defenses held, the Heldu retreated after attempting to charge up the rocky slope. On the way back down, fighting broke out between the two groups and it took some time to separate them and settle them down. Ez's minions cheered and jeered.

But if attacks continued, they would be overwhelmed. Ez knew it, Oatza knew it. It is likely all their warriors did too. They could not hold out until night and even then escape was far from certain. "I must try to use the Eyes," stated Ez. "I have read they can control men's minds."

"They are not a weapon," Phraata said.

"Anything can become a weapon," was the sorceress' retort. She turned back toward the battlefield, and took the Eyes into her hands. The Heldu were again moving forward, in a more organized manner now. The two commanders might have conferred.

Our guard suddenly slumped. A grinning Kagakupa stood over him, bloody knife in hand. Four of his fellows were arrayed behind him. "Help we come!"

Oatza had seen them and leaped toward us, a pair of troll-men following. "Go!" cried the dwarf.

"Not without the gems," I answered. "You go with them Phraata." By now, Oatza and his followers had reached us, facing off against the knives of the dwarfs.

But Phraata did not go. She was staring at Ez and Ez was staring at her, both in some way entranced. Did the two contend in another world? In the Eyes themselves?

"They won't let me in!" Ez shrieked. "*You* won't let me in!"

"You don't belong," came Phraata's calm reply.

"The Eyes must be mine! I won't let you keep me from them." Ez sprang forward, knife in hand.

Only to be greeted by the blade of Kagakupa, thrust into her chest. Ez stumbled back, hurt badly but perhaps not mortally. Oatza hesitated a moment, then drove his own blade into her. "Witch dead," the dwarf said, looking down at her crumpled body.

Oatza held his men back with a curt command, following up on his sudden decision. "We have no use for these baubles now," he proclaimed, pulling the pouch from Ez's grasp. "And no reason to remain here and fight. Dick—go down to the leader of the Kama-tians and ask for a truce. Tell him we are ready to bargain. But, um, best not mention Ez is dead until we speak face to face. Will you promise this?"

I could see no reason not to. Oatza trusted me to keep my word or he would not have released me. I had absolutely no doubt he could not have been trusted had our places been reversed. I went down the slope toward the Kamatians, my hands in the air.

Tepelus at once pulled his men back when I spoke to him. Dyges had no choice but to do the same, though he knew not in what way things had changed. "I will give their leader safe conduct," the Kamatian captain promised. "I will swear an oath if he desires."

"Your word is good enough," I told him, and returned to the troll-man leader. A few minutes later, the two met in the open between their forces. Only I stood with them—none told me I couldn't!

"I will give you the Eyes," stated Oatza at once. "The girl too. And we will add our force to yours if the Asakians give any trouble. In exchange, we ask only safe conduct back to our own home, without pursuit."

Tepelus would not have to do much bargaining. He seemed relieved. "We will inform Dyges," he said, and waved a soldier to him. A whispered exchange and the man was off, toward the Asakians. "I have invited the priest of Asak to join us. He will accept my word as did you, um, Awn. That is the correct term, is it not?"

"The title is meaningless here. Oatza is my chosen name."

The lean Dyges was with us in a couple minutes. He looked rather inconsequential beside the two burly war-leaders. Maybe I did too. "But does Ez agree to all this?" he asked.

"Ez is dead. I lead now."

"Ah." Dyges considered all this. "I suppose I have no choice but to agree. At least the stones of prophecy will be with our people. I should be against that, shouldn't I? I doubt it will serve evil at all." He let out a harsh bark of a laugh. "You will allow me to lead my men home, Captain Tepelus?"

"Yes, go back to your temple now. We will not molest you. And you had best not think of stopping and waiting in ambush for us."

The priest bowed. "I think of it, to be sure, but think it is a bad idea." Within half an hour, he and his troop had disappeared up the trail.

Sixty-five

The demigoddess Kesarra lay yet unconscious, in the camp of the Kamatians. Oatza and his men had gone, melted into the darkness, as had our dwarf allies. A fire blazed; we would journey through the pass tomorrow, into the valleys of the Heldu.

Now, Phraata knelt beside our friend, holding the Eyes of the Wind, though she again assured me it was unnecessary. It might have made her feel more confident to have them close. Already she had once attempted to probe, to follow Kess wherever she had gone. "I'm going to bring her back this time," she promised. "Some of the essence of Asak has taken residence in her. Or maybe some of her essence has taken residence in the realm of Asak. I think both might be the same."

"But you found her," I said.

"Yes. She was—listless. Unresponsive. She might not have recognized me at all or maybe she didn't care. I'm going to take her into the Eyes. I think that'll fix her."

An awake Kess would not at all approve. But what else could we do? What else could Phraata do—I myself was powerless. The girl left us, off into other worlds.

"She is exceptionally talented," remarked Tepelus.

"Yes," agreed Xardes, "and she has had almost no training. I am convinced she is the prophetess who was promised to us."

"At last." The Kamatian gave me another looking over. "And he too is from the ancient book of prophecy?"

"He fits its words."

And the words had reached their end, that story done. I had fulfilled their prophecy, it seemed, and was free to go where I wished, do what I chose. Would I choose to remain with the Heldu? Already, I saw that future would not be as I had hoped only a few weeks earlier. Perhaps I could go back to the coast, become a trader among the Ba'esu. Or on Nagi. I could spend a life sailing back and forth from the Uparhna to Akmem. Ha, maybe with a wife in each port!

And at times my dreams still visited Maranua and her sacred

valley. Dreams—was Kess awakening from hers? Her eyes opened. She sat up abruptly.

"You were far away," said Phraata, an unaccustomed gentleness in her voice.

"Yes, far away. Naught mattered there. I could see only the great void, swallowing all. I was in my grandfather's head, I suppose."

"And he in yours. I had to banish everything of Asak and bring back everything of you."

"With the help of the Eyes. In a way, maybe, I've been carrying around some of him for a long time. My mother too."

"Neither can enter where I led you."

"But I could. I was afraid to before." Kess breathed deeply. "Oesurat is going to be surprised at just how much inner peace I have now."

Phraata giggled. "He won't have an excuse to give you one-on-one lessons."

"No, I do not think I need those any more." A brief smile gave way to something like a sigh. "But I need to learn other things. I am not ready to reside in the realm of Banat, and certainly not prepared to accept the offers of him or his brother."

"Or both?" The girl snickered.

"That is an intriguing idea, Phraata," admitted Kess.

"Will you leave us now?" I asked.

"Not right away."

The next day we all passed through the gap in the mountains and into the land of the Heldu, I with my knife again on my belt and with my questions about the future. The goddess Kesarra walked beside me, wrapped in her own thoughts and questions.

And before us, Phraata and Xardes also walked side by side.

Sixty-six

"I know Phraata and Xardes have a bond now. The Eyes played their part in that but maybe it was also simply nature taking its course."

Kess might have been sympathetic. At least she was willing to listen to me. We sat on the porch of the temple of Banat, a great log house on a hillside. A green pastured valley spread below us. A herd of the long-horned cattle could be spied grazing in the distance.

Beyond, more mountains, more valleys. One could dwell here in peace. I could yet. Someone was coming up the path toward the temple. A big fellow, striding purposefully along. I pointed him out to my companion.

She seemed amused. "It is Lord Banat, come to visit in mortal form. I wonder if the priests will recognize him."

Banat himself? Well, I had met other gods but this one, I was aware, was of several degrees greater magnitude.

"Welcome, my lord," she said, as he ascended the wooden stairs. He was indeed large, though not beyond the human norm. Banat was also, I decided, the most handsome man I had ever laid eyes on. There was a slight golden sheen to his skin; his eyes were large and violet in color.

The god held up a hand. "Name me Vulo, a priest of Vulata come visiting."

"A truth, in its way," she acknowledged. I could see that. Every man should be a votary of his wife, shouldn't he? Gods, too.

"You know I can not lie, Kesarra. Perhaps you should have a new name, for you need no longer be the Hand of Banat."

Kess kept a straight face as she answered, "But that name has been set down in the histories now, Vulo. We mustn't confuse the faithful."

The god laughed outright. "I fear my sons would not understand the jest. Nor my wife." He settled onto a roughly-hewn bench. "The prophecy spoke of a spirit finding peace at last. Even I was not completely sure of the meaning but now I know it meant you."

"Peace. Yes, perhaps I have found some peace. But I am far from content." Kess gave me a quick look. She knew I had not yet found contentment either. Maybe I was not meant to. "The Eyes will remain here now?" she asked.

"They will. The Jewels will be safe enough in this well-defended and well-warded temple. And there will be a prophetess to serve them and our people."

"Until trouble comes again," said Kess.

"As ever it does. There will be peace for a time, so they may prepare. The Heldu rarely fight among themselves and they are far from the coasts where Ez and others have ruled. I see many possibilities, Kesarra, but can not say which are most probable. Not yet."

"So that will be up to Phraata?" I asked.

"Indeed it will. She and her successors will be able to guide our people. This is what I hope and this is one possible future I have seen." He turned to Kess. "He is an astute one."

"Did you not foresee that as well?" she asked. I do not believe she was being entirely serious but Kess remained difficult to read, more often than not.

Banat-Vulo only smiled this time. "I saw some, but Dick came to us from another world, a world even I find nearly impossible to see. He was, in a phrase from his own language, a 'wild card.'"

As, I suspected, was Kesarra. Her mortal side, her free will, played its part in her choice by Banat. Or it didn't. What did I know of gods?

Kess puzzled over the wild card reference for a few seconds. I'm not sure she ever quite grasped its meaning. "I can see, too," she said. "I can see his role and mine are done here."

"That is up to you, my girl. You may remain and interfere in human events as much as you desire. Or you may come home."

"Or I could visit some others of the infinite worlds." Kess turned to me abruptly. "Would you like to come along?"

I was unable to come up with a ready answer. Fortunately, the god stepped in. "This I most certainly never foresaw. Yet it makes sense as the final step to finding yourself, Kesarra. And perhaps you as well, Dick Brown."

I had the sudden thought that this had all been as much for his great-granddaughter as for his people. Those powerful talismans, the Eyes of the Wind, were peripheral, a means to an end.

"I would," I said. "I mean, explore with you." There was much to explore, much more than I could once ever have imagined.

"Very well, Dick. I wonder where the nearest gate is. We'll have to use gates, you know, with you being mortal."

"But I would recommend first spending some time here with the Heldu. You both could use the rest." Banat rose to greet a priest who had come out onto the porch. "Greetings, Brother. I am Vulo, come from the temple of Vulata. Could you show me around?" The two entered the great house.

The other two remained.

Afterword

"Stones in the Sea" should be, chronologically, the earliest of all my Annals of Izan novels, the fantasy cycle set in the world of Exura. The events take place some seventy years or so before the beginning of my first Malvern book, "Coast of Spears." As such, it is, in a sense, a foundational work. It introduces the Eyes of the Wind, the mystical talismans whose story is wound through some of the other novels.

Will there be a sequel? Admittedly, none are planned at the moment, but the stories of both Phraata and of Dick suggest possibilities for one or several. Perhaps you would care to sample some of my other fantasy—or even non-fantasy—work while you wait.

Stephen Brooke